JOHNNY APOCALYPSE

AND THE SKY PEOPLE

MARK ROBIJN

BLUE FORGE PRESS

Port Orchard ✺ Washington

JOHNNY APOCALYPSE

BOOK 1:
Johnny Apocalypse
and the Nuclear Wasteland

BOOK 2:
Johnny Apocalypse
and the Fight for a New World

BOOK 3:
Johnny Apocalypse
and the Battle for Freedom

BOOK 4:
Johnny Apocalypse
and the King of New York

BOOK 5:
Johnny Apocalypse
and the Sky People

Join the Johnny Apocalypse Discord:

ymBcADDZFR

Dedicated to all the fans of
Johnny Apocalypse and the Nuclear Wasteland

ACKNOWLEDGEMENTS

I would like to acknowledge the invaluable inspiration I received from some of my favorite authors who inspired me to write the Johnny Apocalypse adventures, including:

I am Legend by Richard Matheson
The Berserker Wars by Fred Saberhagen
The Martian Chronicles by Ray Bradbury
Call of the Wild by Jack London
The Lord of the Rings by J. R.R. Tolkien
The Stand by Stephen King
Planet of the Apes by Pierre Boulle
The Hunger Games by Suzanne Collins

JOHNNY APOCALYPSE

AND THE SKY PEOPLE

MARK ROBIJN

WHAT HAS HAPPENED SO FAR
IN THE WASTELAND

One hundred years after a nuclear war, Johnny Apocalypse, his friends and family face adventure and danger in a world of chaos and ruin.

Having established a new home in the old city of Washington Deecee and finding it a little too quiet for them, Johnny, Starbucks and their now mates Deb and Super take off on their Harleys for new adventures.

They travel back to their old home Pill-a-delpia where they find a new tribe has taken over. The tribe call themselves Letfreedomring, and they call the city Pelpia. They seem to be friendly and their society is based on the ideals of democracy and freedom, just like Johnny's tribe. Johnny and his friends quickly make an alliance between their tribe and the people of Letfreedomring, and their leader Mayr Restaria.

However, they have little time to get to know each other, for an army from the city of Nork up north attacks Pelpia when Restaria refuses to give them food and supplies.

Soon Johnny and his friends join the people of Letfreedomring in a new battle for their lives against the Nork army.

Meanwhile, Johnny's friend Lady Stabs has also been captured by the Nork army, along with an evil ganger Monsta. Monsta was a member of the Doomsday Prophecy gang led by Johnny's nemesis Ripper who fought Johnny and his tribe in Washington Deecee. When Lady Stabs and Monsta reach the city of Nork as captives, strange beings from the sky attack the Nork soldiers watching them. Lady Stabs is taken captive by the strangers, but Monsta manages to run away.

Johnny, Starbucks and their new friends continue their fight with the Nork army, but suddenly monsters from Ballmor in the south, the Kraken, attack! In a brilliant move, Johnny leads the Kraken to the Nork army and they fight each other, saving most of the people of Letfreedomring.

But at the end of the battle, Deb, Restaria and the half of the people of Letfreedomring are captured. Johnny and Starbucks take after them on their Harleys, hoping to come up with a plan to rescue them. Starbucks turns back after a while to try and find Super, his mate, who was not captured and is nowhere to be found.

What happened to Super? Super and a brave warrior from Letfreedomring named Lightpole took Monsta's Harley and drove south. Super hopes to contact their tribe in Washington Deecee and Johnny's mentor and best friend Misterwizard and get their help to free Deb and the people of Letfreedomring.

And in all the confusion, Deecee, Johnny's beloved dog, is separated from him. Deecee sees Johnny heading north, and he takes off running in pursuit, but Deecee is on foot. Can he catch up to Johnny who rides his fast Harley? Or will Deecee just get even more lost?

The adventures continue in the next chapter of *Johnny Apocalypse and the Sky People*.

CHAPTER 1

Deecee ran on as night fell, bathing the world in darkness. The lack of light didn't bother Deecee, for he could see well in the dark and he ran on confidently. It grew chilly as the Red Eye disappeared, and Deecee was glad for his warm fur. He even began to sweat from his exertion, but a slight breeze blew, helping to cool him.

He ran down the gray ribbon, choked with old rusted hulks of steel, weaving back and forth between the cars and sometimes jumping over piles of rubble. Often, he would see skeletons of humans, and even of other dog-beasties sitting on the seats of the old hulks, their sightless eye sockets staring up at the sky, their mouths open, as if in surprise.

Large walls of concrete rose up on either side of the road, making Deecee feel like he was in some kind of channel. It would be hard to climb up either side, but Deecee didn't want to anyway, he was intent on moving as fast as he could to catch up to his master. Deecee's type was once called a Siberian Husky, and he was big with black fur over his back and head and white fur underneath, pointed ears and bright blue eyes. His thick fur kept him warm in the cold.

Worry slowly crept into Deecee's mind as he loped along. The hard rock beneath his paws made them hurt, and his stomach rumbled with hunger. What if he couldn't find his master? He would have to give up the chase soon and find something to eat, for there was nothing in the old steel hulks and there was no game anywhere on the gray ribbon.

Shame filled his mind, for if he'd been faster, he would have caught up by now. Though Deecee tried to be brave, a whine escaped him, more from frustration and impatience than fear. It seemed like he'd been running forever. He stopped and sat down, Panting. His master was nowhere to be seen. He finally accepted the fact that he would have to eat or drink, or he wouldn't be able to continue much longer. He began to look for a way off the gray ribbon.

Deecee's ears perked up, for he heard something ahead, behind one of the rusted hulks. It sounds like someone eating, the sounds of chewing and ripping filling the air. Slowly, Deecee padded forward, careful to keep a rusted hulk between himself and the sound. As he poked his head around the corner, he saw the source of the sound.

Standing over a dead dear-beastie eating was a huge dog-beastie, what men used to call a wolf. It was gray with a long nose and yellow eyes. It grabbed pieces of a deer-beastie with its sharp, pointed teeth and pulled, ripping small bits off and chewing them.

Deecee's stomach groaned at the sight of the deer-beastie, making him remember how hungry he was. Would the strange dog-beastie let him share its meal?

Deecee padded forward until the wolf-beastie sensed him. It stopped eating and lifted its head. It looked at him, its jaw dripping with blood. Deecee waited for a moment, wondering if the creature was of the sharing kind.

He soon found out, for the wolf-beastie lifted its lip, showing a long, pointed fang, and growled deep in its throat.

Deecee felt something deep inside him awaken, a strange kinship with this beastie, the wild savage creature his ancestors once were. Instead of feeling afraid, Deecee felt bold. Courage and anger rise up inside him. If he had to fight this beastie for some of the meat, he would. He snarled back, even deeper and stronger than the wolf-beastie.

The wolf-beastie's eyes opened wide, and Deecee realized the wolf-beastie was a bit smaller than him, and he could easily take it in a fight. The wolf-beastie seemed to sense this as well, for it backed away and stood watching.

With pride, feeling like the leader of the pack, Deecee padded forward. He stared at the wolf-beastie for a moment, then slowly lowered his head and began to tear pieces off the deer-beastie, not taking his eyes off the watching opponent.

As he tore off hunks of meat from the deer-beastie, Deecee felt the world fall away. He was a wild beastie again, and he had cowed his foe and now feasted. He relished in the taste of the raw meat and blood as he chewed. He found thoughts of his master disappearing, and a feeling of kinship with the wolf-beastie taking its place. For a second, Deecee forgot about Johnny, or any quest, and simply enjoyed the sensations of the cool night and the tasty meat.

The wolf-beastie padded forward, as if asking permission to join Deecee in eating. Deecee didn't react, giving his permission for the other to eat as well. Together they ate, both silent on their task, enjoying their meal.

Deecee wondered if this wolf-beastie was alone, like him, or whether it belonged to a pack. The idea of running with the wolf-beastie and his pack sent a warm thrill through Deecee, as if it would be returning to where he belonged. A vision of him running alongside the wolf pack through the rusted hulks and abandoned buildings, doing what he pleased, fighting and hunting, filled Deecee's mind. He glanced up at the wolf-beastie, and it seemed to be looking at him with a quiet respect and kinship.

Then Deecee heard a deep growl from not far away in the darkness. He stopped eating and looked up. Out of the blackness, another wolf-beastie padded out. This one was much bigger and looked fierce and deadly. Behind him, two more appeared from the darkness. All three peered at Deecee with dark, menacing eyes.

Deecee could tell these newcomers had no intention of letting him join their pack. *It's time to leave,* Deecee thought. He turned and bounded off as fast as he could. The wolf-beastie he'd been eating with snarled, now full of courage since Deecee was leaving and his pack was there to back him up.

The pack of wolf-beasties immediately took off in pursuit, forgetting all about the dead dear-beastie, for now they had a new and entertaining game to hunt.

They passed by the smaller wolf-beastie who joined them running at the back of the pack. Deecee ran fast, knowing he was no match for them. He also knew if they caught him, he'd be their next meal. Deecee wove between the hulks, hoping he would confuse his pursuers and they would lose his trail. Fear squeezed Deecee's insides, for he knew if he didn't escape, he was going to be in the fight for his life. He had eaten now though, so he felt a new burst of energy. He ran fast, proud of himself for his speed and agility. Part of him was confident he could outrun the pack, but the other part kept his heart beating swiftly and told him to run!

Johnny drove his Harley fast, his mind clear and determined. All he could think about was Deb in the hands of the terrible soldiers from Nork, and it drove him on faster and faster.

Having ridden for what seemed like forever now

but was close to a year, he was getting to be an expert at weaving around the hulks of the old cars and occasional tree that grew up in the middle of the long, gray ribbon he traveled. He rarely had to give it a second thought when something stood in his way, just a small turn of the handlebars, a slight lean to one side or the other, and his Harley moved around the object like a fish-beast swimming through the water.

Johnny realized he had no clue just what he was going to do when he caught up to the Nork army. There was only one of him, and who knew how many soldiers. He was sure they would be moving slow, for they had all of Restaria's people to herd along, even though most of the Norkers rode on their strange, horrible rat-beasties.

Starbucks had started out with Johnny, but he had turned around to look for Super, Starbuck's mate who was somewhere back in Pelpia. Now Johnny rode alone, and he didn't know if Starbucks was going to join him again or not. He couldn't rely on his friend, or wait for him. Every minute the Norkers drew closer to their city with their captives, and Deb. Who knew what would happen to them there?

Johnny slowed down, for he saw an amazing sight on the horizon. There in front of him, seemingly so far away they were just an illusion, stood buildings. They towered into the sky, like giants. Some were black, others white. Some had jagged edges, as if they had been touched by the mushroom monsters. Others gleamed by the light of the yellow eye, and one even had the yellow eye on it, as if it was some kind of magic that could capture it and hold it.

Even though Johnny was far away, he could tell these buildings must be enormous, giant steel fingers touching the sky. And there were so many of them! They seemed to go on forever, like a field of grass that never ended. There had been buildings in Pelpia, but nothing like this. They seemed to stand shoulder to shoulder, as if crowded together, like a huge army of tall, silent soldiers. The Norkers lived there? This was Nork? This was where they were taking Deb and the people of Letfreedomering. Johnny had a bad feeling that if he didn't get to them before the Norkers reached home, they might be lost in that giant maze of buildings, never to be found.

There was something even more sinister, more terrifying about the buildings ahead. They didn't look like the buildings of Pelpia or Washington Deecee, and then Johnny realized what the difference was. The tops of the buildings seemed to be covered with some kind of substance that draped over them and went from building to building. It looked to Johnny like the webs the spider-beasties that used to live in the corners of New Sanctuary made to catch fly-beasties.

Johnny's insides felt icky, like he was looking at something so creepy he should run away from it. His muscles froze, as if willing him to turn around. A primal fear inside him said, *It's too late, she's gone. Save yourself!*

The thought made Johnny angry, and he scowled. Johnny steeled himself and sped up, desperation welling up inside. He had to come up with a plan! He had to get Deb away before the Norkers started reaching their city with those horrible webs!

He decided something. All alone, he couldn't save all the members of Letfreedomring. But he could rescue Deb, and then together they could come up with a plan. Johnny knew better what to do now. Save Deb, no matter what. He sped up, roaring his engine. He took off in a flash again after the Nork army. Nothing was going to stop him from rescuing the girl he loved, even if he had to die doing it. He would rescue her at least, no matter what he had to go through to do it.

The tall buildings with their weird web-like coats drew closer and closer, yet still far, far away. Dark shapes in the night sky, they looked like some kind of nightmare vision, a dark forest of steel covered in horror. Johnny had to find Deb and rescue her before she was swallowed up in that strange steel jungle ahead.

Then Johnny saw something that filled him with relief and joy. He had reached the Nork army and their prisoners! Deb was somewhere there, just ahead!

A pang of love and longing filled Johnny's heart, and sorrow as well, thinking what the evil monsters had done to Deb while Johnny wasn't there to protect her.

Anger replaced the sorrow, fierce hot anger. Johnny's jaw clenched and his eyes narrowed.

Hang in there, darling, he thought to himself savagely. *I'm coming to save you. And I pity anyone who gets in my way and tries to stop me!*

CHAPTER 2

Moxie, the leader of the Nork army, rode on his rat-beastie at the back of the slow, large group shuffling down the gray ribbon. The whole procession moved achingly slow, for they were all exhausted, and the road was choked with old rusted hulks, big blocks of broken rock, cracks in the road big enough to fall into and trees that had grown up right in the middle. Luckily, large rock walls rose on either side of the road, so he didn't have to worry about his prisoners running off and escaping. Without the walls, it would be difficult to keep some of them from sneaking off into some of the old buildings. Even here, it was a chore to watch all of them, since Moxie and all his soldiers were also near dropping with exhaustion, and that was during the daytime. Now, as the yellow eye rose high in the sky and light began to fade away, it would be downright impossible. He knew he would have to stop and make camp soon.

Moxie knew he couldn't push the prisoners of

Pelpia much further either, for many were old and weak, and there were women and scrabblers too. It wouldn't be too good to bring the Boss some small, ragged group of people and have to explain that a lot of 'em died on the way because he pushed 'em too hard. And he also knew his men were tired and a lot of them could barely stay in the saddles of their rattys. The rattys couldn't be pushed too hard either, for when they got too tired, they got mean. Moxie knew he was going to have to stop, or things were gonna get out of hand.

Looking forward, he saw one thing that cheered him up. In front of Moxie sat an angel, a beautiful blond haired one who called herself Deb. Even though Moxie was so tired he could barely stay in the saddle, knowing she sat in front of him and he had his arms around her gave him an extra burst of energy.

She was some guy's doll, some joker named Johnny Apocalypse. He also knew the girl hated Moxie's guts. But she would learn to like him. Or not, Moxie didn't care. She was gonna be his anyway. Moxie wasn't worried about this Johnny guy either. Whoever this Johnny was, he was probably dead, eaten by the weird beasties that had attacked his army back at Pelpia. Even if he wasn't, what were the chances he could catch 'em before they reached Nork? And once inside the city, Moxie was home free. Nobody was gonna find her after he got her safe among the giant sky fingers and back to his pad.

Moxie looked up and saw a sight that warmed his heart and made him smile. It was the sky fingers.

They were almost home! They seemed miles away, though, and a pang of homesickness filled Moxie's heart.

The yellow eye shone down and reflected its light off the glass of the buildings, making it look like there were yellow eyes, not just one. The yellow eye was a full circle tonight, which people in Nork said meant if you prayed to it, you would get good luck. Moxie didn't really believe in that wish wash, but just for fun he gazed at it and said a silent prayer anyway. He asked it to guarantee this Johnny mug was dead. He asked it to make sure when they reached Nork, he would get to keep the dame sitting in front of him, and that he would be rewarded and promoted for being such a great soldier. Then he asked, with real urgency, that it would help him stay awake long enough to make it home and no new disaster would happen. Just let him get home safe, and he would pray to the yellow eye every night for the rest of his life!

He decided they had no choice but to stop. He was about to fall off the rat-beastie and it was hissing and twisting its head, a sure sign it was about to rebel. He looked at Deb, and felt a feeling of actual concern for her, for she looked tired and weak. The thought of stopping terrified him, for any delay gave somebody time to attack them, especially those weird beasties they left behind in Pelpia. They were vulnerable out in the open, and the walls on either side, good for keeping the prisoners in, also trapped them like in a big stone cage. Still, he didn't have a choice. He knew he was never going to make it if he didn't stop, he'd drop any second.

Up ahead he saw something that sealed the deal. It was the tunnels. Three openings looking like some kind of silent stone guardians, each one right next to the others. In the twilight, they made a silent hand grip Moxie's heart as he imagined what could pour out of them and attack them while they slept. The tunnels went on for what seemed like forever, but they were the only way to cross the river and get to Nork from the south since the bridges nearby had all been broken. They could have taken the one bridge to the place called Statn I-land, but nobody went there, unless they wanted a quick and painful death. Nobody messed with what lived there.

The only way was the tunnels, or go all the way up north to the bridge at the top of Nork, but then you had to pass through Clancy's Clan, and that was another thing he wanted to avoid.

Every time Moxie and his men rode through the tunnels, he was scared to death, his heart pounding and sweat dripping from his face, wondering what was waiting for them in the darkness. He made sure to never show it, though, for he didn't want his men thinking he was soft. Still, each time he wondered, could there be members of the Cursed waiting to ambush them, or the Sky, or some Gi-ant who had wandered away looking for a person to snack on? Or just wild beasties, or a gang of crazies. Or worst of all, Lurkers. It was always so dark in the tunnels, and he never knew which of the three to pick. It didn't really matter, they were all just as long and full of broken down, rusted hulks, trash and dirt, and the constant dripping, dripping sound.

He knew his men were scared of the tunnels too, but they all tried to not show it. Still, no one talked while inside, they just concentrated on getting through as fast as they could. It was crowded and hot inside, and they were crammed in together, fighting their way around the junky wrecks, annoying little trees that grew up right out of the concrete and trash. In the darkness, they had to trust the rattys' eyesight to get them around the rusted cars in the dark. It was always a heart-stopping, frightening ride, with only the darkness, whispers from the men that sounded like gunshots and the awful squeaks of the rattys around them. Sometimes the rattys would even get stuck and stop, and then others would bump into them and they'd start to fight. You had to turn them or back them up, yelling at them and cursing, so they could move forward again, all the while hoping you didn't fall off your ratty and have it run off without you. Meanwhile, your skin was crawling and you felt claws on your back every second.

Moxie knew it was best to travel the tunnels in the daylight, for at least you could see the end of the tunnel when you grew close. You definitely didn't stop inside, for every second surrounded by the old hulks they were vulnerable to attack. Moxie didn't want to camp so close to the tunnel openings, but he wasn't going to turn everybody around and go back. They'd just have to risk it.

"Everybody, take a load off!" Moxie yelled. "We're getting our forty winks here tonight."

Sighs and loud cheers of gratitude rose from everyone, including the Nork soldiers. The prisoners sat right down on the ground, and Moxie's men climbed off their rat-beasties and made a circle around the outside, without even being told to. They knew the drill, keep your eyes peeled and your weapons loaded.

Bugsy walked up to Moxie. "Too bad we can never take the bridge to Statn I-land" he said, rubbing his eyes tiredly. "If it weren't for the Gi-ants."

"Even if we wasn't too tired," Moxie said, "We're not dumb enough to pick a fight with them mugs."

Moxie climbed off his ratty and scowled. "Go watch the prisoners." He was too tired to have a long conversation, and found Bugsy just plain irritating. Bugsy was always asking dumb questions and making stupid comments, as if always questioning Moxie's decisions. Moxie knew Bugsy wanted something to happen to Moxie so he could take over.

Bugsy nodded and walked off. Moxie raised a hand to help Deb off, but she jumped down on the other side, her eyes flashing with disgust. It made Moxie mad. He'd teach her to respect him, even love him, whether she liked it or not.

Deb ran off to find Restaria, and Moxie hurried to follow her.

"Hey, get back here!" He yelled, wondering how she had so much energy after such a long and exhausting ride. Finally, he caught up to her standing next to Restaria, talking. It made Moxie feel stupid, chasing her, like she was in charge, and it made Moxie even angrier. He grabbed Deb's arm and yanked her around. She yanked her arm, trying to get free, which made Moxie furious. He had half a mind to slap her around a little, but decided he was too tired.

"Listen, girlie, you don't go anywhere without my say so, got it? Unless you want me to slap you around a little and show you some respect."

Deb's eyes narrowed and she yanked her arm free. Moxie stood close to her, his own eyes narrow and threatening. Then she spit on him! Moxie, too tired to react, just stood there, looking like a dope, wiping the spit off.

"You pig-beastie. You'd like that, wouldn't you? Beating a helpless woman. You're nothing but a bully. Johnny is going to do worse than slap you around when he gets here. He'll show you what happens to people like you."

Moxie made a fist, and held it in the air. "Mention that palooka one more time, and I'm gonna give you a fat lip. You're my dame now, capeech? You better get used to the idea and real soon."

Deb laughed! Before Moxie could think, his insides sank and fright filled him. Suddenly he felt like a little scrabbler who'd just had his pants pulled down in front of all the other kids. It was everything he could do to keep raising his tommy gun and filling her full of holes.

"I won't need Johnny to take care of you. Very soon, I'm going to kill you myself."

This dame was something else! Moxie began to

wonder if she was a little too strong for his taste. He liked his dames to be just that, dames, tame and meek, afraid of him and obedient. The type you slapped around and who sat silently until you called on them. He'd never met a girl with so much guts, almost like she was a guy. And he was getting real tired of everybody threatening to kill him.

Deb spoke in a haughty tone. "I'm going to help Restaria with the people of Letfreedomring. They need food, and some need help with their wounds. Don't worry your little pea-brain, I won't run off, not yet anyway. Not until after I've had the chance to stare down at your dead body."

Deb followed Restaria away, and Moxie stood there, clenching and unclenching his fists, not sure really what to do. He'd never been good with dames; they always found a way to make him feel stupid. He lifted one foot and then the other, and finally turned around. He looked around but luckily nobody saw the way she talked to him. *Okay,* he thought, *let her help the people, but she better not try anything else.* Moxie had just won a big victory in Pelpia; why was he beginning to feel like a loser again?

Moxie turned to see Clancy, the huge clansmen watching him with a dark grin. Behind Clancy were his whole clan, thirty or so of them. Clancy had seen what happened between Moxie and Deb. Of all the people, why did it have to be these guys? *Great, that was all he needed,* Moxie thought, *this big ape-beastie seeing him bested by a skirt.* Clancy was big, like a mountain, and he made Moxie nervous. He knew Clancy would kill Moxie in a second and take whatever he wanted, the moment Clancy thought he could get away with it. There was definitely no love shared between them.

"Whaddya you lookin' at?" Moxie snarled. "Go do whatever weird stuff you clansmen do on your own time, like sacrificing to your goat god, and mind your own business."

Clancy chuckled and stared at him, not in the least intimidated, which scared Moxie even more. "Be wary who you are barking at, little dog-beastie, or I'll whip ya and send ya to the corner with yer tail between yer legs. Me men and I are going hunting, and if ye whine and beg like a good beastie, we may bring ye back a bone or two to chew on."

Clancy's words made Moxie realize how hungry he really was, and before he caught himself it showed in his eyes. He tried to look like he didn't care, but couldn't keep the hunger and longing from showing on his face.

"You better get enough for all my guys and the prisoners too, see. That's why we brought you bums on this trip. You want the Boss to keep likin' ya, ya better pull your weight."

One of Clancy's clansmen, a man named Gavin, turned to Clancy with a look of disgust. "You gonna take orders from this dafty eejit, Clancy?"

Clancy just smiled back. "Aye, for now, we'll let this little dog-beastie bark. We need to keep the truce with their king, for now."

Moxie raised his tommy gun and pointed it right

at Clancy, expecting it to make him afraid, but Clancy just stared back. Moxie snarled, "Someday the Boss is gonna tire of you with your strange ways and your silly little kilts. He's gonna rub you and all your lousy people out. And I'm counting the days."

Clancy stared back, eyes showing hatred mixed with humor. "That king of yours is sick in the head, making ye all dress and talk like pictures he saw in a book. T'won't be long before he's drooling on himself and chasing rabbit-beasties in the fields. When that happens, the Clan'll take over for good."

"He's called the Boss. And I'm gonna tell him what you just said," Moxie said through clenched teeth. "Then he's gonna roast you mugs and all your little savage families over a big fire."

Gavan scowled. "Let's finish them right now, Clancy. We can take the prisoners back, and say all his men died in the battle."

Fear gripped Moxie's heart. Would Clancy listen to what Gavan said? He looked at Clancy, and his trigger finger squeezed a little harder on the trigger of his gun.

There was a tense silence. Then Clancy just chuckled. "No, Gavin. I think that Moxie here may not find such a warm reception when he brings home all these new mouths to feed, and I'm looking forward to seeing that. There will be a time for bloodshed. We'll see his insides soon enough. For now, we'll play the obedient pups and bring back what grub my men don't favor."

Clancy's men chuckled. Gavan, one lip curled

said, "He means you can have the hides and the hooves."

Moxie relaxed, and moved his finger off the trigger, but what Clancy said made him wonder. He scowled and said, "You better give us better than that! You better bring us some good meat and lots of it!"

Clancy and his men strode off in their kilts and heavy boots, laughing and talking amongst themselves.

Bugsy walked up again. "What's he mean, the Boss ain't gonna be happy, Moxie?"

"Ignore him," Moxie growled. "That nut in a skirt is crazy."

"Yeah," Bugsy said, staring after Clancy. "Crazy."

"I think these Clan jokers need to have an accident before we get back," Moxie said, grinning darkly. "Maybe in this very tunnel."

Bugsy grinned back. "Yeah, an accident," Bugsy said. "Hey Moxie, why don't we just do it now?"

"They're bringing us food, stupid. Plus, if we miss, they got them big axes."

Bugsy looked scared. "Yeah. Them axes."

"Pass the word along. When we get to the middle of the tunnel, I'll give the signal. Then," Moxie pantomimed with his gun. "Rat-a-tat-tat!"

Bugsy grinned. "Rat-a-tat-tat!"

They smiled at each other with evil looks.

Starbucks rode back into Pelpia, wary of any Kraken still hiding in the shadows. The yellow eye was high in the night sky, and the dark, empty streets showed evidence of the recent battle. The dark shapes of the buildings surrounded him, some just broken piles of bricks and rock, others still standing high into the sky, their empty windows looking like black eyes staring. Dark piles of rock, brick or dirt lay on the ground everywhere. They were the bodies of dead Nork soldiers, people of Letfreedomring and even a few dead Kraken, laying in the street and on the sidewalks.

Worry and fear for Super made every beat of Starbuck's heart hurt. *Super, where are you?* he thought. *Why weren't you with Letfreedomring and Deb? What horrible fate met you, and are you somewhere lying hurt somewhere, with no one to help you?*

Starbucks rode his Harley slowly, its engine making a soft puttering sound. He stared with melancholy at the dark street ahead and into the black pools of night that engulfed the buildings. The night was cool, and he felt a chill run through him. How cold Super must be, all alone somewhere. He never should have left her side. He promised himself, no matter what adventures or dangers they faced again, if he was lucky enough to find her, he would never leave her side again ever, no matter what. He could see her long, black hair, her smart-alecky smile and flashing eyes, and it made his heart ache to hold her again. They had only just become mates a few day cycles ago, like Johnny and Deb. He couldn't have lost her already! It was too horrible to even consider!

He saw the dark shape of a person on his left, and his heart skipped a beat. Could it be Super? He turned his Harley towards them, but remembered to stay alert, for it might not be a friend. He glanced over and made sure his sword was safely in its scabbard on the side of his bike. Then he slowly approached the stranger.

When he grew close, Starbucks could see it was just an old man. The old man leaned on a staff, looking as if he might fall down at any minute. He had long, gray hair that blew in the wind, and a long, wrinkled face. He wore ragged clothing that looked like it did little to keep out the cold.

Starbucks stopped next to the old man. "Hey old man, are you from a member of Letfreedomring?"

The old man peered at him, his white eyes glowing in the light of the yellow eye, two round orbs in a dark, leathery face. The man as if he didn't know whether Starbucks was friend or foe.

"You're black as night!" The old man guffawed, leaning on his staff precariously, looking like he was going to topple over at any second.

Starbucks grinned and relaxed, seeing the old man meant no harm. "I'm not one of the Norkers. I'm a friend. Please, I need to know what happened to my mate! Have you seen a white girl with long black hair?"

"Hair? Nair? Sair? Dare?" The old man repeated, rocking back and forth. "Ambazilla never brought me my stew for dinner! She didn't come back at all!"

Starbucks began to suspect the old man was what at New Sanctuary they called waksy. It happened to some people when they grew old, they started to lose touch with the real world and said wild, funny things. When it happened, they usually ended up drooling on themselves and sitting around, not able to hear or see and not much use to anyone. Sometimes they even forgot who their family were, and acted dangerous.

Back when they lived at the old Sanctuary, if they got too bad, Leader Nordstrom banished them from the tribe, sending them out to die. People in the tribe tried to hide the fact that their old people were getting bad, so Leader Nordstrom wouldn't find out. It was one of the reasons Johnny had worried about his father Foodcourt so much when he used to talk about going to Australia.

"Don't you know they had a big battle here?" Starbucks asked.

"Battle? Wattle? Fattle? Cattle?" The old man peered at Starbucks, as if his eyes were not very good anymore. "If they had some battle, why didn't they give me any? My stomach is empty!"

Starbucks felt sorry for the old man.

"Have any battle on you boy? I could eat a humpalump!"

"A what? Listen old timer, I have a little food on my Harley. Let me take you to your home and you can have some."

"Home, home on the range!"

The old man turned and tried to walk off, but he

looked like he was going to fall at any second.

"Wait!" Starbucks got off his Harley. He walked over and put an arm around the old man's waist. "Come with me, old timer. I'll give you a ride."

"Ride? Bide? Side? Tide? Is that like a cracker?" The old man didn't understand, but Starbucks turned him around and led him to the Harley. With a little effort, Starbucks got him seated on the back. Then Starbucks hopped on.

"Put your arms around me, grandpa, and hang on tight!"

Starbucks felt the old man grip him, one hand still holding tight onto his cane. With a smile, Starbucks took off, looking forward to giving the old man a fun ride.

CHAPTER 3

Super sped down the road, her long, black hair flowing in the breeze. She wasn't aware that it kept flying into Lightpole's eyes, and he had to keep moving his head to get away from it, or even worse, spitting it out of his mouth. But Lightpole, the strong warrior of Asian descent, grinned anyway. He had never ridden on a Harley before, and the pleasure of speeding down the road, the wind on his face and the sound of the engine in his ears, thrilled and excited him.

Super grinned too. She was having the time of her life. This was the first time she'd actually gotten to ride by herself. Always before she sat on the back, holding onto Starbucks. Now she was in control, and having a blast.

"Yee-haw!" She yelled, her voice trying to reach above the roar of the engine. She wove back and forth around the old, rusted cars, bumped over the cracks in the pavement and barely avoided the small trees that had sprung up in the road. "How you doing, Lightpole?"

He grinned and spit her hair out of his mouth. "I am good. This is a strange way to travel." His delight was evident in his voice, and Super grinned wider.

"We're coming up on Ballmor. As Misterwizard says, keep your eyes peeled. There may be Kraken around."

"The horrible creatures with the long, slimy arms?"

"Yes!"

Lightpole grinned again. He loved adventure, and ever since he met Johnny and his friends, it was all he had experienced. He found himself really liking Johnny and his friends, and especially the nice girl he rode with right then. She was wild and unpredictable, but he could tell she had a good heart, just like her friends.

They reached Ballmor. Super slowed down, and the engine's roar became a soft muttering. Then she stopped so they could study the landscape. Before them stood the crumbling buildings and clogged streets of the city. Moss and grass had grown over most of the old cars, making them look like green mounds of some horrible vegetation.

Super looked in all directions. It was late at night, and the yellow eye shone between two of the taller buildings. Super, who had been having fun, now felt somber, knowing that if they were attacked, there was no one to help them. A shiver of fear traveled up and down her spine, as she remembered the last time they were there, and how narrowly they escaped.

It was so silent, even the wind was still, and it made Super's skin crawl. The windows of the buildings were black squares, possibly hiding one of the monsters. She thought about the noise of the engine, and decided if they were going to go through, they had better do it fast.

As if reading her mind, Lightpole said, "Should we not get going?"

"You bet your bippie!"

"What is a bippie? And what is bet?"

"Don't ask me! Ask Misterwizard when you see him!" Super said, as she roared the engine and took off.

She barreled down the street, but then almost skidded on the soft moss on the road. The Harley tipped precariously, and Lightpole yelled.

Super said a bad word she'd heard Johnny's father say once and pulled the Harley back upright. She sped off, the tires slipping and sliding on the wet, slimy surface. She wondered if she was going too fast.

"Too fast!" Lightpole yelled. Super just grinned.

A Kraken appeared in a ground floor window, just as Super had feared. It saw the dark, strange shape of Super, Lightpole and the Harley, just a black shape in the middle of the road, but it knew right away this was something to eat. It shrieked in an ear piercing, heart-stopping way, breaking the silence with dreadful sound.

Its long, gray tentacles poked out outside and touched the ground. It was so big it had a hard time squeezing out of the window, its blob-like body slowly pouring out onto the street.

"Super!"

"I see it!" Super replied. "Jumping Jehoshaphat!" she said, repeating another thing she'd heard Misterwizard say. Her heart beat wildly. She concentrated hard on the road ahead, for now would not be the time to stop or fall over.

The Kraken made it out of the window. It leapt in the air like a grasshopper-bug, landing on the street. Then it took off running at an amazing speed.

Super couldn't look back, but Lightpole did. His eyes widened with fright and urgency. In his mind, he willed Super to go faster as he watched the Kraken bound around cars or leap onto them and down in front of them.

Lightpole didn't speak, he knew it would only distract Super, who was doing her best to get away from their pursuer. He simply gritted his teeth and watched the Kraken silently. He had a sword, and if the worst happened, he and the girl would fight it together.

Monsta hid behind just inside the doorway of an old rotted building and watched the strange attackers as they carried Lady Stabs away. The building was one story and ran the length of the block, with small rooms that had once been shops with doors and windows in a row. The windows were all gone and most of the doors were broken or missing, but the one Monsta hid in still had a door that he hid behind.

Inside the room behind Monsta was moldy trash and old chairs, some standing up but most lying on the floor on their sides, rotted, dirty wooden tables, and a long counter with old plates and silverware strewn about on it. The sign hanging above the door said "Murphy's Diner," though Monsta could barely talk good, let alone read the ancient text and so didn't even bother to look at it.

He peeked out and watched the chaos in the street, as the people of Nork fled from the flaming balls of fire thrown down by the attackers. It looked like things were not all happy and peaceful in Nork, which made Monsta so happy he couldn't help but chuckle.

He thought back to what had just happened, and it seemed so unreal he wondered if he'd just been so tired, he'd just dreamt it. He even saw a few winged beasts flying about in the attack, with large white wings and golden hair. But no, here he was, in this strange new city. Fires still burned in the street where the strange people who came down from the sky had shot their fireballs, so it must have been real. And was that a monster he saw on the side of the building? It was giant and black, and looked like a spider-beastie.

No, it couldn't have been, Monsta thought. But then he remembered the weird beasties in that other city, the ones with weird long arms and suckers at the end. The world had become a strange, twisted nightmare, full of new beasties and strange tribes. Who knew what new weird sights Monsta would see next? It gave him a silent thrill, for this new world was strange and chaotic, one perfect for a soldier of fortune like him.

And now this new strange tribe had dropped from the sky, shot Charlie with an arrow and killed him, and grabbed Lady Stabs and took her somewhere above. Tick-tock had ran off, and Monsta was on his own in Nork.

Monsta tried to make sense of it, but under normal circumstances it would have been hard for him. As tired as he was now, thinking about it made his brain hurt, so he stopped. One thing he did know, it looked like Nork had more enemies, some right there in their own city, and that meant more opportunity for a lowlife scum like Monsta.

He thought about how he could pretend to help one side and get them to trust him, then pretend to help the other and get something from them too. Then when he found out who was the strongest and most likely to benefit him, he'd betray the other and end up on top. It was just what Ripper, the leader of his old gang the Doomsday Prophecy, would do.

It grew late, and Monsta shivered. He was so tired, and so hungry. He realized then that he might have been better off going to the king of Nork with Charlie, at least they may have fed him and gave him a place to sleep. Now he was on his own. He'd have to find what he needed himself, and kill anyone who got in his way. But he was so tired!

And Lady Stabs! She wasn't much, but she was a part of his old gang, the Doomsday Prophecy. Shouldn't he make an effort to rescue her from those weird people with the arrows? Monsta thought about the strange tribe from the sky, their fireballs and their arrows, and that-thing that attacked with them. And the strange flying beasts! No; Lady Stabs was on her own. It was the code of the gang. If someone could help you without risking their own neck, they would, otherwise, you were on your own. He wasn't going to risk his neck to save her. Maybe if he saw a chance later when it didn't put him in any danger he'd help her, but for now, it was time to forget her and think about himself.

He looked back at the room, but it was barren, cold and dirty. No place to sleep, unless he wanted to sleep on dirty, wet piles of trash. He decided no matter how tired he was, he had to go find some food and a decent place to lay down for a while.

He looked out again, and everything seemed peaceful. Charlie's body and those of a few Norkers lay in the street, some with arrows sticking out of them, others smoking and burning. No one seemed to be in a big hurry to collect them, in fact people were all moving about again, as if the attack never happened. What a waksy place! Monsta had a feeling he was going to like it here. He grinned, stood up tall and walked out to explore the city, which looked full of new opportunities for profit and adventure.

Clancy and his clan strode to a high, stone wall at one side of the gray ribbon of road. Below Moxie, the Norkers and their prisoners milled about. Clancy and his men made a human ladder and climbed up the wall, then helped each other to the top. They looked back at the large group below, dark shapes in the night.

One of Clancy's men, Gavan, stood next to him. Gavan was slender, but strong, with a black hair and a black beard. He wore a green kilt, a white shirt that was stained with blood and big black boots. He balanced a large axe behind his neck, holding it with both arms.

"They're weak and stupid, Clancy, like little lambs. Ah dannae ken how much longer I can keep acting like a little, scared wee bairn one in front of them. When will we show them our true strength and take over, Clancy?"

"Keep yer heid, Gavan. We be strong, 'tis true, but they have the numbers on their side. We need to grow a mite, and then things'll be different, I guarantee ya."

Another mate, Finlay, a young man of eighteen with curly brown hair, a sharp chin and a jutting nose, piped in. "Are we really going to fetch them their dinner? That's just plain clatty, if ye ask me."

"Aye," Clancy said. "We'll play along a wee bit longer. But nothing says we have to give them the best of the vittles."

Gavan laughed. "We'll give 'em the hides and the hooves!"

Finlay laughed too. "Let 'em chew on that for

a spell!"

"All except the bonnie lass," Clancy said. "Give her the best shank of meat, mates, I've taken a fancy to her."

"She is right soft on the eyes, I'll give ye that," Gavan said with a smile. "But how you kinder to get her away from that eejit Moxie without creating a ruckus?"

"It's still a little way to Nork, me lads. And there's a dark tunnel just ahead. Bad things might happen to that feller, and for not one of them could ye lay the blame on me."

They all laughed darkly, took one more look at the crowd below, and left to go hunting.

Starbucks rode slowly so the old man wouldn't fall off. The old man's long, gray beard and long gray hair flowed in the wind, but the old man looked over Starbucks's shoulder with an intense gaze. Starbucks began to feel a little desperate. He couldn't spend all night looking for a place for the old man, he had to get back to looking for Super. He was wasting valuable time.

"You have a name, old timer?"

"Rumpelstiltskin is my name, it is my name, my claim to fame!" The old man yelled over the roar of the engine, his cracking voice rising and falling."

"Where do you live, Rumpelstiltskin? Where's your house?"

"Fly me to the moon, I want to ride among the stars," Rumpelstiltskin sang. Starbucks grinned. He didn't know what the old man was singing about, but it was a pleasant song, and the old man sang it with feeling, belting it out in a loud voice. Starbucks wondered if it was something the old man made up, or something he'd heard once.

"I want to see what life is like on Jupiter and Mars."

Rumpelstiltskin definitely was waksy, Starbucks thought. He just hoped the old man would point to his house so Starbucks could get rid of him. He had a scared feeling that the old man lived right where Starbucks had found him, and Starbucks was just wasting time.

"In other words—" Then he seemed to change songs. "Over there! Over there!" He pointed to a big building with long white steps. At the top of the steps stood two stone lions, looking regal and terrifying, even though they weren't real.

"Over there! Over there!"

"What?" Starbucks said.

"See those scrabblers, see those scrabblers, over there!"

Starbucks looked where the old man pointed, and then he saw them too. A whole crowd of small people, obviously scrabblers. They all stood on the steps, watching Starbucks and the old man approach.

One of the scrabblers, a young brown-skinned boy with black hair, seemed to be the leader, for he stood in the front and the rest watched him. Starbucks recognized him. It was Redeye. He was the one who led the scrabblers when Starbuck last saw them, when he was with Johnny. Starbucks remembered how brave the boy seemed, and how he was the one who told him about Super.

Redeye observed Starbucks and the old man approach. Then suddenly he yelled at the scrabblers and they all turned and ran into the building behind them. The leader boy followed.

"Stop!" Starbucks yelled, but the children disappeared like mice-beasties when you tried to catch them. He stopped in front of the steps and gazed up.

"They must have thought we would do them some harm."

"Boys and girls, girls and boys! Little rascals all with toys. Them's the kids of the village!"

"Maybe they know more about what happened to Super!" Starbucks said. "Last time, they said they saw her with Lightpole. I wonder if they've seen her again." Starbucks stopped the Harley and both he and Rumpelstiltskin climbed off.

"Put on a happy face!" Rumpelstiltskin said, dancing back and forth. Starbucks shook his head and took some dried deer-beastie meat out of his saddlebag. "Here, Rumpelstiltskin. Have something to eat. Then will you help me talk to those scrabblers?"

"Talk to the Walrus!" Rumpelstiltskin said, taking the meat and taking a big bite of it. "But my dear, this is Wonderland, and you're not Alice,"

Starbucks sighed in frustration. But then

Rumpelstiltskin said, "Keep your sunny side up! I'll talk to the little ragamuffins."

"Good! Let's go!"

Starbucks motioned with his hand, and together they started up the stairs. Starbucks walked, but Rumpelstiltskin hopped from one to the next, banging his staff on each step, singing, "Little Miss Muffet, sat on a tuffet, eating her curds and whey…"

Across the street behind them, a creature appeared from behind a building. It stared at them with hunger in its eyes. It was another Krakn, and its long tentacles wrapped around the corner of the building. This one had one eye missing from the battle, and one arm tentacle was cut off, leaving a two feet stump with a red, raw end. The Krakn watched Starbucks and Rumpelstiltskin enter the building. Then it disappeared around the corner again. From the darkness, a high screeching filled the air.

CHAPTER 4

Deecee ran swiftly through the dark highway by the light of the yellow eye. He knew he should be afraid, for he heard the growls of the wolf-beasties close behind him, but somehow, he felt alive, free, strong. He even laughed inside, confident in his ability to outrun the pack, and sure they would lose interest if he just ran far enough away.

He saw a crack in the high stone wall that lined both sides of the road. The crack was wide and a dirt path led up to where Deecee could the top of a hill above the wall. Beyond the wall, he saw old, rotted houses and cars. He turned and headed for it. If he could get off the long highway, he'd have a better chance of hiding in an old structure than on the road with nothing but old cars.

The wolf-beasties behind him howled, filling the night air with frightening, beautiful sound. They sounded close. Deecee wondered if they'd seen the crack in the wall too, and were afraid of losing him. Deecee added an extra burst of energy. With relief, Deecee reached the crack. He sped up the dirt road and reached the first house in a row of houses that lined the highway. It had once been yellow, but now was a drab white from the sun and age. The house had a raised porch with columns, a front door and two window frames, one on either side of the door, the glass long gone. Bushes grew up the sides of the porch and covered half of it. The interior was dark, with only moldy black shapes that might have been couches or chairs visible inside. The house looked old and tired, as if waiting for time and the elements to reduce it back to the ground so it could rest.

Deecee stopped in front of the house, pondering whether to try and hide inside, or keep running. Suddenly a figure walked out of the house. Deecee turned in instant alertness and fright. It was a tall thin man with a long, scraggly gray beard, long gray hair that draped over his face, and wild eyes. He held a club in his hands high in the air.

"I told you to leave, and not come back!"

Deecee tried to be quiet. He scrunched down so the man wouldn't see him, but the man turned anyway and peered into the darkness. He saw Deecee and his eyes stared at Deecee with intensity.

"You're not one of them waksy people. You're a doggie. A fine one, too. Come here, fella, I won't hurt you."

Just then the wolf pack came over the horizon. They didn't see Deecee, but they saw the old man instead, and he took all of their attention. They changed course and headed for him. The old man saw the wolf pack and he ran back inside the house. Deecee watched the wolf pack run towards the house.

Deecee knew this was his chance to get away, but something inside him told him he couldn't leave the old man to be attacked. He was torn between his fear and the desire to do what was right.

The wolf pack ran into the house! Soon Deecee heard their snarls and howls inside, and the scream of the old man.

Deecee grit his teeth and decided. The man was not Deecee's master, but he was a man, and that meant he should help him. Deecee sprang into the house, his fangs bared, ready to fight to the death to save the lonely stranger.

Johnny stopped and turned off his Harley, hoping the noise of its engine hadn't already alerted the Nork army to his presence. He was still far enough away that the army appeared like small ants on the road ahead. He noticed they were camped just before three huge dark caves with round tops. The caves looked like dark holes, and all Johnny could see inside were the rusted hulks of cars, just like the ones that dotted the road everywhere. Johnny figured the Nork leader, Moxie, wanted to rest before entering one of the dark caverns. It made sense, for the cave looked frightening, something you definitely would want to enter with only the yellow eye in the sky providing light.

Johnny hopped off his Harley and rolled it to where it was hidden behind a huge, rusty old long hulk that had once been a bus like the ones his tribe had ridden in. He took his sword out of its scabbard on his waist. Then he slowly crept forward, hunched down, keeping an old rusted car between him and the encampment.

He thought hard, trying to come up with some sort of plan. Surely, they would have guards posted. If he killed one of the guards, it would have to be done silently, or the whole camp would be alerted to his presence, and then his chances of saving Deb would be nearly impossible.

Johnny had always grumbled about the old rusted hulks on the road, but now he was grateful for them, for without them, he would be totally exposed. He moved close enough to hear talking. The people of Letfreedomring busied themselves making fires and cooking what little food they had with them. The Nork soldiers stood around the outside of the camp. They sat on old cars, leaned on the tall gray walls of the road channel, or sat on the ground, trying to get some shuteye.

Johnny had to find Deb. How could he do it without getting into the camp? He wished Starbucks was with him, then at least there would be two of them and it might be easier. He decided he didn't dare take out a guard until he was sure where Deb was. He needed time to find her.

Johnny stopped behind another old car. It was small, so he had to scrunch down. Just beyond him, he saw the first guard. The man sat on the ground against another car. His tommy gun was on the ground next to him. His head was down, and Johnny heard the distinct sound of light snoring.

Johnny grinned. The soldier reminded him of the Enforcers back at the first Sanctuary, the old men who stood guard. He remembered the time when he and Starbucks crept out and found the Enforcer sleeping, and how they joked about it. That was the first time they took Deb and Super out on an adventure, and it was just before everything happened and their worlds were turned upside down. It seemed now like that was a whole lifetime ago, maybe just a half-remembered dream. So much had happened, and their lives had changed so much. But some things remained the same—the danger and adventure, in fact they seemed to have gotten even more intense since they left Sanctuary so long ago.

Johnny tried to see past the soldier and into the camp. He couldn't see Deb anywhere. How was he going to get inside to find out where she was? He decided to circle the camp, very carefully, and see if he could get a better look.

Slowly Johnny crept to his right, keeping old cars between him and the camp, his eyes searching for any sign of the girl he loved.

Super sped on, her hair flying back into Lightpole's face. He tried to keep from getting her hair in his mouth so he could yell, let her know how close the monster was behind them. Super's hair made it hard for him to see as well, and he kept trying to move his head so he could get free and turn it and see how close the monster was.

Finally, he was able to turn enough to look behind them. The creature was so close he could see its red, angry eyes! Its long tentacle legs splayed along the ground, and its tentacle arms waved in the air, as if ready to grab as soon as it could. It was a hideous beastie, and it ran like a spider-beastie on its tentacles. What dark pit could had it crawled out of? What nightmare spawned such a creature?

"It's right behind us!"

"I know!" Super yelled back, surprising Lightpole.

"How?"

"The mirrors, silly."

Mirrors? Lightpole didn't know what this meant, but then he saw what she must be talking about. On either side of the Harley there were small round pieces of glass. As he stared at them, he realized they reflected what was behind them! He had seen glass like this before in old buildings, but it was faded and dark. Most of it was found and given to magicians or medicine men for it seemed magic. The ones on this Harley were clean and sharp, reflecting everything! Truly this Harley was an amazing machine!

"Oh, oh!" Super yelled against the wind.

Lightpole looked ahead, and saw two more of the Krakn, one on either side of the road next to buildings!

"We're trapped!" Lightpole said, his voice full of worry.

"Hang on!" Super turned the throttle and the Harley moved so fast the front wheel lifted off the ground. Lightpole yelled and grabbed onto her, feeling himself sliding off the seat. The wheel came back down with a bounce, almost jolting Lightpole off to the right.

They roared down the road, quickly approaching the two monsters. The one behind them screeched, and the other two screeched back in response.

Then they were at the other monsters! The monsters both rushed towards Super and Lightpole. One reached out a tentacle and grabbed Super's leg!

The Harley slowed down and began to tip sideways. Lightpole scowled and swung his sword in an arc. He slashed at the monster's tentacle, again and again. The Harley almost came to a stop! The other monsters were closing in!

Finally, the Krakn's tentacle came free. Super gunned the engine again. They roared forward, and not a moment too soon. The other Krakn reached the spot where they had been and ran into each other, all falling on the concrete in a heap. But they recovered swiftly, and soon chased Super and Lightpole again.

"Look!" Super pointed.

Lightpole looked forward and a glimmer of hope lifted his heart. They were close to the end of the city! The open road beckoned them.

"We're almost there!"

Suddenly in front of them appeared a huge brown beast. This one Super recognized, and even though it looked fierce and intimidating, it was a welcome sight compared to the monsters.

"That's a normal beastie!" Lightpole said, pointing, grinning. "I recognize it!"

Super grinned too, and a warm cheeriness filled her heart. What any other time would be considered a dangerous encounter was now their luckiest break.

Super drove right at the big, snarling bear-beastie. It rose up on its hind legs. Lightpole's eyes widened in fright as it seemed as if Super was going to drive right into it. Then at the last moment, she turned and zipped right around it.

The bear-beastie turned and roared, but it didn't see the three huge Krakn bearing down on it. Super didn't look back but just kept on as fast as she could. It was Lightpole who watched the fierce battle between the bear-beastie and the Krakn over his shoulder. He tried to capture it in his mind. He knew it was something terrible and yet strangely beautiful that he would never see again, something he would replay over again and again in his memory, wondering and marveling at it.

It wasn't long before the battle disappeared over the horizon. Part of Lightpole felt disappointed he couldn't see the whole fight, but most of him was mighty happy they were putting distance between themselves and the monsters.

He smiled and turned to look at Super's face. She had a strange gleam in her eyes, and wore a dark smile, just like he did. Lightpole decided they were a lot alike, both full of courage and a love of adventure. He found himself feeling a deep affection for Super, sensing in her a kindred spirit.

"Did you see that?" Lightpole said, grinning. Super grinned too. "I sure did!"

They laughed as they drove on into the night, heading towards New Sanctuary.

CHAPTER 5

Deecee bolted into the house where the man and wolf-beasties fought. He expected it to be pitch black, but an orange light from one wall gave the room a cheery glow. On that wall there was a square hole. Inside the hole a small fire flickered under a heavy metal pot that hung from a hook above. The yellow fire and orange coals gave off a pleasant heat that warmed Deecee's fur. Something in the pot smelled delicious, and Deecee had to force himself not to get distracted by his hunger. Deecee saw a couch on one side of the room, and an old lampstand and some stuffed chairs on the other. A mirror, long since grayed with age and soot, hung over the square hole with the fire. The room looked occupied, for there were plates with pieces of scraps of food on them and clothes strewn about.

What he didn't see was the old man or the wolf-beasties. He heard wolf-beastie snarls from a back room, down a dark hallway. The fleeting thought entered Deecee's mind that he still had time to leave and not risk getting hurt or even dying, but he fought the urge to run. He had to help the old man, even though they would probably both be killed.

Deecee sped down the dark hallway until he came to a room with cabinets on the walls, a metal table and a white hard floor. There in the corner, the wolf pack had the man trapped. They were all biting at him at once, and Deecee could see that they had already bitten him on the wrist and leg, for blood was seeping from the wounds. The old man was about to fall, and then the wolf pack would make easy work of him.

Deecee snarled and leapt on the closest wolf-beastie. It spun around and snarled back, baring its sharp fangs, and the fight was on. Deecee was large and could be fierce when he wanted to, but the wolf-beastie was wild and used to fighting savagely. It leapt at him, pushing Deecee into the hallway. There it jumped on top of Deecee, snapping its jaws, trying to get a hold on Deecee's throat. Deecee lowered his muzzle and countered the attack, biting at the wolf-beastie's muzzle.

The two combatants went down in a heap of fur and flashing teeth, each snarling and trying to get a bite on the other, rolling and fighting in the dark, narrow hallway. Deecee latched onto the wolf-beasties ear, clamped down and pulled, ripping part of the dog-beastie's ear off. It yelped but then turned even fiercer, and once again threw itself against Deecee, trying to get to his throat. It bit Deecee's shoulder instead, clamped down hard, shook its muzzle and held on. Deecee in turn bit the wolf-beastie's jaw and clamped down hard, but it held onto Deecee's shoulder tight. Deecee let go and instead bit the wolf-beastie's eye, and it finally had to let go.

Meanwhile, the old man had picked up a knife from the counter and held the wolves at bay. Some of the wolf-beasties heard Deecee and the other wolf-beastie fighting. Three ran into the hallway to investigate, and the old man smiled with relief. He didn't know who his new friend was, but he was very glad they were there. As soon as the three wolf-beasties left, the old man took the advantage. He stabbed the nearest wolf-beastie right in the eye! It yelped with pain and fell back, and now it was the old man's turn to attack. He swung the knife in a deadly arc, and the wolf-beasties began to lose courage. Not ones to stay in a fight where they didn't have the advantage, the wolf-beasties began to consider running away.

Meanwhile, Deecee was in the battle for his life. The other three wolf-beasties had joined the first, and all four of them fought for room to bite Deecee. The narrow hallway made them have to crowd together, but Deecee was beneath them, and the sheer weight of all four wolf-beasties made it hard for him to fight back. The first wolf-beasties bit into Deecee's leg, and fear crept into Deecee's heart as he felt the fight going against him.

Suddenly the wolf-beasties that had been fighting the old man bolted out of the kitchen with the old man in pursuit. They sprinted for the door out of the house, some whining in fear, all sporting cuts from the man's vicious attack. But as they poured into the hallway, they ran right into the pile of wolf-beasties on top of Deecee, and soon there was a jumble of fur, snarls of fury and confusion.

The old man ran out of the kitchen, looking woozy but triumphant. He saw Deecee at the bottom of the pack, and realized it was a courageous dog-beastie that had come to his aid, but that now needed his assistance. He ran at the wolf pack with yell and began stabbing them. The wolf-beasties were in full fear mode now, just wanting to escape. They all forgot about Deecee, for all they wanted now was to get out of the hallway and out the door of the house to safety.

Deecee smiled and his courage returned, for he knew the tide of battle had shifted once again. He bit savagely at the wolf-beastie's throat closest to him with relish. He clamped down hard and ripped at the wolf-beastie with all his might, and a large chunk of fur and skin came off in his mouth. Deecee tasted the blood, and it woke something deep inside him, a wild savageness that filled Deecee with a dark, warm pleasure. Something about it seemed right, as if he'd just went through some sort of rite of passage, and he had proved himself to his dog-beastie ancestors.

The other wolf-beasties finally were able to unscramble themselves. One by one they sprinted for the first room and ran out the door into the night. The man continued to stab at the ones who were left, until only the one on top of Deecee, the one who had first attacked him, remained. It lay still, bleeding from its wounds. The man stuck it in the heart with his knife, and soon it was dead.

Deecee climbed out from under the wolf-beastie and stood, his muzzle dripping blood, his heart pounding. Pride and pleasure filled him, and he felt at that moment that he could take on anything and win. His left front leg was weak from the earlier bite however, and he stood on it gingerly, testing his weight on it. It ached every time he tried to put it down, so he kept it bent, just barely touching the floor.

The old man sat down on the floor with relief and rested his back against the wall. He looked exhausted and about to pass out and his breathing was loud and ragged. But then he smiled at Deecee.

"Thank you, brave doggie. You saved us both. You are a mighty dog, brave and strong."

Deecee didn't know what the man said. He stood at a distance, still not sure if he should trust the man. Deecee was tired, and all he wanted was to lie down and sleep, but he didn't dare, not knowing what the man might do if he took his eyes off him.

The old man looked down at Deecee's leg and he frowned with concern. "Your leg is hurt! Oh, no! Come here, poor thing, and I'll fix it for you!"

Deecee didn't move, and the old man looked too tired to come to him. The old man touched the fur of the wolf-beastie.

"I bet you're hungry too. Let's cook and eat our foe, shall we? It's only fitting, since we beat him in battle."

The old man stood with an effort, using the wall to support himself. He winced and touched his leg where he'd been bitten. Then he smiled. He picked up the wolf-beastie by the fur and lifted it up. It was like a limp rag, its mouth open and its tongue lolling out.

"Give me a few minutes to cut this fellow up. Then we'll throw him on the fire and have a good little meal!"

The old man reached out and walked towards Deecee. Deecee didn't move, just watched the man carefully. The old man reached out and petted Deecee's head, stroking his fur. Deecee relaxed slightly.

"What a handsome and courageous fellow you are. I can tell you and I are going to be good friends." The old man walked back towards the kitchen with the wolf-beastie. Deecee watched him for a second, then slowly he limped after him.

Johnny stopped next to an old rusted pile of junk that looked like it had once been a bus, but a small one. It lay on its side, the windows all broken out. It had once been green, and there were still small patches of color, but most of it now was orange with rust, places in the metal shell so worn there were holes you could see through.

Johnny was close to the camp now. He could see groups of men and women sitting on the concrete, huddled together in the darkness. He heard a scrabbler cry, and someone cough. Here and there, fires burned with people circled around them, trying to get warm.

In front of Johnny, right on the other side of the van, two Nork soldiers stood guard. One held some strange white stick in his hand and he put it to his mouth often and then smoke would curl up around his face. The other one held a pack of strange paper squares with faces of strange people or dots in them in his hands, and he kept pulling some of them out and then shoving them back into the rest. Johnny tried to come up with a way to get past them to look for Deb.

"I don't know why we carry these stupid tommy-guns," one of the men said. "Most of 'em don't work. And we ain't got enough of them things that go inside to shoot. We all gotta carry knives and clubs anyway."

The other man laughed a guttural sound full of anger. "Only Moxie's and a few of the bigshots actually shoot. They're just for show, you know, 'just like these stupid outfits we gotta wear, and the stupid way we gotta talk."

"Do you really think the Boss is crazy, like they say? I heard he talks to that big lady statue in the water, calls her his mother."

"Hey, you be careful what you say about the Boss. People here have ears," the other man said. "He may be crazy, but he's the Big Cheese. And he's mad like a foxie, you know what I mean? Just when you think he's goofin', he gives you that look, and you know he's thinkin' real hard, and you're gonna get the worst of it."

"Yeah," the other man said, his voice trembling. "He loves to hear people scream, that's for sure. Just as long as he don't do it to you and me."

Johnny found a rock and he picked it up. Then he carefully threw it towards a dark corner far from him.

The men instantly reacted, pointing their tommy-guns in that direction.

"What was that?"

"Go check it out."

"I ain't going alone."

"Don't be a pansy."

"You go then."

They both looked at each other, lowered their tommy guns and took out their clubs. Slowly, they both walked towards the sound, eyes wide with fright. Johnny grinned and slowly tiptoed the other direction, past them into the camp.

He made sure to keep himself hidden from the groups of people by the fires. He saw a huge white box vehicle, the size of one of the buses. It had square windows on all sides with little curtains on them and a ladder on the back that led up to its top. A light shone from inside and he saw people moving around. Johnny thought it had to be where their leader had Deb, for it was better looking than all the other pieces of junk steel around, and looked warm and cozy.

Johnny had come up with a plan for what he was going to do if he found Deb. He would run with her into one of the dark tunnels ahead. They could easily escape in the darkness, even though Johnny had no idea what else waited in the tunnels and he had no light, so they would be stumbling around in the dark. It was a chance he would have to take, for at least they'd be away from the Nork army. The only question was, how to get her out? The white box vehicle was surrounded by prisoners and guards. He needed a distraction. How he wished he had one of Misterwizard's bombs!

Johnny gazed about and came up with an idea. Now he just needed some fire. He looked and looked and finally found just what he needed. A little distance away there was a fire with three people around it. And they all looked asleep!

He crept towards the fire, searching for a rag or something to burn. He spied an old skeleton in a rusted car. On top of the skeleton was an old, moldy blanket. Johnny grabbed it and stuffed it under his arm. Then he crept to the fire.

Slowly, he put one foot In front of the other and moved closer and closer, his heart beating wildly, his body tense. He looked at each of the people around the fire one by one, willing them to stay asleep. Two were older people, a gray-haired woman with a wrinkled face and an old man. Both snored softly, leaning on each other. The third person was a little girl with brown hair, about six seasons old. Her eyes were closed and she lay in the old woman's arms. Johnny smiled and a warmth filled his heart, for she reminded him of Sephie. He felt sorry for these people. Who knew what horrible fate the Nork army planned for them? Johnny vowed that he wouldn't give up trying to free them, even after he found Deb.

Looking at the couple, and the little girl caused a flood of home-sickness to wash over Johnny. He thought of how long it had been since he and his friends were with their own families. They had meant to take just a short trip, but it had turned out to be much longer than they expected, and full of dangerous adventures.

Suddenly a woman's voice broke the silence behind him, making him jump. Fortunately, she spoke in a soft, quiet voice, as if not wanting to attract attention.

"Who is that, sneaking around our campfire?

Johnny was caught! But for some strange reason, he didn't feel scared or worried, for he instantly recognized the voice. He turned and smiled. There standing behind him was Restaria!

CHAPTER 6

The Red Eye rose over the crumbling ruins in the distance, beginning a new day, as Clancy and his men wearily shuffled up to the camp from the concrete wall on the right. They were bloody and tired, having fought and killed a lion-beastie and chased down three deer-beasties, killing them and cutting them up into pieces. Some of the men carried sections of lion-beastie and deer-beastie meat on their shoulders. The meat was raw and red and blood dripped on their dirty white cloth tunics and green sashes, all the way down to their green skirts and onto their boots, but they didn't care. They were used to being dirty and covered with blood, and always smelled badly, never really being fond of baths.

Clancy was the only one not holding a piece of meat. His hatchet rested on his shoulder, blood dripping from it on the ground. "Moxie twill dance a merry tune when he sees what we brought back."

"Aye," said Gavin. "He'll prance about like a wee

kitten waiting for his saucer of milk."

"You're not really going to give them our meat, are ya Clancy?" Alasdair, Clancy's second in command, a strong man with short black hair, a big, pointed nose and a sharp chin asked. "There's not enough for us and that whole horde down there."

"Aye. We have three deer, and a lion. We'll give them the lion meat and one of the deer," Clancy said, turning and smiling at his men, "But we'll keep the rest for ourselves. You see lads, I have a fancy for that pretty lass Moxie has latched onto. Tomorrow when we enter one of those tunnels ahead, I want that Nork fool to have no suspicions about me. For I'm going to snatch her for me bride. Then who knows, our Moxie might just have a wee accident in the dark."

His men laughed, but one named Finn frowned with concern. "Clancy, I never seen ya take to a lass this way. Are you sure the long trip has not addled your brains? You might start a war with the Nork king, all over a bit of lass."

"'Tis true, I am not one to let a woman cause me sway as a rule, but this one tis special. An angel with white hair and a fire inside. She'll make a bonny queen someday, for me a king."

Finn spoke again. "Isn't she already married to this Johnny character?"

"Twasn not done in a ceremony with the Clan, so it don't mean a thing. And one day, when I separate this Johnny from his head, then t'wont matter anyhow."

Gavin laughed. "And what if she doesn't want to

be yer bride?"

Alasdair chuckled. "When has anyone ever worried about what a lass thinks?" Alastair adjusted the leg of deer-beastie on his shoulder. "But if you kill Moxie, even in the tunnel, the others will see. Won't you be declarin' war?"

"Not if I do it right," Clancy said. "If he falls over an old junker and hits his head, who's to say someone helped him along?"

Gavin stroked his beard and said, "We could simply fight them out in the open. The people of Pelpia would surely lend us a hand."

"But there's only three hundred of them, none armed, only twenty of us and over five hundred Nork men," Gavin said.

Alasdair turned to him. "That's what the dark is for, laddie. A way to even the odds. I'll tend to Moxie. If ye find a way to dispatch one of the others quietly, don't wait for an invitation."

They all nodded with grim smiles.

"I for one am itching for another good fight," Alasdair said. "We have a whole city of mates back home, hundreds and hundreds. It's time we deposed this king and put you in his place, Clancy. Before their mad king decides he doesn't like us anymore and declares war on us."

"Aye," Clancy said. "Our time as allies of the mad king be numbered already. Last time I was in his presence, he spoke of us givin' him a tribute of pretty lasses. We've had just about enough of him and his ways."

"Enough jabbering, let's get going," Finn said. "This deer-beastie leg is getting a wee bit heavy, and I'm wanting to get it roasted."

They all laughed.

"On, lads!" Clancy said. "Tomorrow is going to be a day to remember, for it's the day of war and bloodshed, and the day I take me a fine-looking bride."

They started down the hill back to the concrete road below where the Nork army and their prisoners waited.

Behind them, a strange creature sat on the ledge of a building, high up on the third floor. The creature had huge white wings and looked like a man. It had been listening to all they said. Now it flapped its wings and flew away, just like a bird-beastie.

Super and Lightpole rode on as the Red Eye began to slip down the sky. Then Super saw Washington Deecee ahead! A rush of emotion flowed through her, and she almost sobbed. Her throat felt tight, and she felt all weepy inside. She didn't realize how happy she was going to be to see home again. Images of the joy she was going to feel when she held her mother and father again, and hugging Misterwizard, filled her mind with joy. She only wished her friends were there with her, that they were all home. She wished they'd never left now, for who knew if they'd ever all return safely now.

"Is that your city ahead?" Lightpole asked.

Super couldn't respond because there was a lump in her throat, so she just nodded.

"It is not that far away from our city, is it?"

Finally Super found her voice, and full of emotion she said, "Once this is all over, we'll become one large people."

Lightpole smiled with pleasure and Super smiled too.

"I'd like that," Lightpole yelled.

They rode past houses and broken buildings. Super knew it wouldn't be long until they reached New Sanctuary. Excitement bubbled up inside her and she rehearsed what she was going to say to explain to Misterwizard and the Tribe what was going on. The thought crossed her mind that they might not be willing to help, but she dismissed it. How could they not want to help possible friends and allies? That's what they were trying to do, wasn't it, make new friends and help gather all the land together as a people under 'mocracy again? That's what Misterwizard had always said. They had to help, or they might as well build a wall and plan on being all alone, forever.

They passed by places familiar to Super. She saw the entrance to the underground, now covered in rubble and stone, where Johnny and their tribe had trapped Ripper and the gangers and sealed their doom. Somewhere down in that darkness, the giant robots lay in the water, along with Ripper and his gang. Memories flooded back, of her and Deb's adventures down in the dark with the wolf-beastie. And those horrible other creatures that attacked! She almost imagined, as she gazed at the entrance, that she saw one of those creatures staring at her from the rocks. The past events now seemed distant, as if they were only an exciting dream she made up.

Once again, she felt emotions flood through her, threatening to make her cry. She remembered all the dangers her and her friends had faced. She wondered when she would see Johnny and her friends again. When would she see Starbucks, the man she loved?

She forced herself to stop thinking about it, for it would only lead her to go waksy with worry. She had to concentrate on what she was doing, and hold on to the faith that once again, they would find a way to win and be united once more.

Ahead she saw the wall of cars that made up their new home. They had arrived! She pointed at it.

"Is that your home?" Lightpole yelled. "Impressive structure you've built."

They had reached it sooner than Super expected, for it looked like the Tribe had expanded their territory. Now the structure included a huge part of the city. The Tribe been busy while she was gone. Super felt happy, for it meant that things must be going well. She couldn't wait to tell Misterwizard all about their adventures!

She drove up to the wall and saw in some places, it was now made of rocks and bricks. It rose high in the air, at least twenty feet, and she wondered how she was going to get inside.

"Where's the entrance?" Lightpole said, and it irritated her, for she realized it seemed like he was always saying just what she was thinking.

She didn't have an answer, so she just kept driving next to the wall. It was easy to do, for it looked like the Tribe had cleared out the area in front of the wall as well. Some of the buildings near the wall had even been leveled. Super knew this was so the Tribe could see enemies approaching in all directions. Excitement filled her as she thought how different New Sanctuary must look now too.

She saw someone at the top of the wall, a man walking. He held a rifle in his hands and looked relaxed, at least until he saw her. He jerked as if from a half-sleep, pointing his gun in Super's direction and opened his eyes wide with excitement and alarm. Another man ran up too and they both pointed their guns at Super and Lightpole and peered down at her. They scowled with suspicion, ready to do their duty and protect New Sanctuary.

The men didn't seem to recognize Super. She knew someone would soon. She grinned, thinking about what a ruckus she was going to make when they all realized she was back. Another lump rose in her throat and once again she had to fight down the emotions, scolding herself and calling herself a scrabbler.

She rode on, growing annoyed there was no gate. How were people supposed to get inside?

Suddenly she heard an all too familiar screeching

behind her. Both her and Lightpole turned and looked. There behind them was a Krakn!

It was a huge one too, with red eyes, standing almost half as tall as the wall next to it. It ran fast, coming after them! It must have followed them from Ballmor. Super knew she had to find the gate and get inside, or they would be the creature's snack!

"A monster! Hurry up before it catches us!"

I know, thought Super, irritated, that once again, Lightpole was reading her thoughts.

She sped up, and her joy of the last minute was replaced by anxiousness. To die this close to home would be the worst thing ever, right in the shadow of New Sanctuary, only a short distance away from her family. She didn't dare stop or even slow down, for it was right behind them.

Yells drifted down from the top of the wall. The men had seen it too. She didn't dare take time to look, but then she heard gunfire. The men were shooting at the monster! Hopefully that would make it break off its pursuit at least or slow it down.

"Good! They are shooting at it!" Lightpole said.

Super grinned. She was beginning to like his mind reading, it was funny.

Then with relief she saw the gate ahead! A huge metal gate with iron bars and impressive looking strange metal beasts on either side. They looked like lion-beasties but with wings, and they were golden. Super had never seen anything so beautiful. New Sanctuary was sure getting fancy!

"The gate! Hurry!" Lightpole said.

"No duh," Super said, repeating something she heard Johnny's father, Foodcourt say one time.

They reached the gate and stopped. Super turned to look, frightened by what she'd see. Lightpole looked too, and they both peered down the wall with dark expressions.

The Kraken had stopped chasing them! It was scaling the wall! Its long tentacles snaked over the bricks, stone and old cars, clinging to them like a giant spider-beastie. Its tentacles curled into the cars, finding a grip on the door frames and windows. The men, who had followed Super's path on top of the wall, turned their guns at the Krakn and shot at it frantically. Super knew how fast the Krakn was, and she felt nervous that it would reach the top soon. She tried to think what to do. What would Johnny do? She scowled, and turned back towards the monster. She took off in a roar.

"You're going to try and make it chase us?" Lightpole said. "But we just escaped!"

"Hang on!" Super yelled, grinning darkly at how once again, he'd read her mind.

"You're not Johnny, you know!" Lightpole yelled, which made Super irritated that once again he'd read her mind, and now was insulting her.

"Shut up for once!" She yelled. "Hey monster!"

The Kraken turned and saw her, and its ragged mouth opened showing yellow fangs. Red eyes narrowed with hatred and hunger. The men shot at it again and again, and Super watched the bullets hit it in the head and on its tentacles. It jerked with each hit, and she felt encouraged, thinking the men might actually take it down.

Suddenly the Krakn leapt in the air! As Super, Lightpole and the men watched it flew up and over the wall and into New Sanctuary!

"It's inside!" Lightpole said.

Super turned the Harley around and sped back to the gate. From inside, she could hear yelling and more gunshots. Her heart raced with excitement, as once again she felt the thrill of battle. She had to admit, she was becoming addicted to it.

She grinned and stopped at the gate. She beeped the Harley's horn as she and Lightpole looked up at the massive gate. On either side of them, the golden lion-beasties with wings stood guard, making Super a little nervous.

"Hey!" Super honked the horn again. "It's me! I'm back! Anybody care?"

"They're too busy fighting the monster!" Lightpole said, staring at the gate.

Super could tell he was probably right. She heard the Krakn screech and more shouting.

Then she heard a loud explosion!

"One of Misterwizard's bombs!" She said, and the thought of seeing him made her feel soft inside again. Good old Misterwizard, always ready with his amazing tricks to win a battle.

Suddenly there was silence. Then a loud cheer broke out inside. They'd beaten it! And Super was missing out!

She honked the horn again in irritation and again roared her engine!

"Hey! Dum-dums! Open this stupid gate! Misterwizard! Open Sesame!"

And then, as if she had said the magical word, the gate opened.

Super felt another rush of feeling, and she bit her lip so she wouldn't cry. She was home!

"We're back at your home!" Lightpole said cheerily.

Super was too happy to even feel annoyed. She just nodded, for she couldn't speak. Then she drove the Harley into Sanctuary, as the Red Eye began to rise over the distant hills.

CHAPTER 7

Johnny, standing with the fire to his back, stood in the shadows. As soon as he walked towards Restaria and she recognized him, a smile of joy spread all over her face.

"Johnny Apocalypse!" She whispered. She walked up to him and to his surprise, put her arms around him and gave him a big hug. Warm emotion flooded through him, and he hugged her back with feeling.

"You have come to rescue us!"

Johnny frowned, wishing it was true. "I'm sorry, Restaria, for now, there's only me."

Restaria frowned, disappointed, but then she smiled with understanding. "You're here to rescue your fair maiden."

Johnny smiled grimly. "I promise you my tribe is going to rescue your people as soon as we can. Super and Starbucks are hurrying to tell them about your capture, and then they'll come. Together, will set you free. Meanwhile…"

Restaria put a hand on Johnny's arm. "You're going to rescue Deb. I don't blame you."

Restaria led Johnny over to the fire. The others there looked up at them as they approached. A few of them recognized him and pointed.

"Johnny! He's come to save us!"

The little girl yelled "yay" and her mother shushed her. "Not so loud!"

Restaria found an old cloak and wrapped it around Johnny. "Sit down, and act like you're one of us."

Johnny did as he was told. "Is Deb in that white box over there?" Johnny pointed.

Restaria nodded. "Yes, she's in there with their leader, Moxie. I'm afraid he wants to keep her."

This made Johnny's blood boil, and he made fists with his hands. An even stronger sense of urgency filled him to rescue Deb.

"But if you go in there, you'll surely be captured."

Johnny knew she was right. He noticed with dismay the Red Eye was peeking over the distant hills. Daylight was coming, and he would be totally exposed. He was running out of time!

Suddenly there was the sound of excited voices coming from the side of the camp far away. People ran towards the commotion, smiling with happiness. Restaria and Johnny looked.

"It's those rough-looking men, the ones with the shaggy cloaks and skirts," Restaria said. "They call themselves the 'Clan'. They've brought food back for the camp!"

As Johnny watched with pleasure, Moxie and his men came out of the white box and walked towards the commotion.

This was Johnny's chance! Without another thought, he jumped up, threw off the cloak and ran to the box. Restaria watched him anxiously, alternating from looking at him to looking at Moxie and his men.

Johnny snuck to the door of the white box-like car and knelt down beside it.

Restaria took one more glance at Moxie and the crowd then ran to the side of the box-like car too.

"Hurry, Johnny!" She whispered. "I'll try to buy you some time!"

Johnny smiled at her and nodded. Then he snuck inside. Restaria stood up and joined the throng by the Clan.

Inside, Johnny searched frantically for Deb. There seemed to be a row of cabinets on either side and two chairs near the front where a set of windows looked out. In the opposite direction there seemed to be a small room that held a bed.

"Deb!" He whispered urgently. "Are you here?"

"Johnny?"

Johnny's heart melted with joy at hearing the voice of the girl he loved. Tears came to his eyes and he felt his insides turn to goo, just like they always did around Little Debbie. He peered down the hallway towards the sound, which came from the end of the box where the bed was. Johnny ran down the narrow corridor.

Then he saw her. She lay on a bed surrounded by pillows, leaning against the wall. Her long blond hair fell over her shoulders, her soft, sculptured face was half covered in shadow and her intense blue eyes peered out of the darkness like two shining marbles.

Johnny felt such immense relief in seeing she wasn't hurt. He didn't care if he did get caught, just getting to see Deb again, to hear her soft voice was worth anything. She lay on a bed surrounded by blankets. Her hands were tied with a rope to a ring set in the wall.

Johnny rushed over to her and climbed onto the bed next to her. They grinned at each other in a silly way, both so excited to see the other again. Johnny hugged her and held her close. Her long, blond hair fell on his shoulder and he breathed in her lovely aroma. He closed his eyes and just held her, so full of joy for a moment he couldn't move.

Then Johnny kissed her, hard and long, the touch of her lips the most wonderful thing he could ever remember. She kissed him back and sobbed, tears in her eyes.

"Oh, Johnny!" She gushed, and they pressed their cheeks together. "I missed you so much! Don't ever leave me again!"

"Never!" Johnny said, pulling her closer, holding her.

But then Deb pulled away and looked angry,

even though tears still stained her cheeks. "What are you doing here? You're going to get caught!"

"Rescuing you, Silly!" Johnny said.

He pulled out his sword and quickly cut the ropes.

"There's no way you're going to get me out of here! You're just going to be killed!"

"Don't talk so much. Run!"

Johnny helped her off the bed and they dashed for the door. Then they heard voices outside! It was Moxie.

They stood silently, listening. They heard Restaria talking to Moxie in an irritated voice, saying something about getting more food for her people. He heard her say something about some of her people with wounds.

Then she said, "Come with me, I'll show you!"

She was leading him away! This was their chance.

Johnny slowly opened the door and peeked out. No one was in front of the white box. He turned to Deb.

"Follow me as fast as you can. We only have a few seconds!"

She nodded. Together they leapt out of the box-like vehicle. Johnny saw the tunnels in the distance. He grabbed Deb's hand and together they ran through the morning light as the Red Eye rose in full circle and bathed the world in morning heat.

They weaved around old junk cars and buses, past prisoners from Pelpia huddled around campfires. They ran past a Nork guard who was half asleep. He opened his eyes just in time to see them disappear behind a car. The man turned in a sleepy stupor towards the middle of camp.

"Hey, Boss! Hey Boss!"

The guard took one more look at Johnny and Deb then ran back in a sleepy stumble towards where Moxie was still talking to Restaria.

Johnny and Deb looked ahead, and it seemed like the tunnels were miles away. Deb looked back and more guards were watching them and pointing.

"Run!" Johnny yelled, and they ran as fast as they could. Deb was not as strong as Johnny, and began to grow tired. Johnny stopped, picked her up and kept running.

There were three tunnels. Johnny decided to take the one on the right, the closest one to the camp, hoping they wouldn't see which one they entered. They reached the entrance. Johnny set Deb down. They gazed into the dark mouth, trying to see what was beyond it.

"Are you sure it's safe?" Deb said.

"Just like going up the stairs to Misterwizard's room," Johnny said, though he knew neither of them thought so. "Do you want to turn back?"

Deb put her hand in Johnny's. "I told you, wherever Johnny goes…"

Johnny grinned. Together they ran into the dark, cool tunnel, to face whatever waited inside.

Starbucks and his new friend Rumpelstiltskin entered the large stone building with the lions out front and found themselves in a small room with white stone walls, floors and benches against the walls. In front of them, a large curved archway led to a much larger room ahead. The larger room occupied most of the building.

The small room they were in was only ten feet square. On the walls to the left and right, moldy drapes hung down next to old, faded paintings. An old suit of armor stood in one corner. Starbucks had only seen armor once before in Misterwizard's castle, and it made him nervous. It felt like there must be someone inside it who was going to clank towards them, sword raised, at any moment.

From the room ahead they heard children laughing, a lot of them. Rumpelstiltskin smiled at the sound and rushed into the next room. Starbucks followed a little more slowly, looking around at all the strange surroundings.

As Starbucks entered, he gazed about the room, for he'd never seen anything like it. The room was a big circle, with another doorway at the far end. The huge open space in the middle was full of wooden tables and chairs, some broken and in pieces but others still standing, though covered with dust. At the back of the room, a long wooden counter seemed to go from one end of the room to the other.

But it was the walls that amazed Starbucks. Every one of them was full of shelves, and the shelves were full of old, dusty and moldy blobs of what looked like old books. Some of the paper blobs were green and wet, but other blobs looked intact, and Starbucks realized this must be where people came to read them. The walls went up as far as he could see, and each row of shelves had its own walkway in front of it. Circular stairs at the back of the room led to each walkway.

A large group of scrabblers sat in the middle of the room on the floor. It was their voices Starbucks heard from outside. They played with toys, laughed and talked, just as if there was no danger and it was just another fun day.

"Wow, look at this place, Rumple," Starbucks said, using the new name he'd made up for the old man.

"Look at the little scrabblers!" Rumple said. "How nice!"

Starbucks smiled and walked towards the scrabblers. Rumple followed. Then they stopped for both felt hard, cold steel poke them in the ribs.

"Hold it right there, creepies!"

Starbucks turned to see who was holding the knife on him. It was Redeye!

Another scrabbler held a knife to Rumple and he was younger, only eight seasons. He was a white boy, and looked almost comical as he tried to look tough and mean, for he couldn't have been more than three feet tall and wasn't in any way scary. He looked more scared than Starbucks and Rumple.

"Get on your knees now, before we cut you into little pieces!" the leader said.

As Starbucks watched, more scrabblers approached, mostly older ones, holding spears and clubs they had made. Starbucks realized the older scrabblers were the guards, while all the young ones continued to play.

Starbucks knelt, wanting to gain the young boy's confidence and not make an enemy out of him.

"Hello, young man," Rumple said, smiling at the boy holding the knife on him. "My, that's a nice little knife you have there. You're mighty brave!"

"Tell the oldster to kneel down, or we cut him!" The other boy said.

"Rumple, you better do what they say."

"Oh! Okay!" Rumple said, and with effort he managed to get to his knees. "Though someone may have to help me up again!"

Starbucks looked at the boy in front of him.

"Redeye, don't you remember me?" Starbucks asked. "I was with Johnny Apocalypse. We talked to you."

Redeye relaxed, grinned and lowered the knife a little. "Oh yeah. I remember you now."

Redeye turned to the other boy. "They're all right." The other boy reluctantly nodded and lowered his knife. The other ones with spears and clubs looked disappointed and lowered theirs too.

"I'm here to find out if you know any more about Super and Lightpole. Did you see where they went?"

"Of course, I can!" Redeye said, puffing himself up. Didn't I tell you I was in charge?"

"Well, where?" Starbucks said, wrinkling his brow in impatience."

Redeye pointed to the South. "I was outside looking for food, and I saw her and Lightpole get on a strange metal thing with two round circles." Redeye pointed in the south direction. "Then they drove off that way."

"Why would she take him back to Ballmor? That's full of monsters."

Then Starbucks understood. "She's going to get help from our tribe!" Starbucks' eyes opened wide with excitement. "That means she's safe, at least from the Nork army. But she's heading right back past the Krakn!"

Starbucks turned to hurry back out of the building.

"Where are you going?" Rumple asked him.

Starbucks looked torn. "I have to go find her and make sure she's okay. But I really should be going to help Johnny."

"How will you know which to do?" Redeye asked.

"I won't. I'm going to go find Super. Sorry, Johnny, but for now, you're on your own. Why do we always have to get split up? It's so annoying!"

Starbucks turned to leave again, but Rumple grabbed his arm.

"Let me come with you, help you."

Starbucks shook his head. "I appreciate the thought, Rumple, but I'm afraid you'd only slow me down. Why don't you stay here and help protect these scrabblers until I get back?"

"Hey!" Redeye said, his eyes flashing, taking a step towards Starbucks threateningly. "Super left me in charge!"

Starbucks grinned. He put a hand on Redeye's shoulder. "You are! You've already proved how brave you are. But every leader can use a sidekick."

Starbucks looked at Rumple who laughed silently. Rumple looked at Redeye. "You give the orders, commander!"

Redeye looked even more pleased. He turned to Starbucks.

"I hope you find her and make sure she's all right. She's beautiful. One day, her and I will be married."

"Sorry, Redeye," Starbucks said, his eyes laughing. "She's already spoken for. By me."

Starbucks and Rumple laughed. The scrabblers did too, but Redeye frowned and looked embarrassed.

"I know she really liked you, Redeye, and if I hadn't gotten her first, you'd have been her choice, I'm sure of it."

Redeye looked a little better, but still disappointed.

Starbucks turned and hurried away. "We'll be back soon Redeye, with a whole army to help you get your people back."

Rumple waved at him. "Godspeed, fellow warrior. May the sun always be at your back, and... I don't remember the rest!"

CHAPTER 8

Monsta stared out at the street of Nork from the broken window of an old store, watching the strange people wander by. It was night and the yellow eye was high in the sky, but that didn't stop the people from wandering about, just like it was daytime. Some wore the strange clothes like the soldiers did, with the bowl-type hats and the suits. Some of the women wore round hats with feathers and outfits with dresses. Many of the Norkers were clothed in only rags, however, dirty clothes that were threadbare.

There were so many of them! Monsta had never seen so many people in one place before, and it made him nervous. When he was with Ripper and the Doomsday Prophecy in Pill-a-delpia, the whole city was empty with only a few crazies or widlies hiding in the old buildings. Monsta and his gang owned the city, and it was theirs to explore and plunder, at least until Johnny came along. Here, the people jostled each other just to pass on the sidewalks, and they all looked unfriendly. It made Monsta itch to be back home, back with his gang, when things were so much better.

The room Monsta hid in was full of metal shelves along the walls and in the middle of the room, making aisles between them. On the shelves sat colorful bottles of all shapes and sizes, all full of some kind of liquid. The liquid didn't look rotten, but the bottles were all old and dusty, and Monsta didn't dare open any of them, even though he was very thirsty.

In some places, rotted food and rotted paper objects sat on the shelves as well. On one side of the room there was a wall of tall cabinets with glass, also filled with bottles, rotted food and paper. On the other side of the room a counter stood just in front of the wall. Behind it a shelf held a square cabinet full of little paper boxes. Monsta had seen Ripper with one of those paper boxes before, and from it, Ripper had taken out a thin white tube which he stuck in his mouth. Then he took fire and lit the tube, and smoke came from it. It had always mystified Monsta, and made Ripper seem almost magical, like Misterwizard. Now seeing the paper boxes everywhere kind of disappointed Monsta, lowering his view of Ripper which he didn't like.

Monsta had been in places like this before. The food, if you could find any that hadn't turned to dust long ago, was usually so full of green stuff that if you tried to eat it you would get sick. Once in a while, you found something that was so well wrapped or made of such hard stuff that it was still edible, but even that usually didn't have much taste anymore.

Monsta had run inside this building, his heart

pounding in his chest, fear crawling up and down his spine like a spider-beastie, and he was glad he made it inside alive. The creatures that had attacked came so suddenly, and then the people of Nork were so strange, Monsta was still reeling, trying to come to grips with what had happened.

He had expected to have a great time in Nork, now that he was free and could do whatever he wanted. He was big, huge in fact, and strong, not afraid of anything, or so he thought. Monsta expected to loot and steal and maybe even find a gang to join in the new city. What he didn't expect to feel was the strange, creeping fear that gripped his insides, hiding in a building, afraid to go out.

For the people of Nork were wild, or plain waksy. They walked the streets with strange expressions, looking like hunted animals. They talked to themselves constantly, even arguing and yelling for no apparent reason. And every one of them carried some kind of weapon, a club or a sharp stick, or a piece of sharpened glass. They all needed it too, for, fights would suddenly break out amongst them, and they would attack each other. A crowd would gather, everyone yelling and shaking their fists. The fight would continue until one finally had enough and ran off bleeding or was killed. Then the creepiest thing of all would happen. The crowd would jump on the body, stealing the dead person's clothes or belongings, and then a group would hoist the body in the air and carry it off. Monsta didn't want to think what they were planning to do with it.

Even the little scrabblers were mean and tough and looked like wild beasties, their faces dirty and savage. Some people seemed just plain waksy, for they lay in the middle of the street as others walked around them or clung to the poles with the glass domes at the top and yelled down at the others, shaking their fists.

Everywhere on each block there were big pictures of paper. They all showed the same thing, a man and a woman dressed in odd clothes, the man with the pinstripe suit and hat with the brim, and the lady in a red dress and top with the funny bobbed hat on her head. Monsta figured they were how the king told everybody to dress, and some of the people seemed to try and look like the picture, but most didn't seem to bother.

Monsta ran inside because everyone in the crowd stared at him as he passed. He could tell they saw he was a stranger, and Monsta wasn't sure if that meant he was the next one to be attacked.

Once hiding in the shadows, Monsta saw one of the guards with a tommy gun yell at a boy scrabbler who was only six seasons. Instead of being scared, the scrabbler kicked the guy, hard, again and again. Monsta could tell the guard didn't expect that, and he started getting scared. Soon a crowd gathered, twenty people or more. The guard tried to calm the kid down, but the kid kept kicking him and then bit onto his leg. The guard pointed his gun at the scrabbler, which was a bad mistake. The crowd roared and rushed the guy. It turned out his gun didn't even work, for he didn't even try to fire it, he just tried to beat the crowd back. The crowd swarmed over the guy so Monsta couldn't even see him. When they finally backed off, the guard lay on the ground, a bloody mess, dead. The crowd all smiled at the scrabbler, and it moved towards the guard and knelt down. The crowd surrounded the guard and the scrabbler and watched, so Monsta couldn't see what happened, but then a few minutes later, the scrabbler came out, his fingers and face covered with blood. That was when Monsta decided he'd better hide, and fast. The king of Nork didn't seem to have his people under very good control, and it looked like order was just barely being maintained.

Now, Monsta snuck a glance out the window again. So far, the people outside walking by hadn't noticed him. Then it happened again. The people all looked up at the sky. Monsta knew what was coming. Sure enough, an explosion erupted on the street, filling the night with orange flames and a bright orange and red glow. The people screamed and ran as more fireballs filled the night.

As he watched, more slim, white men climbed down halfway up the buildings, armed with bows and arrows. They shot at the fleeing people. Then he saw strange creatures with large white wings flying in the sky!

"Man," Monsta whispered to himself in awe. "Nork is a waksy place."

Out on the street, one of the Nork guards stepped out with a tommy gun. As Monsta watched with dark glee, shot at one of the attackers on the vines. The bullets found their mark, and the men fell, crashing to the ground. A cheer went up from the hidden crowd. But then one of the strange flying creatures swooped down and grabbed the guard, carrying him out of sight as the guard screamed. His gun fell from his hands and hit the ground with a rattle. A few seconds later, the guard's body came crashing down from the sky, splattering on the hard concrete.

Monsta shook his head, wondering if he was so tired and hungry, he was seeing things. It was just some giant bird-beastie, grabbing the guard for food, it must have been. After all, he'd seen bird-beasties, big ones, swoop down and grab dog-beasties before.

A hiss came from somewhere in the darkness behind Monsta, and his heart skipped a beat. He was getting tired of all the weird things happening and the constant action, and even though he was big and tough, his courage was almost at an end. He put on a look of terror and turned around slowly, the whites of his eyes showing bright in the darkness with fear.

There on the floor, crouched down like a wild beastie was just a little girl scrabbler. Her teeth showed in a snarl, and she stared at him, her hands curled into claws. Now Monsta had seen everything!

A little scrabbler beastie! Monsta burst into giddy laughter, all the tension and tiredness of the last few days making him loopy. A little tough scrabbler girl who couldn't have been more than eight seasons old! He'd better watch out for her! He laughed and laughed, not even stopping as she crawled towards him on all fours like she was a cat-beastie.

When she was only five feet away, he stopped laughing to catch his breath.

"Hi little scrabbler. You're a tough one for sure! But you ain't got all the people outside to help you. Some day you can join the Doomsday Prophecy, would you like that?"

The little scrabbler girl stopped and stared at him, just like a wild beastie, as if she had been raised by beasties. She was thin and wiry, with a cute face all covered with dirt and grim. Her blue eyes peered at him, just like a cat-beastie would.

A mean thought entered Monsta's head: How nice it would be to grab this little scrabbler, choke the life out of her and throw her against the wall. He'd show her who he was messing with and get the frustration and fear of the last few days out at the same time. Maybe, it would be a message for the wasky Norkers not to mess with Monsta, and once they learned that, he could walk around town without any fear.

Monsta motioned to the girl. "Come here. Just a little closer." *Just close enough that I can wring your little neck*, he thought.

Suddenly the girl leapt towards him, so fast and with such fierceness that it took Monsta totally by surprise. He was frozen into immobility as she clamped her teeth onto his leg and bit down hard!

"Aaah!" Monsta yelled, as pain shot up his leg. The leg instantly started to go numb and fear filled Monsta, for she bit down viciously and tore back and forth, trying to rip a chunk out of him.

He shook his leg violently and tried to grab her, but she had a grip on him like iron. Monsta felt desperate as he began to get woozy.

"Let go!" He screamed and made fists to beat her to death.

Then he looked up to see eyes staring at him from the darkness on either side of the metal racks. Five, six, seven, ten sets of eyes. As he fought with the girl, the owners of the eyes crept into view. It was a whole pack of beastie scrabblers! They were all dirty and in rags, and all crawled on all fours towards him, like monstrous spider-beasties.

Finally kicking, punching and screaming, Monsta was able to make the little monster let go. He kicked her way, where she rolled and then hopped up on all fours again, her mouth dripping Monsta's blood.

"You people are not just waksy, you're freaks!" Monsta yelled. He tried to put weight on his leg but it felt like it was going to collapse under him.

Terror filled Monsta as he stumbled desperately towards the door of the building, half sobbing, half yelling. The little scrabblers crawled along the floor towards him. The little girl scrabbler leapt up onto the counter just like a dog-beastie. And then she snarled! She raised her head in the air and howled, and all the other scrabblers snarled back.

Monsta looked back with wide eyes full of terror as he hobbled towards the door, hoping he would make it before the mob of scrabbler-freaks could reach him and all attack. Even outside had to be better than this.

Monsta stumbled out the door in immense relief and slammed the door. Inside, he saw the scrabblers peering at him through the window, looking like a pack of wild dog-beasties. Sobbing in fear and pain, Monsta limped down the street as fast as he could. Each step with his bad leg shot a spasm of pain up it, and the leg threatened to fold.

How he hated Nork! Johnny or no Johnny, he was getting out of this place as fast as he could. Let Johnny come here and get eaten. He was escaping, before someone, or something ate him alive.

Deecee sat in the corner of the first room with the couch and tables and watched the man as he knelt over the fireplace. The room was warm and cheery, and now had the pleasant smell of cooked meat. The old man had dressed and wrapped Deecee's leg wound and, though it throbbed, it felt better.

Deecee's mouth watered and he licked his lips, anticipating the tasty meal he was about to enjoy. The man had placed a metal stick over the fire, and the remains of the wolf-beastie was skewered on it. Quite happiness filled Deecee like a warm blanket, and a sense of pride, for he and the man had beaten their foes and now feasted on one. At that moment, Deecee felt like the king of the wolf-beasties, and he could fight and kill anything. He had momentarily forgotten all about his former master, and in the back of his mind, he toyed with the idea that this was where he belonged, with this lonely man who needed him.

The man smiled at Deecee, and his eyes twinkled. "A little sweet revenge for dinner, my fine furry friend. To the victor goes the meat. We eat well tonight."

Deecee laid down on the couch and put his head on his paws. His eye began to close, despite his hunger, for the warmth and the wonderful smells were like a sleeping potion. His pointed black ears still stood straight up however, for part of him always remained alert, listening for any danger.

The old man took a knife and cut a piece of the wolf-beastie off. He bit it to see if the meat was ready. Then he gazed at Deecee, enjoying the sight of the beautiful dog who had found its way into his home.

"You and I are going to have a fine life, my friend. I know of a big house on a hill. It has two floors with nice, big bedrooms and a huge fireplace. It was once owned by someone very important. Once I get enough supplies, we'll go there and live and leave this waksy city with all its dangers behind." The old man looked content, and his eyes were moist. "We'll have a good life, living out our years in peace. Doesn't that sound nice?"

Deecee didn't know what the man was saying, only that his voice was soothing and friendly. Deecee thought about how he would make a good master. The old man seemed gentle and kind, and Deecee was sure he would feed him well.

Just as if reading Deecee's mind, the man cut off a chunk of meat and brought it over to Deecee. As soon as the meat grew close, Deecee smelt it, and his eyes opened wide. The man held the meat in front of Deecee, and Deecee gingerly grabbed it. He gobbled it up greedily, but then had to spit it out for a second, for it was hot. After waiting a few seconds, Deecee tried again, and this time he was able to chew and swallow the tasty morsel. It was the best tasting thing Deecee could ever remember, fresh and delicious. Instantly strength began to flow back into Deecee's insides, as his body reacted to getting the food he needed. Deecee finished the piece and licked his lips, waiting patiently for another piece.

The old man rotated the wolf-beastie over the fire and little bits of grease dripped from it. They hissed and spattered when they hit the fire, but the sound was somehow pleasant to Deecee, sounding like good food cooking.

The old man cut larger pieces off the carcass and placed them on a wooden plate. As he did, he studied Deecee, enjoying Deecee's handsome body and soft fur. "You are a fine dog-beastie. A husky, they used to call you, I think. I've seen pictures of dog-beasties like you, in old magazines. In the pictures they were up in a place where the ground was all white, and there were many of them all trussed up in some kind of harness. They stood in front of a flat metal thing that I think they were supposed to pull along. It was a very strange picture, with people wearing beastie fur and strange round wooden shoes."

Deecee's eyes began to close, the pleasant droning of the man's voice a lullaby. Somewhere an open or broken window let in a gentle breeze that fought with the warmth and eventually lost.

"My name is Harrald. That's what mommy and daddy called me. They left to get food when I was just a scrabbler, and never came back again. I was only ten cycles then, and had to take care of myself. I've been alone so long. No one to talk to. I almost forgot how. Oh, every once in a while, I'll find someone else, but they don't stay long, or they only want to fight." Harrald looked at Deecee. "Not that I mind talking to you, you understand. But another person would be nice."

Harrald dropped another piece of meat in front of Deecee, which instantly woke Deecee up. Deecee was wiser this time, and he licked it before biting to make sure it wasn't too hot. Then he wolfed it down and laid his head back on his paws and closed his eyes.

Something seemed to happen to Harrald, for he started making strange sad sounds and water came from his eyes. Deecee looked up, curious, wondering if it meant danger. Harrald wiped his eyes with his hand, sniffled and continued to cook the meat.

"I am lonely, doggy. No one seems to be friendly anymore. All they want to do is kill and eat others, so you can't make any friends."

Harrald looked at Deecee. "That's why I'm glad I have you. I shall call you, let's see, Mister Furry. How do you like that?”

Deecee opened his eyes and pondered Harrald. He seemed like a nice man. If Deecee stayed with Harrald, he could have a good life. But something inside Deecee told him no. Deecee thought of his former master. He pictured him now in his mind’s eye, with his scruffy yellow hair, his black leather vest and pants and black boots. The thought of Johnny made Deecee’s heart happy. He remembered the adventures they’d had. He also remembered the beautiful girl his master was always with, and her long blond hair and pleasant smile.

Deecee’s heart hurt. He knew then he could never stay with Harrald. He wanted to find his real master. He realized that he didn’t care if he had to face danger or even hunger. He had to get back to his real master. And he knew where his master went. He was losing time sitting there, and every minute his master might be farther and farther away.

Deecee stood up, watching Harrald. Harrald was still talking, but he wasn’t looking at Deecee. Deecee felt bad leaving Harrald, for the old man was kind and wanted him to stay. But Deecee had no choice. He already belonged to another master.

Silently Deecee backed out of the room. Once he was out of Harrald’s sight, he ran fast towards the front door, silently padding along on his furry paws.
He reached the front door and stopped.

With one last sad glance back at Harrald, he ran out into the night to restart his quest for his real master.

CHAPTER 9

Misterwizard stood in a huge room filled with long benches broken up into two sections, making an aisle down the middle. The benches led to a raised area in front with a pedestal. The room had marble floors and walls, and huge columns in rows stood at the ends of the benches, making passageways on either side of the benches as well. The windows were made of colored glass with beautiful images in them, and the Red Eye shone through the glass, making colorful images on the floor. The marble made the room cold, even though there were small rugs on top of it, but since it had been a warm day outside, to Misterwizard the chill in the air felt good.

Misterwizard wore one of his usual outfits, for he liked to be comfortable: black shorts, a short-sleeved silk shirt with flowers on it, and open-toed shoes called "sandals." His long, white beard was neatly trimmed and his white hair created a fringe around his balding head. Since the latest battle ended, Misterwizard had time to relax and attend to his appearance, and now he looked clean and well-groomed.

Misterwizard sat his short, round body on a wooden bench in front of a huge brown rectangular box. On the front of the box in a semi-circle lay three rows of white keys, one on top of the other. On the floor in front of the bench, the box had four long black pedals. But the most amazing thing about the box was what rose up from inside it. Rows and rows of silver pipes stretched up into the air, almost to the ceiling. Each pipe had a hole in the front about halfway up.

Misterwizard, his eyes sparkling with pleasure, pressed one of the buttons on the top row of the box. He waited a moment, listening. A soft, tired hiss came from one of the pipes, and a bit of smoke issued out of the hole. Misterwizard frowned, disappointed, shook his head, and pressed another tab. This time, a strangled sound came out of one of the pipes, not pleasant at all. It was so loud however it rattled the windows of the building. Misterwizard seemed pleased, and smiled. He tried another key, and this time a much more melodious sound filled the air, a majestic tone that seemed to fill the room and pass through a person's body with sensation.

Misterwizard smiled, pleased. "Wonderful! I'll get this pipe organ to work yet! And then, the tribe will all hear something!"

Behind Misterwizard unnoticed, two people walked in and down the middle aisle in a respectful manner. They stopped behind him silently and waited for him to notice them.

Misterwizard, intent on the keyboard, didn't hear them. He moved his hands over the keys, trying to decide which one to try next.

"Hey there, Misterwizard."

Misterwizard was instantly shocked and delighted, for he recognized the voice at once. His face filled with joy and excitement, and he spun on the bench as fast as he could, almost slipping off the end. There standing behind him was none other than Super!

"Jumping Jehoshaphat!" Misterwizard yelled, leaping off the bench, arms outstretched. He ran to Super, his face full of emotion and relief.

Super was touched as well, for tears fell from her eyes and she looked uncharacteristically sheepish and shy. She bit her lip as Misterwizard ran to her and threw his arms around her, squeezed her hard and picked her up in the air. Super was torn between sobbing and laughing. "Don't kill me!"

Misterwizard set her down and let her go, but she put her arms around him and looked down at his beaming face.

"My dear! My dear! Please forgive me, I grew so excited I lost my countenance. You can't imagine the astronomical delight your return has elucidated in me! My mind is enraptured with joy and exultation to the point of losing rational thought! The adventurers have returned unscathed!"

For a moment, he and Super just held each other, enjoying the pleasure of being together again and too full of emotion to speak.

Next to Super stood Lightpole. Lightpole still wore his metal plates and black skirt, and his sword was tucked in a scabbard on his back. He watched silently as Misterwizard and Super hugged, deeply touched by their affection. His mind couldn't help but think of how much he missed his family who were presently captives of the Nork army.

Finally, Misterwizard and Super let go of each other and worked on wiping the tears from their eyes. Then Super looked sorrowful.

"I'm afraid it's only me, Misterwizard. We haven't come back unscathed, whatever that means. At least not yet."

Misterwizard's brow wrinkled with confusion and concern. He looked at Super with trepidation. "Where are your traveling companions, Johnny, Deb and Starbucks? Most assuredly you would not separate from your companions willingly! Heavens to Murgatroyd, don't tell me they've been slain on some foreign battlefield! Or deprived of their liberty by some foreign entity!"

Super smiled sadly and shook her head. "No, Misterwizard, at least I hope not. Though some of them might be. It's all so confusing right now! We've had so many adventures since we left. We made new friends, but now they and Johnny and Deb and Starbucks are all in real danger. I came home to ask for the Tribe's help!"

Misterwizard stroked his beard, deep in thought. "Without hesitation, my dear. We will enthusiastically administer you any assistance that is feasibly achievable. We have actually created a fairly stable and peaceful society at the present time, which is to say quite a benign and monotonous one. A little more adventure could do everyone some benefit, help us to realize just what we're fighting for. And new allies are always welcome!"

"So does that mean you'll help?" Super said, a little confused.

Suddenly Misterwizard saw Lightpole for the first time. "And who is this brave looking soldier of fortune? He appears to be dressed in the fashion of the warriors of ancient Japan!"

Super put a hand on Lightpole's shoulder. "This is my good friend Lightpole, Misterwizard. He's one of our new friends! Their tribe is called Letfreedomring."

Misterwizard smiled with extreme pleasure and deep interest. "A commendable and magnificent title for a tribe, I must definitely assert. We really need to come up with our own moniker. Constantly simply calling ourselves the "tribe" does grow extremely tedious."

Misterwizard smiled with interest at Lightpole. "You seem to be a man of Asian descent, my friend, like many of the families here in New Sanctuary."

Lightpole smiled and walked forward to shake Misterwizard's hand. "I don't understand a lot of your words, Misterwizard, but I think I am already beginning to like you."

Super laughed. "Welcome to Misterwizard, Lightpole. We've been trying to understand him since we first met him.”

Misterwizard shook Lightpole’s hand vigorously. “Welcome to the United States of America.”

Super frowned. “When did we start calling ourselves that?”

“Just now!” Misterwizard said, grinning spryly.

Misterwizard put an arm around Super and began leading her away. Lightpole followed. “Come, Super darling. Let us talk of sailing ships and sealing wax. Tell me all about your adventures and what the USA can do to help.”

Misterwizard led Super to another room that was much warmer and more pleasant. It had rich green carpet on the floor and gold and purple couches throughout the room. The walls were covered with beautiful but faded paintings. It still had beautiful colored windows though, which gave the room a colorful tint. Lightpole followed them inside.

As Misterwizard and Super sat on a puffy golden couch and Lightpole lounged on another nearby, Super began to tell Misterwizard all about their adventures.

As Clancy and the Clan strode into view of the people on the roadway, a cheer of hungry thankfulness went up from prisoners and Nork soldiers alike. The clansmen all grinned, for they were like returning heroes, but each of them also hid secret dark smiles thinking about their plans for the future.

The Red Eye began its slow climb over the distant horizon to start a new day. The Clansmen carefully climbed down the concrete wall and handed down the meat to each other as the prisoners and guards gathered around them in eagerness. Moxie stomped up to take charge.

"'Bout time you mugs showed back up. Hope you brought enough for everybody, or you're going out again."

Clancy, who had just about had enough, scowled with anger at Moxie, and his face clouded with thunder. He strode up to stand within inches of Moxie, his face dark with fury. Moxie blanched, looking scared, realizing he might have pushed Clancy just a little bit too far.

"Be watchin' that tongue of yours, little mouse, or I'll cut it out and feed it to you instead."

"Look," Moxie said, trying to smooth things over without losing too much face, "It's just, we couldn't go out, 'cause we was watching the prisoners. If there ain't enough food, we gotta get more." Then Moxie tried to act tough again, just to show he wasn't intimidated, even though he was. "And I'm in charge, get it?"

Alasdair cut in. "If there ain't be enough, you and your men can go looking for some, while we have a smoke and lay on our backs for a change. We can guard the prisoners very well."

"Though the truth be told," Finn said with a jaunty grin, "they might be looking for a long time, till we all grow old and gray before they catch anything."

Moxie glared at both Alasdair and Finn. "There's only a small bunch of you. There ain't no way you could watch all these jokers. And you were brought along to do the huntin, since you's always saying how good you is at it."

Clancy and the Clansmen chuckled. The Nork guards bristled and scowled, and it looked like there might be a fight right then and there, but Moxie smiled, trying to ease tensions. "Look, we're buddies, ain't we? You just got a lot of hungry guys here. Let's go cook some of the meat and you can take a load off."

Moxie turned around, and it looked like the confrontation was over. But then Clancy looked at his fellow Clansmen, then back at Moxie.

"My men eat first. Then the prisoners. If there's anything left, your men can gnaw on the bones."

Everyone tensed, sensing another, more dangerous confrontation had just begun. Moxie turned around, and he looked tough, but behind his eyes there was fear and unease. Everybody looked at him, to see what he would say.

Moxie looked around at everyone, then back at Clancy, who grinned at him with relish, not afraid of Moxie at all.

"There better be enough for everybody," Moxie said, his voice tough but strained. "Or when we get back, the Boss will hear about it. He's already on the fence about you freaks and your little green skirts."

Moxie turned back around and now it was the Nork soldiers who grinned. They fingered their tommy guns and turned to follow Moxie. Clancy and the Clansmen watched them leave silently.

"He's going to tell his mother the king, Clancy," Gavin, Clancy's second in command, said mockingly.

They all laughed.

"He's a little worm, he is," Alasdair said. "No man, and that's a fact."

"A little worm who will soon be crushed by our boots," Clancy said.

Then Clancy saw something in the distance, and his whole face changed to a look of surprise.

"Death take him now!" Clancy yelled. The others looked to see what had Clancy so upset.

In the distance Johnny and Deb ran from the box-like car towards the right and closest tunnel.

"That must be the Johnny bloke she was on about," Alasdair said.

"He's getting away with your bonny lass," Gavin yelled.

"No, he's not!" Clancy said. "Gavin, Alasdair, Angus, follow me. The rest stay here and pass out the food. I'm going to finally meet this Johnny lad, and we'll see who ends up with the young maiden."

Clancy grabbed his hatchet and held it high. He took off running towards the tunnel. Gavin, Alasdair and Angus took off after him. The rest smiled at each other, entertained by all the strange events taking place. Then they all headed towards the camp.

Clancy grabbed a torch as he ran from a stick holding it in the ground. He and his men reached the opening to the tunnel where they saw Johnny and Deb go, but Johnny and Deb were already inside.

"You sure we should go in here alone, Clancy?" Gavin said, rubbing his bearded chin. "We don't know what might be waiting inside. There might even be…"

"Don't' say their name or be cursed!" Clancy thundered. "If ye lads be too Lilly livered, ye can turn around. I'm not letting some wee lad steal my beauty from me, just because of a little dark tunnel."

Clancy started into the darkness, and the three others reluctantly followed.

CHAPTER 10

Starbucks walked outside onto the big white steps of the building with the two stone lion-beasties. The morning light shone on the broken buildings and creeping vegetation all over them, which seemed to be trying to reclaim the world and bury it in green. The rows of two-story buildings that lined the streets sat in the piles of rubble from their own destruction. Along with the grass covered streets and the rusted hulks of old cars, the buildings made the world look old and tired, as if it wanted to go to sleep forever.

Rumple walked outside, too, followed by Redeye. All three gazed around at the morning scene before them.

"I love our home," Redeye said, surprising Starbucks with his seeming maturity. "I hate those Nork jerks for coming here and hurting my people."

"So do I, Redeye," Starbucks said, his voice full of anger. He studied Redeye and smiled inside, for he could see the qualities of a leader in the boy.

Rumple nodded. "If I was twenty-two again, I'd teach those rascals a thing or two!" Rumple shook his wrinkled fist in the air, but it didn't look very threatening, in fact he almost fell over. "I'd box their ears and flatten their noses!"

"That's okay," Starbucks said, putting a hand on Rumple's shoulder. "You're just as useful here. Someone needs to help the people still here carry on until Restaria and the other people return."

"Do you really think they will?" Redeye asked.

"Of course," Starbucks said. "My tribe will be here soon. And together, we're going to kick those Nork guys' behinds! They're going to wish they'd never mess with my tribe and Letfreedomring!"

Redeye smiled, and Starbucks grinned back.

The rest of the scrabblers came out of the old building and gathered behind them. They squinted in the morning light. A little scrabbler girl said, "I'm hungry." Redeye walked over to her. "I'll get us some food soon."

Rumple looked in the distance in front of them with interest. He pointed a bony, wrinkled finger. "Speaking of people, here are some right now!"

Starbucks looked too. Coming towards them were two men and a large crowd. Starbucks estimated it must have been a hundred or more. The people ranged in age from old to young, some just scrabblers or even wrigglers held by their mothers. Some were men, Starbuck's age or older, and some were grown men.

"It looks like not all the people were captured!" Starbucks said.

The men, holding hands, walked up to Starbucks and his group and stopped. The two men walked forward to greet them. Starbucks recognized them right away as the two men they had helped fight the Norkers during the battle.

"Hello again, Bargainbin and Jewelrydept," Starbucks said, smiling brightly at them.

"You remember us!" Jewelrydept said, looking pleased.

"You're not easy to forget!" Starbucks, and all three laughed.

"We've gathered all the people we could find who were not captured," Bargainbin said. "Sadly, this is all that is left of Letfreedomring."

Starbucks and Rumple gazed at the rag-tag crowd of people. They looked tired, hungry and scared.

Starbucks motioned with his chin to the scrabblers behind him and Rumple. "Redeye has been keeping these scrabblers safe."

Jewelrydept nodded, smiling grimly. "Redeye is a very brave boy."

Redeye grinned and stuck out his chest with pride. The people of Letfreedomring moved to the group of scrabblers, and began talking to them. Some of the scrabblers' parents were there and happy reunions took place.

Meanwhile, Starbucks, Bargainbin and Jewelrydept continued to talk. Bargainbin looked grim and raised a fist. "We're going to fight and get our people back!"

The crowd heard him and their voices rose in angry agreement. Some shook their fists in the air and others nodded.

Starbucks looked over the crowd that was now mixed in with the scrabblers. Though there were some who looked like they might make good fighters, the majority of them were women, scrabblers and elders. Starbucks figured there might be twenty or so men who might be able to fight.

"It is good that you have the courage to fight," Starbucks said, "but first I suggest you get food for your people and fix their wounds. They'll be much more ready to fight when they're well fed and rested."

Starbucks pointed to the South. "My mate Super has gone to get help from my tribe who live that way in a place called Washington Deecee. It's not that far away, just past Ballmor. I am going now to find her. When I do, we will return here, hopefully with men from our tribe to fight alongside you to rescue your people."

The crowd smiled and looked encouraged. Bargainbin and Jewelrydept smiled warmly.

"I knew you and Johnny were good people. I see the tribe has truly changed. Is Leader Nordstrom no longer in charge?"

Starbucks thought of how Leader Nordstrom met his doom. It seemed ages ago, almost in another world.

"Leader Nordstrom got what all evil men deserve."

Jewelrydept smiled with dark joy. "He is dead

then. He was truly was evil, and unkind. I'm glad."

There was a moment of reflective silence, then Starbucks said, "Misterwizard lives with the tribe now. He has all kinds of fancy tricks to fight with. You'll see when he gets here!"

"But if we wait for you and the tribe to return, our people who are captured will already be in Nork.," Bargainbin said. "We need to try and rescue them before that, or it will be much more difficult."

Starbucks nodded but his face showed regret. "I'm sorry Bargainbin, but they already have a full cycle's march ahead of us. I don't think we could catch them now before that happens anyway. And without my tribe, our small numbers won't have much of a chance. I think the only hope is to get help from my tribe. Misterwizard will now find a way to sneak into Nork and free your people."

Jewelrydept nodded. "Even so, it won't be easy. We are in for a good battle."

Bargainbin nodded too, reluctantly agreeing.

"You are right. But there are so many of them there. I was a spy once and went there. I looked over their fence. They are as many as a nest of ant-beasties. How will we ever manage it?"

The crowd looked at Starbucks to see what he said.

Starbucks rubbed his chin with his hand and thought. "We will do what Johnny does so well. Create a distraction. Then we'll sneak in, rescue your people, and hurry back here. As Misterwizard would say, 'piece of cake'!"

Bargainbin said, "We will do as you say. For now, you are in charge. We will help the wounded and get food. Then we will organize those who can fight. When you return, we'll be ready."

As everyone watched, Starbucks walked over to his Harley and climbed on it. The people gathered around in excited curiosity. Starbucks grinned, as if putting on a show. He put the Harley in neutral so it wouldn't take off when he started it, flipped the kickstand up, grabbed the clutch and flipped the on switch. Then just to give the crowd a thrill, he gunned the engine. A loud roar, familiar now to Starbucks but totally new to his audience filled the air. The scrabblers all put on looks of delight, and so did most of the   older people. Starbucks chuckled. He never got   tired of the sound of his Harley, and the reaction it caused.

Suddenly over the sound of the Harley they heard another sound, one loud and shrill and not at all pleasant, filled the air not too far away. The looks of joy and pleasure quickly switched to those of fright and dismay, for it was the screech of a Krakn.

"More monsters!" Redeye yelled as he pointed towards the sound, his eyes wide open with excitement.

Starbucks looked towards the sound. There in the distance he could see not just one Krakn, but two! The Krakn had seen the crowd and galloped towards them, their mouths open showing sharp fangs. They ran on their lower tentacles, and waved two in the air, as if looking for something to grab. They looked like something out of a nightmare. They were medium sized, but still formidable and at least eight feet tall.

"Just what we don't need." Starbucks turned to Jewelrydept. "Jewelrydept, get all the people inside!" He turned to Redeye, who was already herding the scrabblers back towards the building.

"I know," Redeye said. "Back to hiding again!"

"What are those?" Rumple said. "They look scary!'"

"No time to fill you in," Starbucks said, as he hopped off his Harley and took out his sword, getting ready to fight.

As Redeye herded the people towards the building with the two lions, Bargainbin and Jewelrydept stayed. Bargainbin put on a fierce determined look. "This is our home, and we're going to defend it!"

"Okay," Starbucks said. "Nothing can ever be easy!"

Deecee loped along through the empty, moss-covered streets, past broken houses with such high grass and trees in their yards some of them were barely visible. Moldy, rusted cars lined the sides of the streets, as if their owners had only just parked them there and went inside the homes, though really, they were long dead.

The Red Eye brought light and a small amount of warmth to the day, lighting up the land, as if trying to wake it up. Deecee felt rested and well-fed, thanks to the old man, and the wound on his leg barely bothered him at all. He found he could now put his weight on it, as long as he was careful. It still throbbed, but it was a tolerable pain he could live with.

He found a puddle of water and stopped to drink. The world around him was peacefully quiet, as if he was the only thing alive in it. Deecee liked that feeling, though he knew if it were really true, he would grow lonely quickly. He liked having a master to take care of him, and was glad it wasn't true, and he longed to see his master and his master's beautiful blond-haired friend again.

Deecee kept his eyes open and stopped drinking every few seconds to raise his head and look around for more wolf-beasties or anything else that would cause trouble. He knew there were scarier and meaner things than even wolf-beasties, ones with claws and big, sharp teeth. There were even some that stood on two legs like men, but covered in black hair. Those ones you definitely didn't mess with, for they were big and fierce.

He finished drinking and ran on. He came to a four-foot concrete wall. Beyond it lay a sandy beach that led to a big body of water. The city seemed to curve around the water on both sides, but in front of him, the water went all the way to the edge of the horizon.

Deecee hopped down the concrete wall and walked in the sand of the beach for a while. Then he lay down in the sand and put his head on his paws. The beach was littered with trash and old bits of clothing, and seemed like a sad place to Deecee. Maybe it seemed that way because he was growing sad, not really sure where to go to look for his master.

The morning wind caused waves to dance on the water. The waves looked pretty, but Deecee was becoming so gloomy that he couldn't enjoy them. Should he go in the water? Where did it lead? Could his master have gone out there? He could never swim across it. It seemed silly to try, for surely his master didn't go this way. The breeze off the water ruffled his fur and made his eyes water, but it felt good.

Where to go, where to go? His master could have gone in any direction. Finding his master seemed as hopeless as swimming in the water until he reached the edge of the world.

He lifted his head and looked to his right. There he saw something interesting. In the far distance between the buildings, he saw a ditch made of concrete. Just over the edge of the ditch, he saw a wide road going in both directions. The road was filled with the old rusted mounds that seemed to be everywhere in the city, but there was nothing else, no buildings or metal boxes or any of the other things lying about. It seemed this was a special place just for the old metal mounds.

Deecee gazed at the ditch, and something inside said that this was where his master had gone. He didn't know why, but he felt sure of it. With no other better ideas, Deecee figured he might as well go there. He hoped he wasn't growing farther and farther away from his master, but he had no way of knowing. He had to stop thinking that way, for it made him sad and frightened.

As Deecee grew close to the ditch, he heard voices! There were people down in the ditch! Deecee crept forward until he could just see over the edge of the wall without being seen.

A whole camp of people! They sat in groups next to fires, talked and joked. Seeing them made Deecee feel joy, for even though they were not his master, they were men, and that meant friends. But then he realized the people in the middle were being guarded by others who looked cross around the outside. Deecee's natural instincts told him that this might be a dangerous situation, and he'd better proceed with caution.

Deecee scanned the area and saw there were three large tunnels in the distance, their round black openings looking scary. He also spotted a large white box-like thing at the end of the camp, and light came from inside. More of the guards ambled around this box, as if it was an important place.

Deecee scanned the scene below, looking for his master, but he didn't see him. Then suddenly the noise increased. All the people stood up and looked towards the opposite side of the ditch. Deecee looked too.

A group of large burly looking men in strange looking green skirts and white shirts walked up. They carried big hatchets and clubs, and looked like nobody anyone should mess with. More interesting to Deecee, the men were bloody and carried large chunks of tasty-looking meat on their shoulders. Even though he wasn't that hungry, the meat still looked mighty tasty and he licked his lips in response.

The burly men in skirts stood at the edge of the ditch as the people below cheered them. Even the guards seemed happy.

Deecee glanced around, to make sure he hadn't been spotted. He saw one man come striding forth, and the crowd parted to let him through as if he was someone important. He wore a funny brimmed hat and a striped suit and carried a strange metal thing with a pointy end and a round disc in the middle. When he reached the spot where he could talk to the burly men, he yelled up at them, and they spoke back in gruff voices.

Deecee looked around again, and his heart leapt inside himself with joy!

He saw his master! Deecee's ears went up and he was instantly alert. He stood up, forgetting about concealment. His tail wagged and he let out an involuntary whine of excitement. His master and his master's blond-haired companion had just come out of the big box-like thing. But they were running away, towards the big round tunnels!

Panic filled Deecee. He knew he had to get down there and catch up to his master or risk losing him again! He sensed that his master was trying to stay hidden from the man with the hat however. How to get down there fast and not cause his master to be discovered?

Carefully, as quietly as he could, Deecee padded down the side of the ditch and ran towards his master, hoping no one saw him and was alerted to his master. Deecee ran as fast as he could, faster than he'd ever run before, his heart pounding with panic, hoping to get to his master before his master reached the tunnels, for that was clearly where his master was going. Deecee didn't want to have to try and find his master in the dark.

CHAPTER 11

Moxie watched in shock, his mind numb, as Clancy and three of his men handed off the meat they carried to other clansmen and took off in pursuit of Johnny and Deb.

Finally, he managed to yell, long after everyone else had already realized it, "Hey! They're getting away!"

Everyone looked at him and grinned, and he realized how stupid he looked. He ran over to the white box, as if trying to inspect the scene of the crime, and stood there, looking stupid again. He turned and squinted at the tunnels in the harsh morning light that looked like three open mouths waiting to eat something. He saw Clancy and his three men. They were already halfway to the opening on the right, and Johnny and Deb were nowhere in sight. They'd already run into the tunnel and disappeared.

He stood still for a moment again, willing his slow brain to work, come up with a plan. He didn't really know what to do, things happened so fast. The other

Clansmen stood in a circle nearby, surrounded by the prisoners and guards. They seemed unsure what to do next either, and the people just kept waiting for them to give them the meat. All around the camp, everyone seemed to be shocked into a state of immobility.

Moxie decided to take it piece by piece. He looked at the ground and thought. "The Johnny guy took the girl and ran into the tunnel. Got it. Clancy and three of his men ran into the tunnel after them. Capeech. The other clansmen were back with some grub, and you're starving. Right-o. You should go after that dame, if you want her."

Moxie shook his head. "No way, that Johnny guy was tricky. Better to let Clancy fight him, bring the dame back, then you take her from him. But that ain't gonna be easy once he's won her in a fight." Moxie nodded his head silently. "Yeah, there is that."

"So, what are you gonna do?" Moxie thought some more. "Go in there, run ahead of Clancy and fight the guy first? And what happens when Clancy gets there? You know what happens! He offs you, and then comes back and makes out like it's an accident!"

No way, Moxie thought. He'd let Clancy take the heat, and maybe, just maybe this Johnny would kill him instead. The dame was a fair price to pay to see the big, dumb clansmen out of the way. And if Clancy won, well, he'd deal with that later.

"But if this Johnny wins, will he be ahead of us in the tunnel somewhere, waiting to ambush us and get the prisoners back?" Moxie wondered. He made a scoffing sound to himself and dismissed that idea. He was just one guy. He ain't gonna take on the whole Nork army.

Moxie smiled inside, happy that he'd made some decisions, which showed he wasn't so dumb after all. He'd go back, make sure the dumb clansmen gave everybody some food, and chill out until Clancy came back, or maybe didn't.

Moxie turned with a scowl of importance and strode over to the clansmen, who still stood motionless surrounded by the prisoners and guards.

"What are you guys, statues?" Moxie barked. "Start cookin' that meat and feeding ever-body."

A large clansman with wild black hair and wild eyes glared down at Moxie, instantly scaring him. 'We take orders from Clancy, not you!"

"Well," Moxie said nervously, "I'm in charge until he returns, capeech?"

One of the clansmen scowled. "What is capeech? Are you insulting us?"

"No, stupid, it means 'you understand?' It's from an old language from before. The Boss likes to say it."

"You ain't smart enough to be in charge of your own behind," the clansmen said.

The other clansmen laughed, and Moxie scowled.

The clansmen all glared at him, and for a moment Moxie wasn't sure if they were going to listen to him or not. He dreaded the thought of another fight just then, for he was tired and hungry and just wanted to stop thinking for a while

"You want I should show you what I show you what I can do, wise guy? You want to start somethin' you can't finish? Your boss-man wouldn't like that."

The man stared daggers of hatred at Moxie, but he seemed to give in. "Nae. We'll let you play boss for now. Clancy is simply biding his time. When he's a ken to, he'll whittle a few inches off of your top to show you what a real man can do when he's a mind."

The clansmen walked away towards the nearest campfire, and Moxie bristled, wanting more than anything to grab his tommy gun and fill the dumb, dirty clansmen full of holes. "*Do it,*" he told himself! "*Now's your chance! Kill them, and then when Clancy gets back you can easily kill him and his men that are left!*"

Moxie wanted to listen, wanted to do it. He could call his men and they could fill the clansmen with holes. Then they could wait at the entrance of the tunnel for Clancy and his men and it would be a cakewalk to put them in the grave. But he kept hearing a little voice that told him, "*The Boss won't like it, they're our allies, you can't make a decision like that!*

"*But you can tell the Boss they died in battle! He'll never know!*" another voice in his head replied.

"*But what if I fail?*" the real Moxie replied to the voices in a scared whisper. "*What if they kill me instead?*"

In the end, Moxie's cowardice prevailed, and he decided the odds were still not good enough. No, he had to get a chance when there was no chance of losing, when it would be like shooting fish in a barrel. He hated

Clancy, but when he got back to Nork, he wouldn't have to see him anymore anyway, right? So why push it? He decided if he got a chance, he would take it, otherwise, he'd concentrate on protecting his own skin. He just hoped Clancy didn't decide to force his hand and try to put the hit on him first.

As Moxie walked over to see how the cooking was going, he thought how he'd wished that this Johnny character had killed Clancy before in the battle of Pelpia, and he hoped with all his heart that Johnny would kill Clancy in the tunnel now. If that happened, he might even thank this Johnny if he ever met him again, before killing him of course.

Johnny and Deb ran from the early morning light into the darkness, and soon it enveloped them like a thick, smothering blanket. The red eye outside shone in a short distance, illuminating the first ten or so old hulks, but beyond that lay utter black.

Johnny didn't think about what lay ahead or what they were running from. His mind was full of the joy of feeling Deb's hand in his, again. Her hand was warm and soft and so fragile, like a beautiful rose petal that he had to be careful not to damage. He vowed right then, for what must have been the hundredth time, that he would never leave her alone ever, ever again, Just the feel of her presence next to him, filled his heart with a warm pleasure, and all he really wanted to do was find a quiet place to hold her and kiss her for hours. He told himself he had to wait, wait until they were safe, then there would be time, but he found it hard to concentrate.

"Johnny, look out!" They ran out of the light into utter darkness and right ran into a cold, steel hulk. They stopped and Johnny reached out with his left hand, the one not holding Deb's hand, and touched the cold, dirty, rusted steel. It felt somehow alive in the dark, like a sleeping beast in front of them. Johnny moved them to the left, feeling the side of the car, looking for the end. He felt something sharp, and reminded himself to be careful, for many of the old cars had ragged edges that cut fast and deep.

Johnny looked behind them. He could see the curved opening of the tunnel, a white round shape, already seemingly miles away. Beyond it, he saw something alarming. It was members of the Clan running their way!

Distant shouts came from beyond the entrance. Deb's disappearance had definitely been discovered.

"Johnny!" Deb said, her voice shaky, affected by the lack of sight and the feeling of being lost in an inky void.

"I hear them!" Johnny said, his voice seeming to echo in the vast tunnel and get swallowed up by the darkness at the same time. "We have to move!"

Johnny found the end of the car and they stumbled ahead around it. The ground felt slippery from grass and moss, and was littered with trash that threatened to trip them.

Deb felt something run over her foot and away she involuntarily up in the air for a second, feeling queasy. *It was a rat-beastie,* she thought, *but at least it seemed to run away, not bite.* She felt another one, and this time its long tail dragged across her other foot and she couldn't help but let out a small squeak.

They finally passed that car and walked between it and another they could sense further on their left. Deb already felt as if they'd been in the dark too long, for her eyes felt weird, and her heart thumped. She dreaded thinking how long they'd still have to be in it. Deeper and deeper they went, into the black, into who knew what?

From the entrance behind them, a deep, booming voice exploded, like a megaphone. The sudden sound sent a shiver through them.

"Hold it there, laddie! You be taking my new bride away from me!"

"Who's that?" Johnny whispered to Deb, a disembodied voice in the darkness.

"Clancy!" Deb whispered in a high-pitched voice. She spoke as if she was an expert on the subject. "He's a Clansmen. They fight with the Norkers."

Johnny nodded. He remembered meeting one of the clansmen and fighting them with Starbucks. Johnny recalled the Clansmen seemed bigger and fiercer than the Nork soldiers, a fact that didn't make Johnny happy, since the Clansmen were right behind them.

Johnny and Deb tried to speed-walk between

cars, bumping into them and feeling their way, stumbling over small bushes and trash, weaving this way and that, trying to put distance between themselves and the loud booming voice behind them. They had no idea how far behind them the Clansmen were, and both Johnny and Deb fancied they felt Clancy's hand reaching out to grab them at any second. Deb's long blond hair floated in the soft breeze created by their speed, unseen in the dark.

"What does he mean, his bride?" Johnny whispered, knowing the answer wasn't going to make him happy.

Deb looked towards Johnny in the dark. She couldn't see him, even though he was only a few feet away, and it scared her, but she tried to be brave. "He tried to steal me from Moxie, who also wanted to have me."

"None of them are getting you! You're mine!" Johnny spat out in anger.

Johnny's angry words made Deb chuckle, and she smiled in the darkness, for some reason finding his response funny. But it made her feel better, safer. She knew Johnny would never let anything happen to her if he was there to stop it. And she was with him now. A burst of love coursed through her like one of Misterwizard's bombs blowing up inside her stomach, and she wished she could kiss Johnny all over his face and never stop. She knew she'd have to wait, but when she had the chance...

Johnny and Deb moved farther, farther, into the

darkness. Deb's cheery mood began to disappear again. "Johnny," Deb whispered, "what if we get stuck on something? Or what if…?"

"We won't," Johnny whispered back, but he didn't sound that confident. Now they were feeling their way, reaching out and taking one step at a time, feeling for objects in their way. It seemed like there were more cars, some piled on top of each other, making it impossible to go forward or in one direction or the other.

"This is worse than going up the stairs to Misterwizard's room in his castle," Deb said, trying to make a joke, but her voice sounded hollow.

Something moaned somewhere in the darkness. They both stopped, their hearts thumping, their eyes wide in the darkness, frozen in sudden fear.

"What was that?" Deb asked, her voice high and shaky with fear.

"I don't know," Johnny said, trying to sound brave, but just sounding unsure.

In the darkness behind them in the direction of the entrance, a flickering orange sprang up. Orange light danced in shadows on the top of the tunnel and off the old, rusted hulks.

"Clancy's got a flame stick!" Deb whispered. "He'll see us!"

The sudden light hurt their eyes at first, but only for a second. Then they could see the tunnel around them. The rusted, mangled, broken cars stretched behind and in front of them like a scrabbler's toys thrown into a pile. Some still had glass still in the windows, others had none and looked like metal skulls with sightless eyes. A few were smashed together, their bodies tangled like giant metal beasts that died in a fight.

Another moan shattered the silence, somewhere in the darkness ahead. It sounded different. It didn't come from the same source!

Johnny looked ahead to try and see who, or what the moan came from. All he could see was more cars stretching for what looked like forever ahead. There seemed to be no end to them, and the orange light behind stopped after a few cars to show nothing but darkness again beyond them.

Johnny couldn't see the opening of the tunnel that must lie ahead of them somewhere, it was still too far away. Here and there, trees had grown up between the cars, seeming out of place in the middle of the steel jungle, casting their own long shadows and looking like sinister tall ghosts. Green moss covered everything, like a living creature swallowing everything in the tunnel, eating it.

"He's up ahead, men," Clancy said, his voice somewhere behind them, much too close. "Catch the little rat-beastie and bring back my lady fair!"

Clancy and three of his men crept into the dark

tunnel, their eyes wide open and their faces drawn with apprehension. Behind Clancy came Gavin, Alasdair, and Angus. Alasdair was a tall, strong man with long black hair and a long face. Angus was short and stocky, like a dwarf of old lore, with a bushy red beard and hair. They walked slowly in their kilts, white shirts with red sashes and big, heavy boots. Clancy and his men scanned the area in front of them as far as they could see in the torch light, looking for possible threats.

Even though Clancy held a torch, it only lit up a small area in front of them, and the old cars and rusted hulks blocked the light from shining very far. In fact, it made the cars look more sinister, for the light danced on them, bringing them into the light and then back into shadow. The light made dancing shadows everywhere, which looked like monsters with big claws and sharp teeth, waiting for them around every corner.

Clancy and his men fancied themselves as brave and strong, and so they acted as if they were unfazed by the darkness and cramped space, but inside each was nervous and anxious, and filled with quiet fear. None of them liked the idea of being trapped in the small, dark space, walking around the rusted cars that would block their escape from whatever was in the tunnel.

After a few moments, Gavin looked back. He could barely see the outline of the tunnel entrance now behind them. If they kept walking it wouldn't be long before it disappeared altogether, and they'd be swallowed up in the cramped, dark, foreboding tunnel, only the torch light to save them from utter darkness.

Gavin stopped, and they all stopped and looked at him. Gavin's face, drawn and white with fear in the dancing light of the torch, stared back at them.

"Clancy," Gavin whispered, as if afraid to speak too loudly. He spoke the sentiment the other two men were thinking, but didn't have the courage to say. "Is this lass really worth risking our lives for?"

"Don't tell me you're afraid of a wee bit of darkness Gavin Oleary," Clancy spat out. "I took ye to be more a man that that."

"I'm not afraid!" Gavin replied in anger, but his anger was short-lived, replaced by the cold dread. He tried to think of what to say that might make Clancy turn around. "I'm just thinkin' that this be a bonny place for that rat-man Moxie to ambush us, is all, just the four of us being all alone."

Clancy turned to look at Gavin, and his face in the torchlight was grim and hard. "I be in charge of this Clan, Gavin, and someday be king of Nork. And I already ken ya this lass was special. If you've not got a backbone for it, go back join the old ladies ladling out the soup. I'll deal with this on me own."

The other men all chuckled. Gavin at them all for a moment, then he nodded somberly and started walking towards them down the tunnel again. Clancy watched him for a second with grim satisfaction and continued on down the tunnel himself, his men slowly following him.

Ahead, Johnny and Deb moved faster, deeper into the tunnel, their hearts pounding in their chests.

CHAPTER 12

As the Red Eye peeked over the distant horizon and day dawned, it was witness to a strange new sight, in a world where, ever since the mushroom monsters came, strange sights occurred daily.

A girl dressed in leathers with long, black flowing hair roared down the highway on a strange two-wheeled vehicle, its engine filling the air with sounds that echoed off the old, rotting buildings. Sitting behind her was a man of Asian descent dressed elegantly in silk robes. He carried a sword at his back and looked like a warrior. He wore a tight but happy smile, and stared forward, as if at attention.

Behind them a parade of odd vehicles followed of all shapes and sizes. The first three vehicles were long yellow buses, their exteriors rusted and dented, their windows broken out. The buses had metal plates fastened on the front in a 'V' shape. Faces of men and women could be seen at all the old window openings, staring out at the world with happy, excited smiles. From the windows they could be seen holding weapons, guns or swords or clubs and some sharp sticks. They were an odd collection of characters, for some appeared like normal men and women, dressed in simple clothes, others appeared dirty and ragged, with long, unkempt hair. Still others had strange, white skin and dark eyes, though most of these people stayed in the middle of the buses and covered themselves with blankets.

Behind the three buses followed other cars of all different shapes and sizes. One had the word "Jeep" on it and had no top, and four people bounced along in it, holding clubs, laughing and grinning as if they were on a great adventure. One of the other vehicles was big, orange and shaped like a box and said, "U Haul" on it. Its back door was open and inside, a whole crowd of people sat on the floor. Weapons sat on the ground next to them, and one large gun with a long five-foot long barrel stood in the middle. The people inside sat around it and passed little white papers to each other, for they were playing some sort of card game.

And right next to the girl on the Harley was the strangest sight of all. On a small little two-wheeled contraption sat a short round man with wispy white hair, a white beard and bushy white eyebrows. Dressed in a khaki green jacket that was open and flowing behind him, a short-sleeved shirt with flowers that said "Bahamas" on it, a pair of lime green shorts, and big floppy black boots that seemed too big for him. He wore a funny leather helmet with flaps over the ears and a pair of round goggles over his eyes.

Super rode along, full of excitement and quiet joy, a big smile on her face. She had just enjoyed a wonderful reunion with her parents, and Starbuck's parents as well and she didn't realize how much she was going to love seeing Misterwizard again. She told them all about the battle of Pelpia and all the events that happened, and of course they all volunteered to come and fight. That's what their new society was all about, wasn't it, making friends and defending freedom? Now they were on their way, back to Starbucks, and Super couldn't wait!

Super found out that while her and her friends had been away Misterwizard and the Tribe had been busy, creating a new society based on the principles of the old democracy. Foodcourt had been appointed 'pro-temp presdint', whatever that was, until they could have 'lectons', whatever they were, and Misterwizard was trying to educate the people on all the old ways. From what Super could gather, it was slow going, for the people were more interested in playing and finding food then learning.

Foodcourt and some of the other men had stayed behind to protect New Sanctuary, but most of the Undergrounders and many of the old wildies had volunteered to stay, letting many of the men of the tribe join the fighting party.

Foodcourt told Super some of the wild things Misterwizard was teaching him, things like the 'tree branches of govmint', the 'presdinshal', the 'legslatoff' and the 'chewdishal'. He also told her about something

Misterwizard called the 'constushon' and the 'declarashun of indeependens'. Super was glad her and her friends had left on an adventure, or Misterwizard would be trying to teach them all that junk too.

"I'm glad we're heading back now!" Lightpole yelled up to her, and she grinned. He was doing it again, reading her thoughts. She began to think her and Lightpole were kindred spirits, and would always be good friends.

Now Super knew they were heading for another battle, and once again might all be killed. For some reason, it filled her with happiness, as if being in a dangerous adventure was where she belonged. Best of all, she was back with Misterwizard and her people, and somehow deep inside, she knew they would once again come out victorious. Misterwizard knew, he always knew what to do. He'd teach those Norkers a thing or two, and it would be a blast watching how he did it. Surely, he would have some magical weapon or trick that would light up the night sky, or frighten the Nork into submission. And that big gun he found! Super couldn't wait to see it in action!

They were also heading back to Johnny and Starbucks, which excited Super more than anything. She missed Starbucks so much, she could barely stand each moment without him, and she worried that he might be fighting at that moment, or already dead before she got back to him. If Starbucks was going to die, Super wanted to die next to him, holding his hand. The thought of never finding him again was too horrible, she couldn't even think about it. It would mean her life was not worth living.

Super, Lightpole and Misterwizard, the funny little man on the Moped, could weave around the cars. But the buses were bigger, and so when they reached a car they couldn't go around, that's when the strange metal plates came into play. The first bus rammed into the old rusted cars, pushing them aside so the rest of the strange caravan could get through. It was slow going for some of the cars were large and the bus would have to push hard to knock them out of the way. Every so often a vehicle would be too big, and everyone would have to stop while they figured out a way to get it off the road. Sometimes this took what seemed like hours, and finally they would get going again, Super and Lightpole both impatient the whole time.

As they rode down the highway, Super kept her eyes open for those horrible monsters, the Krakn. Super had told Misterwizard and her people about them after the Tribe had fought the one inside their gates, and how they would have to face more of the monsters if they passed through Ballmor to get to Pelpia. Now she studied every dark doorway of the houses in front of them and on both sides of the road, and listened for the horrible telltale screech that would mean a Krakn was heading their way.

Super looked over, laughed, and shook her head. Misterwizard was grinning wide, singing a song to himself. She only knew because she saw his lips move, she couldn't hear anything over the roar of the Harley and all the other cars, but he seemed to be having a grand time. Super remembered that Misterwizard loved adventure too.

Super waved her hand at him trying to get his attention, but he was concentrating like she was on avoiding the trees, trash and cars in their way. She frowned, becoming irritated, for she had to stop trying to get his attention every few seconds and weave around objects herself just to keep up with him. For a little "Moped" his vehicle seemed to go quite fast, and was even more maneuverable than the Harley.

Finally, she remembered that the Harley had a thing called a "horn" that she could use. Johnny had said never to use it, for it attracted beasties and other enemies, but she decided she'd have to risk it.

She found the button and pushed it. The horn sounded, loud in the morning air, but still barely louder than the Harley's roar. Misterwizard didn't even look over. She honked it again and again, and finally he turned his head and saw her waving.

He smiled at her with a big grin, and she couldn't help but smile back. His cheerfulness was contagious, and she loved him so much and was so happy to be back with him. Then she made herself frown with urgency and made a motion for him to stop.

Misterwizard seemed to get the message and he stopped his moped, much to Super's relief. She stopped the Harley, and its roar lowered to just a soft rumble. Misterwizard turned and signaled to the buses with his hand, and the first one stopped, making the others behind it do the same.

Misterwizard raised his goggles and grinned at her, his wrinkled face making him look like a cheerful weathered apple.

"Greetings, my beautiful and brave fellow adventurer! I perceive by your remonstrations you request a momentary suspension of our forward progress to have a brief consultation."

Super felt irritated but amused. Sometimes she thought Misterwizard simply used big words because it impressed everyone, or maybe even to annoy them for his amusement.

"I wanted you to stop!" She yelled.

Misterwizard chuckled. "And so, we have, dear Super. Do you have a specific motive for pausing our forward progression, or were you just desirous of a moment of refreshment and restoration?"

Super felt more irritated again. "I just wanted to let you know we're getting close to Ballmor. Do you think we should go around, or right through? The Krakn are no joke!"

Misterwizard looked thoughtful and rubbed his beard with his hand. "My strongest inclination would be to avoid the city you call Ballmor and avoid any unpleasantries. But if what you say of the dire situation for the people of Pelpia is true, every zeptosecond of delay delivers the prisoners into deeper peril. Traversing the outskirts of the city would take precious time that we would be imprudent to squander. I believe, in the interests of expeditiousness, we should proceed in the straightest direction possible to our destination, despite the potential for hazardous interactions with the current residents."

"What did he say?" Lightpole asked.

Super huffed and looked grumpy, ignoring Lightpole. "So, what do we do, Misterwizard?"

Misterwizard frowned, not sure why she wasn't understanding him. "Move forward, dear companion in adventure, and face the consequences!"

Misterwizard lowered his goggles again with a flourish, turned on his moped, raised his hand and motioned forward then puttered on.

Suddenly from the front bus came shouts and exclamations. Super, who had been just about to start her Harley, stopped, and turned around. So did Lightpole. They stared at the bus, wondering what was going on.

As they watched, the driver, who was Microsoft, Sephie's father, a tall man with gray hair and a beak-like nose, came off. He held onto a scrabbler's hand and dragged her off too. With surprise, Super saw it was Sephie!

Super climbed off and walked over to the bus, just as Misterwizard puttered back to see what was going on.

Microsoft was busy scolding Sephie as Super reached them. Just then another scrabbler came off the bus, the brown-skinned boy named Wheaties.

"...whatever were you thinking, hiding in the bus?" Microsoft was saying.

Sephie had her arms crossed and she looked stubborn and angry. "I can fight, just like everyone else!"

"You're still a scrabbler!" Microsoft said.

"No, I'm not!" Sephie yelled. "I'm seven seasons! I'm almost a grown-up now!"

Super marveled. How did time go by so fast? Had it been that long since they started their adventures? Sephie was getting so old! It made Super feel like an old maid, even though she was only sixteen seasons still, almost seventeen.

Microsoft turned to Wheaties. "And you, you snuck on with her, did you?"

Wheaties smiled, looking tough. "We go everywhere together. I'm eight. We're fellow adventurers."

"Oh, you are!" Microsoft said, looking irritated.

Super smiled, seeing there was more than just a friendship between Sephie and Wheaties. Young romance was blooming. She decided to say something in the young peoples' defense.

"Microsoft, they were only trying to help!"

Microsoft turned to her with a frown. "I can handle my own daughter, Super, if you don't mind."

Misterwizard walked up, chuckling. "I see we have some stowaways! Little Captains Courageous, wanting to join in the battle and share in the glory."

"Misterwizard," Microsoft said, "they are just scrabblers. They're going to get themselves killed!"

"I'm not a scrabbler!" Sephie said, her face red. "Stop calling me that, daddy!"

Misterwizard stroked his beard and chuckled, though he was careful not to let Microsoft see it. "I'm afraid the hour is too late to take them back now. As long as they stay in the bus during any altercations, I'm sure they will be relatively protected from any injurious effects."

"You hear that?" Microsoft said to both Sephie and Wheaties. "You stay in the bus, no matter what?"

Sephie smiled, like a crocodile-beastie. "Of course, dear father. We wouldn't think of leaving, for any reason."

"We'll do whatever you want!" Wheaties said. "As long as we can come along!"

Microsoft looked skeptical. Everyone laughed, including the people watching from the bus, everyone except Microsoft. "If your mother Abercrombie gets wind of this, she'll feed me to the wolf-beasties."

"Move 'em out!" Misterwizard yelled, a cheerful smile on his face. He remounted his Moped, pulled down his goggles, started his engine, drove until he was pointed north again and took off. Microsoft led Sephie and Wheaties back onto the bus, still scolding them.

Super laughed and hopped back onto her Harley.

"Courageous young children!" Lightpole said with a grin. "They will make great warriors someday!"

Super scowled then grinned. "Hang on again!" She said to Lightpole. Then she turned the key, gave her Harley gas and it burst forward.

Super's mind turned to what lay ahead. She just hoped they weren't all riding right into a Krakn's nest.

CHAPTER 13

Johnny and Deb walked into the darkness, holding each other's hand. To Deb the darkness felt like something alive, as if she could feel it touching her, grabbing her like a living thing. Her breath came in short, frightened gasps and her legs seemed weak and wobbly. It was hot and stuffy in the tunnel. They stumbled along, feeling the cold steel of the cars in front of them, finding the end of the car and slowly shuffling their way around it. They constantly kicked bushes or clumps of grass, unseen on the ground, making them stumble or stop. Sometimes the cars lay on top of each other and the wall of steel continued all the way to the tunnel wall. Then Johnny would have to help Deb up onto an old car's hood, which often made a loud crumpling sound that would set both their hearts racing for fear something would hear them. Then they would both have to carefully slide off the car on the other side so they didn't twist a foot or land on something sharp.

Another moan, now in total darkness, and it

sounded as if it was right next to them! The moan was a sick, horrid sound, like something dead or unworldly. Deb shrieked and squeezed Johnny's hand hard, her voice echoing in the tight tunnel. Johnny stopped and turned towards the sound, his blind eyes straining to see anything in the dark.

"Johnny!" Deb yelled in fright, her voice sounding like a cannon shot, right next to her but somehow sounding far away. Johnny didn't answer. He led Deb the opposite direction as fast as he could, like two people swimming in a dark sea to get away from an unseen predator. They felt their way along the side of a car, trying to go fast but stumbling, frightened. There were old car parts on the ground at their feet, old square headlights and tires, as well as small shrubs and other trash, almost tripping them and making them stop to find footing next to them.

The moan came again! It was just behind them, terrifying in the total black. It sounded like a man, but there was something wrong with him, as if he was sick or dying.

Then came the sound of shuffling feet. A scrape-scrape scrape on the ground, as if the man couldn't pick his feet up and just dragged them over the dirt and trash. Johnny and Deb peered back as they hurried along.

"Johnny, do you see that?" Deb asked, her voice sounding confused and wild from the darkness.

"Yes," Johnny said, pulling her along. They'd both seen it, a strange, green glow emanating from the darkness behind them. The glow was not bright enough to see by, it just gave everything a sickly green tinge that was somehow worse than the darkness by itself.

They reached the end of the nearest car and started to go forward. Someone stood there, blocking their path!

The person, for that's what it was, moaned! It was a different moan than the one behind them. They were surrounded! The person, for it was too dark to see if it was a man or woman, shone with a soft, green glow. The only thing they could see was the soft white of the person's eyeballs, terrifying in the darkness.

Deb screamed, this time in total terror and Johnny quickly turned and tried to go back the way they'd come. A disgusting smell of death and rot assailed their noses, making them gasp and feel sick.

Johnny and Deb stumbled back, and right into another person. This person moaned, and they could tell it was the same as the first moan they'd heard.

Deb screamed again and Johnny kicked out with his left foot at the person on the right. He connected with the body and could feel the person was thin and frail, only flesh and bones. The person fell to the ground and Johnny climbed onto the body and to the other side without hesitation, dragging Deb with him.

Deb screamed even louder, sounding as if she was losing touch with reality. Johnny looked. The other person had grabbed Deb's wrist from behind. Deb punched at the hand with her free wrist. Johnny stomped back and made a fist himself. He punched at the face of the figure somewhere in the dark. He connected with a cold, slimy face that felt like ragged bits of flesh over bone. But the person didn't let go.

"Johnny!" Deb struggled against the grip. Johnny pulled his sword out in the dark, but he was afraid to strike, for fear he'd hurt Deb. More moans came, from all around them.

Johnny squinted to see as best he could. He slashed his sword at the arm of the one that held Deb. He slashed it again and again, as Deb pulled to get away. The arm came loose from the body, still the hand still holding Deb's wrist. Deb screamed and pried the fingers off.

"Deb!" Johnny yelled.

"It's off!" Deb yelled back in a shaky, scared voice.

Johnny yanked Deb to the right, running into another figure in front of them and bowling him over. Other moaners shuffled after them in pursuit.

"Johnny, let's go back!" Deb yelled, but Johnny knew that would only mean capture again. He felt his way until he found an opening between the cars and pulled them around it.

The moans followed, close. Deb felt woozy, the fright and heat making her feel as if she might pass out at any moment. She'd never wanted to get out of anywhere more in her life. She felt like she was in a giant pit of dirt, struggling to get out as thousands of bug-beasties crawled towards her. She could sense Death in the tunnel, stalking for them, like a live beastie, trying to get its kill.

Johnny felt the heat and the danger as well. He began to wonder if he had led Deb into a place where they would both die. It was so frustrating, to be in such total darkness where you couldn't even see your enemy! If he could at least see his opponent and have a chance, but to die in the darkness, without even knowing what killed them, that would be a horrible death indeed.

How long did the tunnel go on, Johnny wondered. It seemed to be nothing but pitch-black forever. He had never really been afraid of the dark before, but this was different. He remembered Misterwizard talking about a mythical place called Hell, and he wondered if this was what it would have been like, a dark, hot place, with something in the dark tearing you apart that you didn't even see.

Johnny knew their best chance was to keep moving, and he hoped that in the total darkness he wouldn't get turned around and end up simply going in circles, not knowing which direction they were even going, until something caught them. The thought made a pang of fear shoot through him, and he tried not to think about it.

Behind them, the shouts of Clancy and his men were almost welcome. Johnny turned to see the light of Clancy's torch far in the distance. Johnny smiled, for without meaning to, Clancy had shown Johnny the right direction to go, and for the moment Johnny felt confident enough to keep walking. He also was encouraged by the fact that Clancy and his men didn't know what they were walking into, they didn't know about the moaners, yet. Soon they would meet them, and with any luck the moaners would turn and be interested in Clancy, giving Johnny and Deb a better chance to escape.

Johnny looked at Deb, for now he could just see her in the torchlight. Her eyes were open wide, trying to see and her face looked drawn and scared. Even though it made him sad to think she was scared, for some strange reason, he thought he'd never seen her looking so beautiful. He chalked it up to his love and concern for her, but the feelings helped, for suddenly he was angry and determined again. Seeing her brought his courage back. He was going to get her out of there!

Johnny stopped, put an arm around Deb and held her for a moment and she turned, finally able to see him smiling. The fear on her face faded and she smiled back. She hugged him back tightly, burying her head in his chest.

"Come on," Johnny said. "We're getting out of here!"

"I love you, Johnny," Deb said. Her words shot an arrow through Johnny's heart, and without any reason, a tear fell from his eye. Johnny grabbed her hand tight and pulled her forward, this time full of a strange hope and determination.

Suddenly ahead of them they heard moans, lots of them There was a whole crowd of the moaners heading their way. There was no escape.

  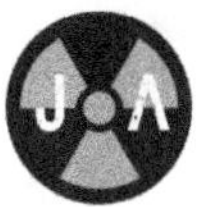

Deecee loped into the right tunnel, from light into darkness. Even though it was still not yet totally light outside, the change from outside to inside the dark tunnel made it hard for him to see. His beastie eyes could see better than people though, so they quickly adjusted to the dark. He saw the hulks of the car strewn everywhere, but they didn't bother him. He simply leapt onto the first one and down onto the other side. He had to weave around some of the cars, and a few times he had to jump into a car and out the other side, careful not to cut himself on the broken glass of the windows.

Deecee couldn't see his master, but he knew he was somewhere ahead. For the first time in a long time, Deecee felt hope and joy fill him, excited to see his master again.

Deecee heard voices, but they didn't belong to his master. He saw the light of a torch coming from the same place as the voices. To Deecee, the voice didn't sound very friendly. He wondered if these men meant to do his master harm. A low growl escaped Deecee's throat, and his lip curled showing a sharp fang. A dark pleasure coursed through Deecee's heart, pleased with the thought that he would once again get to fight for his master, making his master happy with him. He realized he liked danger. After the fight with the wolf-beasties, something had woken up in him, a strange dark pleasure for adventure and battle.

Deecee made sure to stay out of the torchlight, and he padded his way along, trying to get ahead of the men with the torches. They were moving fast though through the darkness, as if they were chasing someone. Deecee was sure now that they meant harm to his master. He put on an extra burst of speed and leapt onto the next car, then down the other side, then around another car.

He reached the spot where the men were and watched them carefully. They were right in the middle of the tunnel, making it hard for Deecee to pass. Deecee followed behind them, staying hidden in the darkness, looking for his chance to sneak by.

Suddenly Deecee heard a scream far ahead in the darkness. It was the sound of his master's girl! Forgetting caution, Deecee leapt on a car next to the men and then down the other side. One of the men spied him and cried out.

"Clancy!" Gavin yelled. "There's a beastie in here with us!"

Clancy stopped, and all the men stopped too.

"What kind of beastie?" Clancy said, lifting his torch high and looking in the direction Gavin was looking.

"I don't know," Gavin said, his voice full of concern. "But it was furry and white and black. It might have been a dog-beastie."

Clancy chuckled, lowered his torch and went back to walking.

"A dog-beastie, ye say. We better get to yon lass

before that dog-beastie does, or it might hurt her. If that happens, you'll see thunder from me, I guarantee it."

Clancy and his men quickened their pace.

Suddenly a moan drifted on the air in the distance. Clancy and his men stopped instantly, frozen in fear.

"Clancy," Gavin whispered, his eyes wide with terror. "Is that what I think it is!"

"Saints preserve us!" Alasdair yelled. "There be Lurkers in here!"

Clancy stared ahead, trying to see in the torchlight.

"Don't be daft," he said, but he didn't sound too sure. "How could they get in here? They're all trapped in Nork's subway."

Alasdair piped up. "Lassie or no, I'll not be risking my neck with any Lurkers. Sorry to say Clancy, no bit of skirt be worth that."

"I agree," Gavin said. "We have to go back to Clancy!"

"How could Lurkers get in this here tunnel?" Clancy said. "It was just a moan from some daft crazy, 'tis all."

"Maybe there's an opening in the subway somewhere," Alasdair said. "Maybe they learned to undo locks."

"How could them with no brains left learn to undo locks?" Clancy spat out in contempt. "They be dead and gone, just walking corpses. They ain't going to be learning new skills any time soon."

"Well, one thing's for certain, Gavin said. "If the Lurkers found a way out, it's a bad thing for everyone. They'll be infectin' everyone, and it won't be long before they come for us and our families."

"Then we should destroy them, and seal up the opening!" Clancy said, more because he wanted to keep looking for Deb than because he believed what he said.

"I'm going back," Angus said. "I'm no hero, not I. And I've not keen on getting turned into an undead."

"Clancy, tis only the wise thing," Gavin said.

"I'm not leaving, 'til I'm sure!" Clancy said. "It might just be a man in there, one who's hurt his leg or has a fever, or just likes to sing!"

"That ain't no singing, Clancy, and you know it!" Angus said, his voice urgent.

Clancy grinned in the darkness. "Let's go a wee bit more. If it be Lurkers, then we turn tail like little girls. But if we find it's just some ordinary joker, you're all going be bowin' your heads and saying your apologies to Clancy, who was right."

Gavin shook his head. "For a truth, this lass has stolen your brains away. I sure hope we don't all be livin', or dyin' to regret it."

CHAPTER 14

When they reached Ballmor, Misterwizard again raised his hand, and the buses and other vehicles behind him all stopped. Super stopped too, and looked over at him expectantly.

Misterwizard grinned at her with a comic serious look, but one that held a scrabbler's excitement at adventure.

"We shall halt our forward progress for simply a nanosecond, long enough for myself to initiate a moment of solitary reconnaissance. I singularly will scrutinize the city ahead and document the current state of its occupation. When I have sufficiently ascertained the level of threat to our cavalcade, I will return and elucidate our next course of action."

"You're going to check it out?" Super said, too tired to try and figure out what Misterwizard said.

"Indubitably. Keep the troops entertained, my dear. I shan't be a moment!"

With that, Misterwizard turned the throttle on

his little machine and sped ahead. Super watched him, and it occurred to her that she would be much faster on her Harley. The little Moped of Misterwizard's was good for scooting around old cars, but if you needed real speed, the Harley was much faster. Then she told herself that Misterwizard would never have agreed to her going instead, so it didn't really make any difference.

Super and Lightpole climbed off the Harley. Super stretched and yawned. Lightpole gazed around. "Do you think he'll meet those monsters?"

Super didn't want to think about it, and she hoped he wouldn't. If he did, she hoped he found a way around them. She simply replied, "I don't know."

Super decided to see what kind of food they might have in the bus behind her. As she walked up to the bus, the driver opened the sliding doors. Sephie hopped out to greet her, making Super smile. Sephie ran into Super's arms and Super hugged her. Then Super gave her a mock reproving look.

"You're a little troublemaker!"

Sephie grinned and then frowned with bravado. "No, I'm not, I'm just an adventurer like Johnny."

Super shook her head, remembering all the wild adventures this little scrabbler had already been through. It was no wonder she had the same thirst for adventure that her hero did.

Microsoft walked out, and soon the whole bus piled out, all welcome for a moment to stretch and stand up. The buses and cars behind them emptied out as well, and soon there was a whole street filled with an odd collection of people.

Super always liked Microsoft. He was the type of man who would always stop and think about something before answering, as if he had to come up with the answer from somewhere in his head before replying.

"Sephie, don't wander off! Hello again, Super! What's the plan?" Microsoft asked.

Super thumbed at Ballmor ahead and climbed aboard. "I told Misterwizard about the horrible creatures that live in Ballmor. Misterwizard is going to check it out and make sure it's safe, and then come back. Do you have anything to eat?"

Microsoft paused, thought and then nodded. He climbed back on the bus and in a few moments came back. He handed her a cloth bag. She took it curiously and looked inside to see brown strips of what looked like leather.

"What's this?" Super said, wrinkling her nose.

"Misterwizard made it," Microsoft replied. "He calls it 'bef grki'. He said it's great for long trips. It's tough, but very tasty."

Super shrugged and took out a piece. It looked tough all right. She sniffed it, then bit down on it. It didn't tear, and she held it in her mouth and looked at Microsoft. He watched her intently, as if studying her reaction.

"You rip a piece off with your teeth. Then you chew it!"

Super pulled on the grki with her hand, biting down on it, and a small section ripped off in her mouth.

She chewed, wondering if she was going to regret it, and slowly it grew softer in her mouth. Then she began to taste the juices of the meat, and began to see it was actually quite tasty.

She smiled at Microsoft and he grinned. Then in a questioning voice he said. "It's good, isn't it?"

Super shrugged. "It's tough," Super said. "But not bad."

Microsoft paused, thought for a moment then said, "It grows on you. Here."

Microsoft handed her a bag made out of a beastie-bladder. "Have some water."

Super took the bag, lifted it to her mouth and gratefully drank. Then she handed it back to him and chewed some more grki.

Microsoft looked ahead, his brow furrowed. "How long will we have to wait?"

"I suppose it will depend on what Misterwizard runs into," Super said.

Lightpole's face filled with excitement and he pointed with his finger. "There's your answer!"

Super looked where Lightpole pointed, and her mouth dropped open. The bad of grkl fell from her hand.

Racing towards them down the main street was Misterwizard on his moped, and behind him were two huge Krakn.

"Why am I always right!" Super groused! "Everybody on the bus!"

Microsoft motioned to the people frantically. "Get back in your vehicles!" Then he grabbed Sephie's hand and rushed back onto the bus himself. The people slowly saw what was happening and began to yell and scream. They all rushed for the doors of the buses, creating a jam, but slowly they all stumbled back aboard. The people in the other cars did the same.

Super sprinted for her Harley and leapt onboard. Lightpole jumped on behind her. Super turned the key and the engine roared to life.

"I'm really getting tired of these creatures!" Lightpole yelled.

Me too, Super thought silently. She just hoped they weren't all going to be Krakn grki soon!

The moans of the strange creatures surrounding Johnny and Deb echoed off the walls and hurt their ears. There were so many of them now, it seemed like they were everywhere, and all only a few steps away.

"Johnny, what do we do?" Deb yelled, her voice shrill with terror and a detached quality. There seemed to be no way out. They were surrounded by darkness and couldn't even see where the moans came from. The moans came from everywhere.

Deb wondered if going back to Clancy and his men was the only way. "Maybe we should just go back!"

The moaners were close! Johnny could smell the evil stench from them, like a wall of disgusting horror about to knock them over. Deb put her hand to her right ear, then let go of Johnny's hand and put her other hand on her other ear. Then she moved her right hand to her mouth, for the smell made her feel like she was about to get sick.

The first moaner in front of them appeared out of the darkness. It was thin and old, dressed in a ragged black suit that was half gone. To their amazement, they saw half of the skin on the man's face was gone. They could see his jawbone, rotted teeth and eye sockets, for it had no eyes. It was as if his skin on his face was a blanket that had been pulled back to reveal what was underneath.

His pants were torn at the knees and Johnny could see bones underneath, with no skin at all. His hands were skeletal as well, with only a small strip of skin covering a few of the fingers.

"Johnny, it looks dead!" Deb screamed.

Johnny didn't answer. He held his sword high. As the creature reached him, Johnny slashed at it with all his might. Johnny hit its arm, and as Johnny watched, the whole arm fell off at the shoulder. The creature looked over at its missing limb, then back at Johnny, as if nothing had happened.

"Johnny, run!" Deb yelled, as she frantically scanned the darkness, trying to see which way to go.

Johnny scowled and struck again. This time he hit the creature right on the neck. As Johnny watched in amazement, the head fell off and lay on the ground. The creature staggered for a second then finally the body fell in heap to the ground. Johnny looked down and saw the creature's mouth opening and closing on the head. It looked like it was still alive! A strange green glow emanated from the dark sockets where their eyes should have been.

Johnny and Deb backed away. Suddenly creatures came from all directions. They were surrounded!

Then Johnny heard something, a sound that seemed totally out of place in the dark, dismal tunnel. It was the bark of a dog-beastie! And even though Johnny's mind was woozy, he was almost positive it was Deecee!

Deb heard it too, and she turned with excitement towards the sound.

"That's Deecee!" she yelled, her voice trembling.

"Deecee!" Johnny yelled, louder and with more confidence.

Out of the darkness Deecee appeared. He barked again, his eyes twinkling with joy at seeing Johnny and Deb again. He ran up to them and stopped, looking at Johnny with happiness.

Johnny and Deb felt tears of joy fill their hearts at seeing him again. Then they remembered their danger. They turned towards the closest monster.

"Run, Deb!" Johnny said. He found her hand and grabbed it.

Deecee saw the monster approaching. He snarled and showed his fangs. He leapt at the monster and bit his leg, ripping at it, pulling it.

The monster turned towards Deecee. Deecee bit

its leg in a tight grip and began yanking and tearing. As Johnny and Deb watched, the monster's leg ripped off and Deecee backed off with it, shaking it in his mouth. The man fell to the ground, thrashing about.

"Good dog-beastie, Deecee!" Deb yelled.

But then the rest of the monsters reached them. Deecee dropped the leg and barked at them. The monsters turned towards the sound.

Johnny knew this was their only chance to escape, though he hated to leave Deecee. After just finally finding him again, it would be heartbreaking if he left Deecee in here with the monsters and it ended up causing Deecee's death. But Johnny didn't see any choice. He had to save Deb. He pulled Deb ahead,

They circled around another junk car and hurried on, towards what they hoped was the other opening, away from the battle between Deecee and the monsters. Johnny looked back. In a faint green glow and in a tiny bit of light from the faraway torches, Johnny could see the shadows of the monsters. There were at least ten of them, and though he couldn't see Deecee over the cars, he could hear Deecee's bark.

"Johnny, we can't leave him there!" Deb yelled her voice full of sorrow.

"I'm sorry, Deb," Johnny said, his voice tinged with sadness as well. "We have no choice. He's helping us escape."

Johnny and Deb looked ahead, and to their relief they finally saw a welcome sight. The round archway of the other entrance to the tunnel beckoned ahead! The

Red Eye was higher in the sky, and the bright light outside beckoned.

"Johnny, we made it!" Deb said, her weary voice full of relief.

Johnny's heart sang. He'd rescued Deb! They'd not only escaped the Nork army they'd escaped the clansmen and the strange monsters! A triple rescue! Soon, they would be free! They weren't going to die in the dark, horrible tunnel after all! Relief flooded him, and a feeling of victory too, for he had fought both three foes for his fair maiden and won. It made Johnny feel strong and brave, like one of the knights from one of Misterwizard's stories.

They ran faster, their excitement giving them an extra burst of energy, despite how tired and dizzy they were.

Johnny pulled Deb outside the tunnel into the welcoming sunshine. It was cold, for the time of the year had come when the leaves fell off the trees and the water fell from the sky, though neither of them had seen or experienced either of those things. Still, the air felt good after the stuffy enclosing darkness of the tunnel.

They stopped running, walked over to the road wall and leaned on it, catching their breath almost in shock they had actually survived. Deb sat down, exhausted, her mind slightly numb from shock, and Johnny sat next to her. They held each other, overcome by their recent ordeal. Now they were out, but they were all alone in Nork. Their new friends were still back behind them, prisoners of the Nork soldiers.   And they were on their own to face whatever lay ahead.

Johnny looked ahead of them, and once again on his adventures he was treated to an amazing and strange sight.

Just as the road rose up to the city, a giant wall, bigger than any Johnny had ever seen, rose up, so high Johnny had to crane his neck to see the top of it. The wall was made of steel wreckage, old cars and bits of rubble, all held together with steel wire. Hanging from the wall were also skeletons, some still dressed in ragged clothes, others just bones or skulls. But there were bodies too that looked as if they'd just been killed, and Johnny could swear he saw some of them moving, as if they were still alive. He even saw a few that looked dead and rotting but moved, and looked like the creatures they'd just faced.

Beyond the wall he could just see the tops of three and four-story buildings that seemed to stretch in both directions as far as he could see, and beyond them taller buildings, ones that rose up and seemed to touch the sky.

"I've never been so tired before, Johnny," Deb said. Then she smiled at him. He smiled back. She put her arms around his neck. He looked at her, and she kissed him, deep and hard. They kissed for a long time, finally getting to enjoy their reunion. When they finally stopped, Deb put her cheek against Johnny's.

"I knew you'd save me."

Johnny's heart filled with happiness, and emotions filled him, threatening to spill out into tears.

"Of course, I did, silly. I'll always rescue you Deb. From whatever danger you face, no matter what happens to me."

Deb looked into his eyes with love. "That's why I'll always love you, Johnny. You're the only man for me, forever."

Johnny felt foolish again, like back in Sanctuary when he saw Deb on that day, they left for their first adventure. He tried to change the subject so he could recover.

"We'll rest here. I don't think Clancy and his men are going to brave those monsters to get to us."

Deb kissed him again, and Johnny began to think he could get used to it. Deb's face grew sad, and tears came to her eyes as she looked back at the tunnel. "Poor Deecee. He just found us again, and now..."

Johnny's heart was torn as well, thinking of his beloved beastie being torn apart by the monsters. Johnny looked back at the tunnel too, and though he tried to answer Deb, his throat was constricted with grief. Tears came to his eyes too, and for once he didn't care.

Clancy and his men inched forward, their white eyes full of fear, their faces grim. Clancy held the torch high and in front of them, as if it could ward off evil spirits.

"Clancy," Gavin whispered.

"Keep quiet and listen!" Clancy whispered back savagely.

Ahead of them, shadows from the torch danced on the cars, making them look like ghosts. A chill ran up and down Gavin's back, and his knees grew so weak he was sure they were going to buckle any second. He chided himself for being like a little scrabbler, but only a little for he knew he was smart to be afraid. If what they thought was in the tunnel was really there, it was more than scary, it was terrifying.

Angus moved faster without meaning to, accidentally getting in the lead. Clancy, Alastair, and Gavin watched as he disappeared in the darkness in front of them.

"Angus!" Gavin whispered. There was no answer. He glared at Clancy.

"Where be he going in such a daft hurry?"

Clancy didn't answer. He was staring intently ahead of them as all three crept forward at a snail-beastie's pace.

As the light slowly exposed more of the tunnel, they came to Angus standing by himself next to an old bus. The door was open. Angus seemed to be hesitating, as if once he was out of the torch's light, he couldn't see. His eyes appeared sightless as if he was blind. They stopped a few feet away from him and stared.

"Angus!" Clancy whispered.

Angus turned his head, and in the torchlight his face was strained and serious. "I heard a bark!" Angus looked towards the darkness ahead again. "There be a barker in here, that's certain!"

"I wonder if that's all we heard before," Alastair, who was taking up the rear, said.

"Don't be daft," Clancy said. "There be a big difference 'tween a moan and a bark."

Suddenly Angus' eyes went wide. His face lost all color and expression and he pointed.

Clancy and Gavin saw it as well, and their faces fell in terror as well.

From the open door of the bus, a skeletal hand, with a piece of flesh hanging off it, moved towards Angus.

"It's a Lurker! Get away!" Clancy yelled, forgetting to whisper.

Angus didn't understand for a moment, and just frowned. Then he turned and saw the hand. He yelled and tried to get away, but the hand grabbed hold of his hair in a tight grip.

"*Aaahh!*" Angus screamed. He grabbed the sides of the bus door and tried to pull himself away, but the hand held on tight. It yanked him up the bus steps.

Suddenly in all the windows of the bus, skeletal heads appeared, as if they were an otherworldly group of travelers. They stared out the windows, flesh hanging off their faces, some with eyes and others with only sockets.

One of the skeletons began climbing out a window! It wore a tattered purple suit. Inside the suit jacket, they could see what was left of the flesh over exposed ribs. There were eyes in the eye sockets, but they were shrived and small, like rotted raisins. And it had a wisp of gray hair on top of its head, like fuzz. The creature's mouth opened, showing jagged, rotted, yellow teeth.

The hand continued dragging Angus onto the bus. He screamed in terror. The others ran to help him, raising their axes.

"Let him go, you dark fiend!" Clancy yelled as he raised his axe. Clancy chopped at the creature's arm, and it broke off, but still held tight onto Angus's hair.

Suddenly moans came from all directions. As the men spun gazed about in terror, creatures came at them from all directions.

"Clancy!" Alastair yelled. "Lurkers there be!"

"We're goin' to die!" Gavin said, all pretense of courage gone. A creature that may have once been a girl with ragged black hair, half a face and no nose wearing a yellow cotton dress grabbed Angus with both hands on his arms from behind.

"Red Eye save us!" Gavin said. He stumbled back the way they'd come. Clancy followed, but before they could get very far, they had to stop and swing their axes at the creatures who pressed in on all sides.

Angus, with the arm still clinging to his hair, ran to follow, shaking his head to try and free himself from the grisly grasp. Angus shrieked and fought, but the girl creature held him tight as two others moved in from the front. Soon five of the creatures stood around him as he fought hard, slugging them with his fists, for he didn't have time to pull his axe out.

Clancy, Gavin and Alasdair made it through the creatures barring their way and leapt around the cars as fast as they could.

Gavin yelled as they ran. "What about Angus? We can't just leave him!" But he continued running away.

Clancy yelled back, sorrow in his voice, but mixed with hardness. "Aye, poor Angus. The Lurkers have him! He wouldn't want us to die too!"

Before Gavin could reply again, the creatures were right behind them. They could do nothing but run. Alasdair was in the lead, for he no longer had any pretense of being brave. His eyes widened with terror and he ran, heedless of where he went, as long as it was away from the monsters. The hand finally fell off his head and rattled on the ground.

Clancy and Gavin followed close behind Alasdair, and in his haste, Clancy dropped the torch.

The men ran in the darkness, screaming, any courage forgotten, using their hands to feel their way, running into cars with their bodies and bouncing off then running on again, just as long as they were moving in the right direction.

A strange green glow shone from the creatures as they slowly shuffled after them, their feet making scraping sounds on the concrete, horrid moans echoing from them in the darkness.

CHAPTER 15

Misterwizard on his little moped weaved between cars and soon reached Super, just as she got her Harley started. Before Super could speak, Misterwizard drove up next to her and yelled.

"I must acquiesce to your foreknowledge and insight, Super! There are indeed very unpleasant and carnivorous creatures inhabiting this metropolis! Follow me if you please!"

With these words, Misterwizard sped past her. Super looked up. The Krakn were only a half a block away! This close and in the light of day, Super could see how terrifying and fierce the creatures were. Their black eyes were narrowed with fury, and their ragged mouths were open, showing their sharp teeth.

Super had to steel herself so she didn't freeze up in fright. Quickly she gave the Harley gas, her mind numb, spun around in a circle and followed Misterwizard. Misterwizard drove on the right side of the buses, past the first one and soon the second. Then he turned in a half-circle, and headed back towards the Krakn!

Super could barely think, but in her mind somewhere, she thought, *We're heading back towards them?* She didn't have time to ponder though, for Misterwizard left no time for it as he roared on with his little Moped, pushing it as fast as it could go.

Super, on her bigger Harley, sped up and soon caught up to him. Lightpole held onto her tightly, a grin of adventure on his face. Super looked over to see him intently staring forward, his goggles on his eyes, a look of concentration on his face.

"Misterwizard!" Super said, wondering if the Krakn were right behind them. "We're heading right for them!"

"We must lead them away from the buses!" Misterwizard yelled, his voice barely heard over the roar of their vehicles. "We are the proverbial sacrificial lamb to lead the wolves away from the flock!"

"I don't want to be a, whatever you said!" Super yelled, but she followed Misterwizard as he sped off to the left down an alley.

Super glanced behind them, and wished she hadn't. The Krakn had turned to follow them, just as Misterwizard hoped, but they were right behind them, so close Super could see the saliva dripping from their mouths. Their tentacles reached out, only feet away, and Super was sure they could grab them at any moment.

Misterwizard and Super sped past old cars and piles of trash in the street. A bus lay right across the road, and Misterwizard veered to the right, up onto the sidewalk and past it. Super had a harder time on her larger Harley, and bounced up the curb, almost falling off. She yelped, Lightpole yelled, and she gave the Harley gas, speeding around the bus.

The Krakn didn't bother to go around the bus. They just crawled onto its top with their tentacles and slid down onto the other side.

Suddenly in front of them, Misterwizard and Super saw a crowd of wildies. The dirty, mangy crowd stood in the middle of an intersection. There seemed to be about thirty of them, standing in a circle, men, women and scrabblers. They seemed to be looking at something in the center of the circle, gazing at it intently. They didn't even seem to hear the loud roar of the engines or the screeches of the Krakn. It was almost as if they were in some kind of trance.

How could they not see the bizarre sight almost on top of them? Super thought.

"Misterwizard!" Super yelled, her long black hair flowing in the breeze.

"I see them!" Misterwizard raised his goggles and frowned at the crowd ahead, still speeding towards them on his moped. "Confound our misfortune!"

Super knew Misterwizard felt the same way she did. They didn't want to lead the Krakn to the helpless wildies, but things were happening so fast, they didn't have many choices.

One Krakn shrieked, then another. Super was sure it was because they saw the wildies ahead, and were licking their chops at an easy dinner.

Super wished with all her might that the wildies would hear, look up and see them and the Krakn coming, but to her dismay they kept looking at the center of their circle. Super wondered if they couldn't hear, like one girl hadn't back in New Sanctuary. People had to make motions to her so she'd know what to do.

There was no more time to talk, or even think. They were almost on top of the wildies, and they were going so fast, Super wasn't sure if she could stop before running into them.

"Exit, stage right!" Misterwizard yelled as he turned his Moped to go down the side street.

Super turned her head to look at him with dismay. She was going too fast! Her Harley couldn't stop as fast as Misterwizard's Moped. She looked ahead. She was right on top of them!

And then the wildies did something totally unexpected. They looked up at her and the Krakn. Super realized instantly that they had heard the noise, they had just been pretending.

In a flash, the wildies in the front of the circle ran to join the others on the far side. Super tried to turn the big handlebars on the Harley to the right to follow Misterwizard, but the Harley barreled ahead.

She looked in front of her and saw what was hidden by the wildies. There on the ground was a circle of some kind of cloth. It was large, at least twenty feet across. What was it?

As Super rode over the cloth, it dawned on her

what it was, but too late. As the cloth gave in and she felt the Harley start to sink, her mind told her what it was: Trap!

Super screamed as she and the Harley fell. She caught a glimpse of a forest of sharp spikes and then the light from above disappeared. She felt a terrific jolt as the Harley's front tire slammed into the side of the pit. Her ribs hit against the handlebars, knocking the wind out of her and making her woozy. Lightpole went flying off to land somewhere else in the pit.

Super fell off the Harley and landed on her back in the hard dirt of the trap floor, and everything went black.

Starbucks ran towards the two huge Krakn, and then suddenly he realized how dumb he was being. Even with Bargainbin and Jewelrydept, there was little chance they could kill both the giant Krakn. He turned and watched Rumple and the people enter into the white, stone building with the lion-beasties.

Starbucks turned and studied the Krakn racing towards them. They were big ones, with slimy gray skin and dark, black eyes. They ran like spider-beasties on their four tentacles, fast.

Starbucks realized he had to do what that girl in Ballmor had done, even though it would put him at risk, just like it did her. He'd have to lead the Krakn on a merry chase, away from the people of Letfreedomring.

As fast as he could, Starbucks turned and ran back to his Harley. *But what about Bargainbin and Jewelrydept?* he thought. Hopefully, the Krakn would follow Starbucks and ignore them. The Krakn were close! Could he get his Harley started in time? And where would he lead them?

He didn't have time to think very long. Turning the throttle and hitting the gas, his Harley roared to life. Thinking to himself how since he started his adventures with Johnny, he was always doing something dangerous, he sped right towards the Krakn.

The Krakn were almost on top of Bargainbin and Jewelrydept. The men looked brave, but terrified. Their eyes were wide open with fear, and their faces were white. Starbucks knew they wouldn't have a chance against the monsters.

Starbucks pulled out his sword and rode right in front of the Krakn. As he did, the Krakn saw him and for a second, they stopped.

Starbucks, his heart in his throat, thought to himself, *Who do you think you are, Johnny?* Then he rode right at the Krakn, sword held high. He reached the first one and swung his sword at the nearest tentacle. The sword hit it and cut a slice across it. The Krakn shrieked and rose up on its two back tentacles.

Starbucks took the chance to turn to the men.

"I'll lead them away. You men run and hide."

But the men didn't listen. Instead, Jewelrydept and Bargain bin yelled at the top of their lungs, raised their clubs and ran at the Krakn. Starbuck's bravado had bolstered their courage. The Krakn, shrieked again, and turned to run. Starbucks realized that being only primitive creatures, the show of force and the larger numbers had scared them. They turned and retreated, scampering back over the junk cars and vegetation, down the street.

The men cheered and raised their weapons, big smiles on their faces. Starbucks stopped and gave himself a chance to catch his breath, not believing how lucky they seemed.

"We showed them!" Jewelrydept said.

"But they'll be back," Bargainbin said. "We have to hunt them and kill them."

Starbucks thought for a moment. "They were heading back towards Ballmor."

"Good riddance!" One of the other men in the crowd said.

But Starbucks was worried. "That means they're heading right for Super and our tribe."

"What do you want to do, Starbucks?" Jewelrydept asked.

Starbucks looked at him. "I have to kill them. I can't let them attack Super."

Jewelrydept and Bargainbin looked at each other and then at Starbucks.

"You mean we have to kill them."

Starbucks opened his mouth to protest, but Bargainbin raised a hand. "Your people are coming to help us. And those things have invaded our home. We want to help you kill them, and we won't take no for an answer."

Starbucks grinned, glad to have the men's help. "Okay, but I'm going to be riding my Harley. How will you keep up?"

"We have our biciclee," Jewelrydept said. "Show him, Bargainbin."

Bargainbin grinned and walked over to a building not far away. As he did, Jewelrydept kept talking. "They may not be as fast as your Harley, but we can ride them pretty fast too."

Bargainbin came from the building, rolling a strange vehicle next to him. It was made of metal and stood waist high. The metal looked like long metal poles stuck together, and in front and back there were round objects with metal spikes in the middle.

"What is that?" Starbucks asked, laughing.

"It's called a biciclee," Bargainbin said. "Watch, I'll show you how it works."

Bargainbin put his leg over the vehicle until one leg was on either side. Then he sat on a black seat in the middle. He raised his feet and put them on two flat pedals. As Starbucks watched with a smile, the round metal things began turning. The strange pedals went around in a circle as well, and the vehicle started moving.

"You make it go with your feet!" Jewelrydept said.

"We had some of those in New Sanctuary," Starbucks said, "though they were all rusted and there were no black things around the circles.

"You need the black things to make it go," Bargainbin said, as he rode around them in a circle. "And you have to fill the black things with a long tube. It shoots air into them!"

Starbucks was amazed, watching the biciclee drive around. He thought how Misterwizard could surely explain the vehicle better. It looked like a lot of fun.

Jewelrydept watched Starbuck's reaction with pleasure. "You have to make it go yourself, so it's a little slower. But you can get going pretty fast!"

Starbucks shook his head. It seemed there was always something new and strange to discover in the ruins of the old cities.

"Do you have one, too?" Starbucks asked Jewelrydept.

"Oh yes. We have many of them, though all of them don't work as good as this one."

"Well, get it and let's get going. I don't want those monsters to get too far away."

Jewelrydept nodded and ran off to fetch his Swin. Bargainbin kept riding around Starbucks in a circle which for some reason, Starbucks began to find a little annoying. He smiled anyway, and waited impatiently for Jewelrydept to return. They had to stop the Krakn before they found Super and the tribe and kill them, no matter how dangerous it was.

CHAPTER 16

As time slowly ticked by, Moxie grew impatient, and a little scared. He didn't know what to do if Clancy and his men didn't show back up. It seemed like forever since Clancy and his men took off after that Johnny character and the girl down the right tunnel, disappearing into the darkness. What did they find there in the dark, foreboding place?

Everyone had eaten now, most having at least enough to keep them going. There was even some leftover meat rotating over one of the fires. Moxie may have hated the clansmen but he had to admit they were good hunters. The Red Eye was climbing high into the sky, and everyone grew restless. The prisoners grumbled loudly, and his men milled about, looking bored. Many of them looked at him, as if wondering why he wasn't telling them to do something.

Moxie didn't think the prisoners would try to attack, but they might find ways to sneak off one by one, especially as his men grew less attentive. The worst thing would be if they had to shoot one, which might start a whole rebellion, which would turn into a real mess. He had to make a decision what to do and soon.

As if reading his mind, one of his men walked up. "Hey Moxie, what we gonna do? Everybody's bored, all this standin' around. Let's go home!"

Moxie decided to stall. "Get everybody up and ready to move." Doing that would take time and give Moxie a chance to figure out just what he was going to do. He thought about taking a different tunnel, and leaving Clancy and that Johnny character to duke it out on their own. The other clansmen would surely squawk though, for leaving Clancy and his men behind. So that was another fight Moxie wasn't keen to have to engage in.

Something finally happened. As Moxie watched with surprise, Clancy and two of his men sprinted out of the tunnel, hot and sweaty. Moxie studied them, and small alarms went off inside, for he'd never seen clansmen looking like they did. They looked actually scared! He'd never seen Clancy frightened of anything, but now Clancy's eyes were wide open with good old-fashioned fear! Was that Johnny guy that tough? Or did they meet something else in the darkness?

Everyone turned to stare at Clancy and his men, and the sight of them caused all talk to died down. Quickly it was replaced by frightened whispers, for the clansmen looked terrified and ran fast, as if trying to escape something.

The three ran out and stopped just outside the

tunnel. One of the men actually fell down, shaking! What was going on? They looked back at the tunnel, as if expecting something to pursue them. They hugged each other and talked in scared voices. Moxie began to feel really scared. Something really bad had happened. Moxie wondered if this trip would ever be over. It was just one nightmare after another, and Moxie began to fear he was never going to see his home again.

Reluctantly, Moxie walked towards them, feeling like he didn't have any choice, for people stared at him as the leader, expecting him to do something. The last thing he wanted now was to walk towards that tunnel, and would have preferred letting the clansmen come to him. As he grew closer, he noticed expressions of grief and fright on the faces of Clancy and his men. Their faces were white and drawn, as if they saw a spirit.

Moxie decided to play it tough, even though he felt anything but tough. He walked up and in an irritated way groused, "'Bout time you jokers returned. Where's the girl? Did you mugs to lose her to that little punk?"

They totally ignored Moxie! They just talked to each other in low tones, not even looking at him. Moxie felt insulted and humiliated, like a little scrabbler that was being punished. It didn't help that he was scared as well. His face flushed with embarrassment and he looked back. Sure enough, everyone was watching and smiling. They'd all seen the clansmen insult him. He had to show he didn't take that kind of treatment, that he was in charge. Moxie screwed up his face and in his toughest voice yelled, "HEY! Stupids! I'm talking to you!"

Clancy and his men ignored him again! Instead, they stood up and started walking away.

"Hey!"

Finally, Clancy turned to him with a grave look.

"Good luck with ye prisoners, Moxie. We be partin' ways now, for me and my men are going a different way."

Moxie's face went blank with surprise. He stammered, "Wha-wha-wha-duyaa mean—"

But Clancy and his men were already walking away, fast. Moxie watched as Clancy and his three men ran to the crowd. Clancy spoke loudly to his clansmen, and they answered him back. Then as Moxie watched, in a stupor, the clansmen separated from the rest and walked towards the left wall of the road. They were leaving!

Moxie realized he'd better do something fast, or the clansmen were gone. What had happened in the tunnel? He stomped after them and caught them just before they reached the high wall on the left side of the road. He moved to stand in front of Clancy. Clancy and his men stopped, but they looked dangerous, as if they weren't going to put up with being blocked for long.

"Who said you could take a powder? You're here to help us, and you take orders from me!" Moxie pointed a finger at Clancy, not sure just how Clancy was going to respond.

Clancy grinned. Then all the clansmen grinned!

"Ye be in charge all ye want, Moxie. You be in charge until them things come, and then we'll see what ye do. As for my men and I, we be leaving, and if ye try and stop us, I'll be cleaving your head from your shoulders right quick."

Those things. Moxie's mind raced, wondering what Clancy was talking about. A cold hand gripped his heart. What things were coming?

"What things?" Moxie yelled, a thin, tough hand gripping his heart and making it pump hard and fast. "If somethin's comin, the Boss is gonna have somethin' to say to you, desertin' us when we're in danger."

Clancy stared at Moxie, unmoved. "There be times when a man has to look for himself, and to the dark, hot place of lore with any that stand in his way.

Clancy walked around Moxie, and his men followed. Moxie knew there was nothing he was going to be able to do to stop them. He turned and watched them walk away.

"Hey! Tell me what happened in there! You got to at least tell me that."

Clancy and his men stopped and turned. It wasn't Clancy that answered, but his second-in-command, Alasdair. "Lurkers in the tunnel, mate. And they be headin' your way. Good luck dealing with them, with this big crowd ye have here. I'd be turnin' back and finding a way out of this here trap, with its high walls, if I be ye. And ye ought to be doing it right quick, if ye value yer skin."

They all walked again. Moxie stopped, trying to think, his dull mind trying to comprehend what Alasdair had said.

"Lurkers? You're off your nut. Them's all trapped in the subway. The Boss sealed up every way out."

"Seems they found a way," Clancy said. "They took the life of my good man Angus. They'll take all of you 'ere long, I wouldn't wager."

His men and him had reached the far wall and begun to climb up.

Moxie's lip quivered. "What about the girl, and that guy Johnny?"

Clancy uttered a short, guttural laugh. "I venture they be one of them by now. You know when the Lurkers bite you, they pass their poison into your blood. You want the girl, just wait. She'll be comin' for ya any moment."

Moxie rubbed his forehead, knocking his hat off and onto the ground as terror shone in his eyes. "Heavens to Murgatroyd," Moxie said, a phrase he learned from the old book about mobsters the Boss had read to everybody when they started acting like them.

Clancy and his men reached the top of the wall.

Moxie's lip curled in anger. "I thought you guys was supposed to be so brave!"

Clancy didn't answer Moxie, but Alasdair called down. "There be a difference between bravery, and sheer foolishness, friend."

Moxie made one more half-hearted appeal. "But there's no other way into Nork. You'll have to go all the way around to the West gate."

"We not be going back to Nork," Clancy said. "We be going home to grieve our fallen brother. When a sufficient time be passed, you'll see us agin."

The Clan moved away, leaving Moxie to stare after them, totally frightened and without a clue what to do.

"The Boss is gonna kill you!"

But the clansmen were gone. Moxie turned to see his men standing there, staring at him. Behind them, the prisoners watched as well. As soon as Clancy had said the word "Lurkers", his men heard it and so did the prisoners. A buzz immediately began of voices raised in fear and alarm, and soon the whole camp filled with fear.

Some of his men kept watch on the prisoners, but everyone looked terrified.

What was Moxie going to do? That rotten Clancy and his men had deserted them, just when they needed them most. He would tell the Boss about their treachery. But for now, he had to act, and act fast.

Moxie ran down to the front of the camp again, as everyone watched him. His men followed him, their faces white with fright, their guns only half-heartedly trained on the prisoners.

"Moxie!" Bugsy, Moxie's second-in-command, came alongside him. "Is there really Lurkers inside them tunnels? What we gonna do?"

Moxie, irritated, snapped back, "What do I look like the answer man? Give me a moment to thing, will ya?"

Bugsy didn't look happy, but he shut up, and just walked next to Moxie.

Moxie slowly walked up to the entrance of the cave, his mind racing, trying to think what to do. He looked back at the camp and the prisoners. He had seen what Lurkers did to people when they caught them. They grabbed them in an iron grip. Then as the person screamed and fought, they bit them, spreading the green goo from their mouths right into the person. Pretty soon, the person's eyes began to glow green too, and they got a fever and couldn't see. It wasn't long before they turned into a Lurker too. You couldn't kill Lurkers, only shoot them in the head or cut them in pieces so they couldn't come after you anymore. The best way was to burn them, but when they burned, they gave off a terrible smell that could make you sick, and if you breathed enough of it, you would become one, just from smoke.

Nobody, but nobody, messed with the Lurkers. They came from the underground, where one of them big bombs landed by where the old trains used to run. The water down there became all green and glowing, and anyone caught down there became one of them. The Boss had blocked off every way out of the underground, and kept guards on every entrance so nobody would be dumb enough to try and get inside.

If the Lurkers had found a way out and were in the tunnels, did that mean they were in the city too? Or was it just in the tunnels? Either way, they were sitting ducks, just like Clancy said, with the concrete walls on either side.

But the only way into Nork was through the gate

up ahead, unless you traveled forever to the gates on the West and East sides, or all the way around the city to the gate on the North. The thought of leading this big group all the way to one of the other gates made Moxie sick. He was already tired of the prisoners, and was looking forward to his warm bed in Nork.

Moxie knew he was not smart enough to figure out what to do, but he had to, they were all waiting on him.

He gazed at the dark openings of the tunnels. The thought of going in them had already been scary to him, now it was terrifying.

Moxie felt his head start to feel light, and he was getting dizzy. Sweat broke out on his forehead, and he realized that he'd lost his hat, as the heat from the Red Eye began to warm the top of his head. He had to think, think, think. What to do?

He gasped. Was that a groan he heard from inside the tunnel?

His knees felt weak and he thought he might wet himself. The thought of just leaving them all and saving his own skin came to him, or just grabbing his men and high-tailing it up the hill and leaving the prisoners to fend for themselves.

Both ideas had great appeal.

It came again. He was sure he heard a groan.

The Lurkers were coming.

Misterwizard hopped off his moped, his face a mask of worry. He ran over in his shorts and flower shirt to the side of the pit, ignoring the wildies surrounding it. The wildies stared at him with wide eyes and looks of fright, having never seen anyone that looked quite like him before.

Misterwizard peered over the edge of the pit, and the wildies joined him and did the same thing. Now that he was closer, Misterwizard could see the wildies held crude spears and clubs. They reminded him of old pictures he'd seen of cavemen, and they resembled them in dress as well, with ragged clothes and dirty faces. He suspected that their language wouldn't be much different than cavemen either, having no one to teach them and being little more than savages.

At the bottom of the pit, Super lay unmoving. Not far away, Lightpole lay still as well. Super's Harley lay next to her, the engine still muttering, making a soft purring sound. Misterwizard saw now that the pit was lined with sharp spikes. There in the pit not four feet from Super lay one of the Krakn, impaled on one of the spikes. It writhed around, not totally dead yet, its yellowish blood seeping down the spike onto   the ground.

That creature didn't worry Misterwizard, but not far away lay the other Krakn. It had not hit a spike, but had simply fallen in just like Super and been knocked out. Misterwizard instantly realized how much danger Super was in, for if the creature woke up first, it would surely attack her. He had to do something fast!

The wildies yelled and screamed, shaking their spears in triumph at having trapped the Krakn. Misterwizard realized, without really taking the time to think about it, that the wildies must have done this before, and they lived off Krakn they trapped. It showed them to be very resourceful and brave, but at the moment, Misterwizard didn't really care to investigate their society. He had more important things to worry about.

One of the wildies, a big man with matted black hair that looked like a black rug sitting on his head, dark bushy eyebrows and a hairy chest partially covered by a gold vest, stomped up to Misterwizard. His face and body were dirty and he scowled at Misterwizard in a way meant to scare him, then shook his spear in the air.

"Or kill! No yors!"

Misterwizard turned to the man with a look of disdain and anger. "My dear aborigine friend, I believe you are trying to say that it is 'your kill, not mine'. Please try to enunciate your speech in a way so that an intelligent person has a rudimentary chance of understanding you. I have no intention of engaging you in a proprietary dispute over the ownership of your dubious but surely satisfying kill. I only wish to ensure the safety of my companions, who have inadvertently fallen into your clever and well-hidden trap."

The wildie, who looked even more like a caveman up close, looked even fiercer. "Or kill!"

All the other wildies yelled in agreement, all

looking threatening and shaking their spears.

Misterwizard shook his head. He had no intention of taking their grisly meal away from them. He called down to Lightpole.

"Lightpole! Are you incapacitated?" There was no answer. Misterwizard studied Lightpole's inert form, and was alarmed to see that Lightpole had landed on one of the spikes. It looked as if it had shot through his left leg. The wound looked superficial, but blood seeped from it in a very serious way.

"Super! Can you hear me?" Super didn't answer either.

Misterwizard knew he had to quickly extricate Super and Lightpole from the pit, for the wildies and their angry leader would surely only grow more threatening the longer he remained. He needed rope, but alas, did not have any. The pit looked like a place where the road had simply collapsed, leaving a deep hole in the ground. It was round and sheer on all sides and at least a ten-foot drop.

Misterwizard looked around at the buildings nearby, trying to spy anything that might be of help. He saw some old curtains through a broken window on a building half a block down the street and smiled. They would work! He would have to tie them to his Moped, and then-

"Or kill!" The caveman wildie broke into Misterwizard's reverie by pushing him on his shoulder with his hand. Misterwizard reluctantly turned his attention to the man, who now glared at Misterwizard with murderous intent. The other wildies walked towards Misterwizard, and it became apparent they intended to do him bodily harm unless he retreated.

Misterwizard realized with irritation the immediate threat of the wildies would have to be dealt with first. He just hoped the time spent did not mean doom for Super.

Misterwizard backed up, keeping his front towards the wildies. The caveman and his wildies companions, encouraged their threats had made Misterwizard back away, smiled and continued to walk towards Misterwizard.

Misterwizard saw something in some of their eyes, a hungry look, and with alarm he realized they thought Super, Lightpole and himself might make a tasty snack as well. They seemed to think the Krakn were already caught, and so they would concentrate on the round and chubby man who might make a good, hearty meal.

Misterwizard reached his moped. He knew it was time for a little magic to impress the natives. He reached into the saddlebag on his Moped and pulled out a long stick. Then he took out a small steel square box. On the side of the box there was a picture of a large ship and the words, "USS NIMITZ".

The stick was what in the old days was called a "sparkler", and the box was called a "lighter", but not even Misterwizard really knew this. He just knew how to use them. Misterwizard pushed on the top of the steel box and it opened, revealing a small wheel. As the wildies watched in curiosity, Misterwizard spun the wheel with his thumb and tiny little sparks of light appeared. The wildies, beginning to be fascinated, grew silent, and watched intently, for they had never seen anything like it before.

As Misterwizard spun the wheel, suddenly fire sprang from the middle of the box. It was a small fire, but it elicited a large gasp of amazement from all the wildies. The caveman wildie looked a little scared, and not as sure of himself. He looked back at the others to see their reactions, and seeing they were the same as his, didn't feel so foolish. He looked back at Misterwizard, then down at the flickering flame again. His eyes went wide with amazement.

As the wildies watched, Misterwizard moved the stick over to the flame. Suddenly there was a loud hissing, and streaks of fire began shooting out of the stick!

"Get back, you malefactors!" Misterwizard thundered.

The wildies all gasped and put their hands up for protection. They slowly backed away, talking loudly in fearful tones to each other.

Misterwizard smiled grimly at the reaction, just the one he'd hoped. He put the steel box away and holding the stick high, he advanced on the wildies.

"There now! See the wizard with his phenomenal power and magic! Skedaddle, you felonious cannibalistic rabble, before I put a curse on you, dooming you to eternal misfortune!"

The wildies did retreat, slowly backing up, their eyes all fastened on the strange hissing stick shooting fire into the sky. The stick hissed and spat, and sometimes the streaks grew longer, and other times stopped and restarted.

Misterwizard glanced at the caveman in front, knowing he was the leader, and the one Misterwizard had to impress the most. To his dismay, the caveman didn't look as afraid as the others, in fact his eyes were dark and he wore a grim smile. Misterwizard began to worry his little trick might not be enough to make the man turn and run, and time was running out.

Still, the man retreated with the rest, and Misterwizard advanced. "Evacuate the immediate vicinity, you uncivilized and illiterate troublemakers! Back to your dark pits of decaying remnants from yesteryear. Scamper into your dens like frightened rabbits!"

Misterwizard reached the pit again, and the man and the wildies circled around the sides. The man was still in front, standing three feet from Misterwizard, which worried Misterwizard. He began to wonder if he was going to have to take out his rifle and actually do the people some harm to cause them to leave. Misterwizard hated the thought of doing that, for he held no animosity towards the wildies, they were only trying to feed themselves, and were actually doing a service killing the Krakn. But if it came to a choice of them or Super, he wasn't sure if even for her, he could harm them. He dreaded the possibility he would have to make the choice, and silently wished for them not to force the issue on him.

"I don't want to harm you," Misterwizard said to the man, voicing his thoughts out loud. "But I cannot allow my companions to remain in distress or possibly be savaged by the strange beasts you have snared. Please do not force me to face this unpleasant conundrum!"

The man simply stared at Misterwizard with a grin. Misterwizard sighed, and decided to go ahead with his plan and hope they understood what he was doing along the way.

Misterwizard strode over to the store with the curtains. The Red Eye had risen high in the sky, and the day began to be warm and bright. *A cheerful day for such dark doings,* Misterwizard thought.

The man watched him walk to the store, then followed. The crowd of wildies all tagged along behind, grinning and laughing, enjoying the strange spectacle.

Misterwizard reached the store, whistling jauntily, hoping he would not feel a club on the head at any moment. He walked into the store and the caveman and wildies watched what he did from through the broken store windows. With dismay, Misterwizard watched the sparkler fizzle out. He threw the remnant on the floor of the store and the caveman walked over and stared at it.

Misterwizard hurried over and grabbed the dusty blue curtains hanging in the display window. As the caveman and the wildies watched with amusement, Misterwizard pulled on them hard until they ripped from the hooks holding them and came down in a dusty pile.

The dust rose in the air, and Misterwizard stood back, waved his hand in front of his face and coughed. The caveman and the wildies laughed, big grins on their faces, pointing at him. The caveman turned to the crowd and pointed at his head with his finger. Misterwizard interpreted this to mean he thought Misterwizard was waksy. The wildies erupted in laughter. Little scrabbler wildies stood in front of their parents' legs, pointed and giggled behind their hands. They were obviously enjoying watching this strange man and his waksy antics, Misterwizard couldn't help but chuckle a little himself. He admitted to himself, he must have been a strange sight to them, and they probably didn't get much to laugh about in their hard existence.

With bustling efficiency, Misterwizard walked over to the other curtain and did the same thing. As the curtains fell to the ground, he was wise enough to stand back from the cloud of dust this time, and waited until it had dissipated before returning to the curtains.

"Or kill!" The caveman glowered at Misterwizard again.

Misterwizard shook his head. *Caveman or civilized,* he thought to himself, *some men were stubborn and pig-beastie headed and all the same.* He grabbed up the second set of curtains and then the first, and headed back out of the store.

When the caveman saw he was heading back to the pit, the caveman grew more intense, as if Misterwizard were challenging his authority.

The caveman moved to stand in front of Misterwizard and stop his progress.

"You!" The caveman pointed at Misterwizard with a dark scowl. "Or kill."

Misterwizard understood perfectly what the caveman meant. It looked like he soon would have no way to avoid a confrontation.

Suddenly there was a screech from the pit. All eyes turned towards it and the wildies ran over to look. The caveman left Misterwizard and ran to look too. Misterwizard hurried as fast as he could with the curtains, fearing the worst.

He was right to fear, for the second Krakn was indeed awake. It snarled from the pit, waving its arms around. Green blood poured from a cut over its left eye, dripping down its face, and making it look even more terrible.

Super stirred! As Misterwizard watched anxiously, Super sat up and rubbed her head. Lightpole lay still, not moving. How long before the monster saw Super? It could only be seconds!

CHAPTER 17

Johnny and Deb held each other and looked back at the three tunnels. The Red Eye was high enough in the sky that they could see clearly now. The tunnels stood like three open mouths; monsters disappointed they had lost their prey.

Johnny and Deb had escaped, but instead of being happy they were overcome with grief, their hearts in pain at the thought of poor Deecee being killed by the horrible creatures in the darkness.

"Why did he have to find us now, Johnny, right at the moment those things were attacking us?"

Johnny pulled Deb's head to his chest, and hugged her. Tears spilled from her eyes. Deb closed them and held Johnny, full of sorrow.

"If he didn't, we'd be dead," Johnny said. "I hate to lose Deecee, but he gave his life for us. He was a brave dog-beastie."

They stood up, still holding each other, heedless of the danger they were in. Despite the loss of Deecee,

Johnny couldn't help but enjoy the wonderful feeling of holding Deb again. Mixed emotions tumbled around inside him, sad at the loss of Deecee, but overjoyed at feeling Deb's soft body in his arms, her soft blond hair close enough to touch.

Deb looked up and back at the tunnels.

"What were those things, Johnny? They looked like people, but rotten, almost like people who were killed by the Mushroom Monsters."

"I don't know, Deb. They must have been changed by the Mushroom Monsters. I slashed one's arm off, and it just kept coming. It was almost as if they weren't alive anymore but still moving."

"Poor Deecee," Deb said softly, biting her lip. "They're probably…"

"Don't think about it, Deb." Johnny held her close. "There was nothing we could do."

Then Johnny looked at the tunnel and his whole face changed to one of joy. It was Deecee! He bounded out of the right tunnel into the sunshine!

"Deb, look!"

Deb turned and as soon as she saw Deecee her face filled with happy surprise. She wiped her tears away with the back of her hand and in a shaky voice yelled, "Yay!"

Deecee ran up to them good-naturedly, his tongue lolling and his eyes laughing, as if nothing out of the ordinary had happened. Both Johnny and Deb knelt down and grabbed him as he bounded into their arms. They held him, stroked his fur and kissed him while he tried his best to lick them both at once, his tail wagging so hard it looked like it was going to fly off.

"Good boy, Deecee!" Johnny said, his voice full of emotion. Deecee whined with happiness, so glad to be reunited with his master and his master's girlfriend again.

"He must have run away from the monsters between the cars, Johnny! Oh, Deecee, smart dog-beastie! How I missed you!" Deb said, crying again but now with tears of happiness.

They held Deecee for a few more minutes, hugging him and grinning at each other like idiots. Finally, they were done and then they started thinking about their situation again. Johnny reminded himself they were wasting valuable time. Monsters or no monsters, Moxie and the Norkers would be coming. They had to find a place to hide or escape, or they were back in the same predicament as before.

Johnny looked ahead towards Nork. What he saw filled him with awe, and a sense of foreboding. Deb gazed towards the city too, and then Deecee joined them. All three stood amazed at the giant wall.

The concrete road rose from the three tunnels upwards until the concrete walls ended at the street level. Here the city of Nork began, and a few buildings stood on either side of the road, which continued until it reached the huge wall.

Johnny took Deb's hand as they continued to study the amazing sight. The wall was fascinating but grisly and horrible at the same time. The bodies on the wall gave the wall a gruesome look, and it incited fear deep down inside, as if it was something they should run away from.

"Johnny, it's horrible!" Deb said, her voice soft and full of awe, saying just what Johnny was thinking. "Look at the bodies on it. What kind of people would make a wall like that?"

Johnny agreed. Something about the wall and the horrors on it filled him with foreboding. What kind of people were the Norkers?

"It's huge," Johnny said, his voice tense. "It must have taken years and years to build it."

"How could anyone build something so big?" Deb asked. "Do you think they know how to use the things from before? How else could they make it so high?"

Johnny nodded. "The Norkers may be more advanced than us." The thought of the Norkers being able to use the things from the time before worried Johnny. If they were, it would mean Johnny's tribe, and maybe even Misterwizard, would be at a distinct disadvantage if there was a battle. It might even mean they couldn't win it at all.

The Red Eye shone on the wall, showing clearly that the hands and heads of some of the bodies moved. Johnny knew one thing; he didn't want to look at it anymore.

"I don't see any way in," Deb said. "It goes up as high as the sky."

Johnny looked both directions along the wall. "I

don't see any way either." Johnny turned to Deb. "But we don't really need to get inside. What we really need to do is find a way to help Restaria and the people of Letfreedomring escape."

Deb nodded, but looked unsure. "What can the two of us do, all alone? And we don't want to be captured again."

"That's true," Johnny said. Johnny thought, trying to decide what to do next.

Deb glanced back at the tunnels nervously. "One thing's for sure, we don't want to be caught again."

Johnny nodded. He didn't know which he'd rather face, the strange monsters or Moxie and the Clansmen. He decided they should leave before either came looking for them. "For now, let's just check out the wall and see if we can find a way in. It might help us free the people of Pelpia somehow."

Johnny and Deb started forward slowly, holding each other's hands. Deecee followed them, his bright eyes looking ahead with quiet happiness, for the world was good now that he was back with his master.

They walked up the road until they reached the surface and began to be surrounded by buildings. The ones closest to them seemed to be totally deserted, just empty shells. Most were made of brick and two stories high, with no doors or windows. Inside them, trash, broken glass and furniture lay, all covered with dust.

They reached the wall and stopped, not sure what to do. Then Johnny saw something.

"Deb, look!" Johnny ran over to a spot, and Deb

and Deecee followed. There on the wall was a metal tube, with a strange cup-like thing on the end. The tube ran into the wall.

Johnny looked at Deb. "I bet this is how to talk to the people on the other side!"

Deb looked frightened. "We don't want to talk to them. They'll just grab us."

"True," Johnny said. "But it means there is a way in. We just have to find it before…"

Johnny turned and his mouth opened in shock. Deb turned, and her expression turned to one of surprise as well.

On the side of the wall thirty feet from the bottom, a door opened. Johnny, Deb and Deecee walked over to where they could see the inside of it. They saw long vertical iron bars on the inside, keeping anyone from entering the door.

From inside, two men peered down at them. One was one of the shortest men Johnny had ever seen, only four feet tall. He wore a pinstripe suit, black leather shoes and a brimmed hat, but they all looked hand-made and slightly comical. He looked even funnier because the man next to him was huge in comparison, taller than Johnny. The big man had a square body, a square head, flat black hair and an empty gaze. He reminded Johnny of old pictures he'd seen of a creature Misterwizard called the "Franknsein Monser". They pointed tommy guns at Johnny and Deb, and grinned.

"Hey, Larry, look what we got here," Tiny, the short, comical one, said in a high squeaky voice, grinning and showing a gold tooth.

"Yeah," Larry, the big one said in a slow plodding voice that made him seem a little mentally slow, said. "Two guys and a doggy want to come inside."

"Should we indulge 'em, you think?" Tiny said.

Larry nodded, nodding his head up and down slowly. "We sure should, Tiny."

Tiny laughed in a high, toy-like voice, and Larry joined him in a deep, ponderous one.

"We mean you no harm," Johnny said, making something up. "We are simply travelers here, looking to join your tribe."

Tiny and Larry seemed to find this even funnier.

"Larry, they want to join our tribe."

Larry looked confused. "What's a 'tribe'?"

"Heck if I knows. I think it means they want to become Norkers."

"Should we let 'em?" Larry said, unsure.

"Of course not, ya dumb palooka. We don't know anyting about 'em!"

They both laughed then, staring down at Johnny and Deb with big grins.

Johnny turned to Deb. "It was worth a try."

Deb shrugged. "Maybe we'd better leave before they decide to attack us."

"I think you're right. I didn't really think it would be that easy."

Johnny put an arm around Deb's shoulders and they turned to the right to walk away.

Suddenly the air filled with a strange, bizarre

sound. It was the ruffling of feathers coming from somewhere in the sky, as if a huge bird was swooping down on them. Tiny and Larry's faces transformed into looks of panic and fright, for they seemed to know what it meant. They quickly slammed the door shut.

Johnny, Deb and Deecee all looked to the sky to see what was coming. What they saw was so strange, it was like nothing they'd ever seen before.

Descending from the sky came a man with giant white wings! Before Johnny could react, the man swooped down, put his arms around Deb's waist and carried her up into the sky!

"Hey!" Johnny yelled, running to the spot where Deb had been, but he was too late. As he watched in horror, the man-creature flew away with her!

As Johnny looked at the man, he saw he was a young man, about Johnny's age. But he wasn't like Johnny. He had long white hair, a strong, muscular body and giant white wings! He flapped them, making a strong wind and a loud whooshing sound as he flew higher and higher with Deb.

"Come back here!" Johnny watched with horror as the boy flew higher and higher away with Deb, Johnny helpless to do anything about it. Johnny tried to think, but it had happened so fast he was temporarily in shock.

Suddenly another wing-creature swept down. This one was a young girl with long, golden hair. Johnny saw they were both dressed in white cloth with gold ropes around their waists. She giggled in a high voice, wearing an impish smile. As Johnny watched she grabbed Deecee and flew away with him!

Deecee yelped as he rose in the air and looked terrified. What was going on?

Johnny watched, his heart sinking. He watched in quiet dread as both Deb and Deecee disappeared over the wall, high in the air.

Another of the winged creatures appeared, flying towards Johnny. Johnny gritted his teeth and took out his sword, ready for a fight.

This one landed five feet away from Johnny. It was another teen, a young man Johnny's age or maybe even younger. This one also had yellow hair and also looked strong for a boy his age.

Johnny raised his sword, but the creature raised his hand and smiled.

"You are Jonni Pocklips."

Johnny was once again taken aback. So many strange things had been happening lately his mind was buzzing, not sure if he was dreaming.

"It's Apocalypse. How do you know my name? And where are you talking Deb and Deecee?"

"I am Mantayo. Don't be afraid. We are your friends. We are the Sky. We mean you no harm. We are taking you to see Pantina."

Johnny didn't move, wary. "Who is Pantina?

Mantayo put out a hand. "Come. All will be explained."

Johnny didn't know who this strange being was, but he could tell he had no real choice but to comply with the stranger's wishes, if he wanted to see Deb and Deecee again. He walked forward. The creature walked behind him, grabbed Johnny by the waist, and flapped his wings.

With his heart in his mouth, Johnny felt himself rising up off the ground. Johnny and the strange winged creature rose into the sky. Johnny held his breath and watched the ground shrink beneath him. He was flying in the air! They rose higher and higher, and soon Johnny and the strange winged boy were just pinpoints in the bright sky.

CHAPTER 18

It wasn't long before the moans of the Lurkers could be heard from inside the right tunnel by the whole camp. Everyone stared at the tunnel, the prisoners of Pelpia with looks of curiosity and alarm, the soldiers of Nork with pure panic, for they knew what the moans meant. Soon panic spread through the camp like wildfire. Shouts and screams of fear started to pop up everywhere, and soon the whole camp was yelling or talking.

Sweat broke out on Moxie's face as the fear spreading all over his body and making him stand frozen in place threatened to swallow him whole. What to do, what to do? He looked at the camp, his mind once again slowing to a crawl, pondering. *We can just run and leave these Pelpia jerks to their fate!* he thought. The Lurkers would be distracted by the prisoners long enough for Moxie and the Norkers to make a beeline. But if he returned to the Boss with nothing, he'd be toast! The Boss would give him a visit with his guards, two guys you didn't want to meet. They were the Boss's "entertainers", and they did things to people that lived in your nightmares. They could make a guy beg for death. And then the Boss would probably feed him to the Lurkers anyway. Unless he planned on taking it on the lamb for the rest of his life, he had to come up with a better plan.

As if reading Moxie's mind, Bugsy ran up to him, his face full of fright.

"Moxie, what we gonna do? Dat sounds like Lurkers comin'!"

"I know dat, Stupid," Moxie said, feeling as if he might wet himself at any moment. His heart beat like a hammer, and he wondered if he was gonna pass out. This was not the time to pass out!

"Well, what we gonna do?" Bugsy said, his voice rising in panic and sounding like a little child without his mother.

Think, Moxie, think! Moxie said to himself. He scrambled to do just that, then simply pulled something out of the air.

"M-maybe they're only in the right tunnel. Move everybody to the one in the middle."

Bugsy nodded, looking slightly relieved that they at least had a plan.

"Get the lead out, Stupid!" Moxie growled, feeling a little more confident and pleased with himself that he actually came up with something.

Bugsy nodded and ran to pass the word onto the other soldiers. Moxie silently willed him to hurry, for the thought of even seeing a Lurker made Moxie's hair stand on end. He'd only seen one once before, one they took out to kill for sport. He'd been only ten seasons then, but he still remembered how terrifying the creature looked. It had green slime from the subway coating its black hair that was all wet and clinging to its skull-like face. Its skin hung from it like it was two sized too big, and its eyes were sunk in. It was the scariest thing Moxie ever remembered.

Some men had the thing in a metal pen, with big walls so it couldn't get out. It wore a tattered gray suit, a shirt that was gray but had once been white and black shoes whose fronts were gone, showing the creature's moldy toes. Moxie remembered in his mind how it moaned and reached out with its arms, trying to grab the men around it. It almost did grab one man's arm, and the man yelled and ran back, falling to the ground. Moxie remembered grinning, a thrill of fear shooting through him like an arrow.

Lurkers were nothing to mess with. And now they were coming for him, and there was no pen between Moxie and the Lurkers to stop them.

Moxie thought he saw a figure in the darkness of the right tunnel heading towards them! It was the shape of a man, darker than the darkness around it. Moxie ran over to the crowd being pushed towards the middle tunnel. It was chaos as people screamed and yelled and tried to run in all different directions. The Nork soldiers were chasing them back and herding them but it was taking way too long! Moxie didn't care if they lost some, just get most of them in the stupid tunnel! Moxie joined in yelling pushing the backs of people to get them moving. Then he grabbed Bugsy's arm. Bugsy turned to him

"Listen," Moxie said with a dark, cold scowl. "You send them Letfreedomring jokers ahead of us. That way, if there is some Lurkers…"

Bugsy grinned evilly and nodded, understanding. "Smart, Moxie. Real smart. Let them take the bite. Then we know to skedaddle."

Moxie nodded and smiled. It wasn't for no reason he was the leader of the Nork army. He knew how to hedge his bets, that was for sure. He ran to help push the people again, but was stopped by Restaria, the Mayr of Pelpia. She stared daggers of suspicion at him. "Where are you taking us?" She pointed at the right tunnel. "What's in that other tunnel?"

You want to know, go down there and check it out, Moxie thought, but he didn't say it because he didn't want to raise suspicion. Instead, he said, "Ain't nothin' in there. We're just tired of sittin' around, and want to get movin'. So shut yer trap and move yer caboose, before I get irritated and start shootin' people."

Restaria didn't budge. "You're lying. My people are not going any further until you tell us what we're up against."

Moxie was in no mood for this lady. He raised his tommy gun and pulled the lever back, making a loud, ominous sound. "You get movin', sister, or you're all gonna be not movin' anymore, get it?"

Restaria was about to respond, when something happened that made both of them forget their argument.

Lurkers poured out of the right tunnel! Everyone saw them. Their faces filled with terror and the air filled with screams. There were four Lurkers, but to Moxie it looked like a giant horde. As they came into the Red Eye's light, their ghastly appearances shone in grisly detail. The man in the lead was nothing more than a skeleton with patches of skin attached, the jaw of his skull opening and closing as if he was talking. His yellow teeth clamped and unclamped together, making a chattering sound.

Behind him came another, what had once been a woman. She wore the remnants of a silver dress that had once been beautiful, but now it was dirty and torn. She seemed to have more skin than the man, but it was blackened as if it had already started to rot.

The other two, both men, were just as horrible. One wore a business suit and had a rectangular shaped black box attached to his wrist with a chain. The box swung about with his arm as he shuffled forward, dragging one foot that was turned sideways. The other man wore a green uniform of some sort, with colorful ribbons on his chest. He wore a green hat with a black brim and a gold metal leaf in the middle of it His lower jaw was missing and he turned his head from side to side, as if searching for a victim with his eyes, which lay on his cheeks, held only by long strings coming from his eye sockets.

"That's what's comin!" Moxie screamed. He forgot all about Restaria or the prisoners and bolted for the tunnel. He wasn't alone, for suddenly everyone ran for the tunnel at once, yelling and fighting each other for space.

Gone was any semblance of order or definition of prisoner and guard, everyone was simply trying to escape the monsters.

The crowd reached the tunnel and ran in, heedless of the darkness or what danger lay inside. Moxie ran next to his men, not thinking about anything but escaping. As he reached the tunnel, something in the back of his mind tried to remind him it was dark inside and might be dangerous, but his mind was too far gone to listen. The front part of his brain told him simply to escape. He had become, like all the others, just a wild primitive beastie, desperate to escape its pursuers.

Bugsy wasn't as mind-numb as Moxie. Standing next to Moxie as they ran, he yelled in a breathless voice, "What if there are monsters in this one too? I thought the prisoners were supposed to go first!"

"Shut up and run!" Moxie said, angry that everybody kept asking him for answers when he was just trying to save his own skin.

The four Lurkers saw the crowd and turned towards them. This made the people crowding to get into the tunnel even more terrified, and they fought the people in front of them to get in.

Three more Lurkers exited the tunnel, two

women and a little scrabbler who looked about six seasons old, holding a moldy teddy bear. She had long black hair in ponytails and wore a pair of pajamas. She looked lost and alone, even though she had no expression on her white face. She followed the others, as if they were leading her back home.

Moxie fought his way past everyone, pushing them out of the way, even knocking some down to get around them.

Then for Moxie, darkness swallowed the light from the Red Eye. The whispers and shouts of the people in the tunnel echoed off the high curved stone ceiling in a deafening roar, hurting Moxie's ears. The voices had a muffled quality, as if sound itself didn't work in the tunnel.

The heat hit Moxie too, for the Red Eye above had already baked the ground on top of the tunnel, and the air inside was stuffy and stale. Moxie looked back to see a crowd of people all rushing to get inside, so many he could barely see any light for they blocked it with their bodies.

Moxie turned and looked ahead. In front of him he saw the rusted hulks of cars, intermingled with the dark shapes of Nork soldiers and prisoners. The people ran through the darkness, weaving around cars. As soon as they were more than ten feet away, they disappeared into the darkness. The realization came to him then that they didn't have any torches, and would be stumbling around in total blackness until they reached the light at the other end. They were heading into a nightmare, and it wouldn't end for a long time.

Moxie felt more terrified than he could ever remember being before, and unsure if he was going to survive the next few minutes. He shuffled forward, dreading leaving the only light behind, but knowing he had no choice, those things were out there, heading his way. His only hope was the darkness, but what waited for him in it as well? Was he just running into the arms of more Lurkers?

Forced between two equally horrible choices, Moxie stumbled forward, his heart crying like a little kid, surrounded by dark shapes that bumped into him or kicked his shins, making him almost fall. He felt his way like a blind man, arms out in front of him reaching desperately for something to feel, to touch things before he ran into them. The sound of shuffling surrounded him. There was nothing in the dark, hated tunnel he liked, it was all horrible sounds and feelings and terror. And people kept talking, filling the air with annoying shouts or the whining of scrabblers. Moxie had never hated people as much as he did just then.
How long could this dark, terrible tunnel last?

Monsta limped as fast as he could, but each time he put his leg down, a shooting pain shot through it, making him gasp. How could a little scrabbler bite so hard? She was like a little monster, and not only that, a cannibal.

Monsta tried not to think about her. There were too many horrible things he'd had to face lately, ever since the Doomsday Prophecy lost the battle to Johnny and were disbanded. Monsta didn't think a big, strong man like him would ever be afraid, but now he was so afraid all he wanted to do was find a place to hide.

As he limped along, he tried to stay near the buildings on one side of the street to be as unnoticeable as possible. He eyed the empty storefronts with an uneasy tension, hoping nothing jumped out to attack him. Most of the stores had their windows mostly smashed, and the stores looked like dead skulls lined up in a row. Each store's interior was dark and full of trash, some of it wet and moldy, others covered with moss or even grass. Each time he passed a new one, a thrill of fear coursed through him like an electric bolt. Monsta couldn't remember feeling so lonely and wretched before.

And just where was he going? He didn't want to have to pass through that city with the black tentacled monsters. And the thought of limping all the way back to Washington Deecee, or even Pill-a-delpia, made him feel weak and weepy. It would be a lonely and miserable trek, and what would he find when he reached there? Nothing but emptiness and more loneliness. He'd never make it! And what about Johnny? What about his revenge?

The thought of leaving Nork with his tail between his legs, defeated, made Monsta angry and his courage returned. Suddenly his fear seemed to melt to be replaced by his old bravado and he scowled. He wasn't defeated, not yet! He was going to kill Johnny even if it meant facing a thousand little monster scrabblers and a million weird black monsters. Even if he died, which was looking more and more likely, no matter what he did.

He looked down at his leg and sneered at himself. What are you a man or a mouse-beastie? A little scrabbler bit you. Poor baby! You should have bit her back!

He snorted and forced himself to stop limping. He looked around. It was quiet as death, not a sound or beastie stirring. It was almost eerie how quiet it was, but he forced himself not to get scared again. He had somehow wandered into an area that was deserted.

He had to start searching for a weapon, that was all. A good, heavy club or some old piece of metal with a really sharp point. Then he'd find that little scrabbler who bit him again, stick her with it and cook her for dinner!

The thought made him chuckle and he grinned. Then he heard a strange sound behind him, a clicking sound. He tensed, knowing something or someone had caught him.

He slowly turned around. Standing there were two Nork guards in their suits with funny brimmed hats. They each held a tommy gun, pointed right at him.

One wore a blue suit with white stripes, but it was tattered and worn with holes at the elbows. He was short, four-feet tall with a thin face and a pencil-thin mustache. The other man was big and round, like a walking ball, with a small round face on top and eyes that peered out of his face like raisins set in a batch of dough. He black suit didn't fit him at all. The pants were too short, showing his ankles, and the suit jacket didn't fit him so his large belly showed in front under a white shirt that didn't fit either. Monsta would have snickered at the guy, but he knew it would probably get him drilled, so he kept his mirth inside.

The short guy with the mustache had a tiny pointed piece of wood in his mouth that he kept moving around with his tongue. He's the one who spoke first.

"Freeze like an icicle, ya big lug or we'll ventilate ya, got it?"

Monsta wasn't sure what the guy meant, but he got the general idea by the guy's tone. He raised his hands nice and slow so he wasn't shot.

The round, funny guy spoke in a wheezy voice as if he had breathing problems and was about to pass out at any moment. "Start singing like a canary-boid, buster. What you doing in Nork and how'd you get past the gate?'

Monsta knew he wasn't getting away from them, they looked as if they just couldn't wait to start shooting. He concentrated on thinking, as if having to turn on a dusty old machine and hope it spit out the right information. Then he came up with something. The truth!

"I was with Charlie and Tick-tock. We got attacked by some strange people from the sky. They was taking me to your king!"

The two men didn't look too bright, and it was obvious neither of them had been expecting to have to think either, for they both frowned. Monsta could see the wheels slowly turning in their heads, and he just hoped they were as dumb as they looked.

Finally, the one Monsta dubbed "Mustache-man" spoke again. "You mean the Boss? You was attacked by the angels, was you? What happened to Charlie and Tick-tock?"

"Charlie got shot with an arrow. I think he's dead. Tick-tock ran off."

The men looked at each other.

Wheezy-fat-man, as Monsta dubbed him, said, "The Boss ain't gonna like Tick-tock running around by himself in Nork. You know how he feels about his type."

Mustache-man said, "Yeah. He only let the guy join the guards 'cause he was big as a house, and Moxie vouched for him."

"What's wrong with Tick-tock?" Monsta asked, curious.

Wheezy-fat-man spoke again in a breathless voice, so soft Monsta had to listen close to understand him. "Never mind. Did the angels have one of them scary spiders with 'em?"

Monsta realized he must have been talking about the giant spider-beastie that climbed down the wall. "They sure did!"

The men looked satisfied, and Monsta relaxed. Maybe things were gonna turn out okay after all.

Wheezy fat man said, "How come you wasn't killed?"

"I ran away too!" *How dumb was this guy?* Monsta thought.

"Okay," Mustache-man said. "we ain't sayin' we buy your story, but we're gonna take you to da Boss. If nuttin else, he'll get a kick out of killin' ya and hangin' ya on the wall. Act like a little lamb and don't do nothin' to make us nervous. Hoof it that way."

Mustache-man pointed back towards the heart of Nork again with the butt of his gun. Monsta limped along, his leg really hurting now from standing for so long. He wondered if he was finally going to get lucky or if he'd been better off staying in Pill-a-delpia and minding his own business.

CHAPTER 19

Misterwizard knew he had no choice. He had to save Super and Lightpole, no matter what happened to him. He grabbed his bag of bombs and the old rifle he kept on his moped and hurried to the edge of the pit. The rifle was a single action type and it had quite a kick when it fired. Misterwizard had oiled and polished it and found some bullets for it, but only a precious few. It was one of his favorite possessions and when he had time, which was rare, he liked to target shoot at old windows.

The cave-man and wildies watched Misterwizard as he set his bag and the rifle down. He tied the two curtains together. Then he tied one end to the bumper of a nearby car and threw the other end over the edge of the pit. He wondered if they would attack him at any second, or even wait until he was down inside the pit to loosen the curtain so he too was trapped.

"Supercalifragilisticexpialidocious!" Misterwizard yelled as loud as he could, calling Super by her full name, hoping to wake her up more. "Lightpole!"

With dismay, he saw it only seemed to wake the Krakn up more. It peered up at him and screeched in its horrible way. Misterwizard picked his rifle up again. He stopped at the edge of the pit and aimed it at the Krakn. Wildies or no wildies, he wasn't going to stand by and watch the Krakn eat his friends!

Super's eyes opened! She reached up and felt her temple, where blood was, evidence of a cut. She looked up at the sky, as if not sure where she was.

"Super! This would be an excellent moment to regain your senses!" Misterwizard yelled. "And you too, Lightpole!

The second Krakn moved! It flailed its tentacles around and peered up at the wildies surrounding the pit, but it was pinned on the spikes. It seemed weaker, but still, anger showed from its eyes. It began to push its lower tentacles towards the ground to lift itself off the spikes. The wildies yelled, some in fear, others in excitement. As Misterwizard watched, a feeling of joy filled him, for the wildies started throwing spears and rocks at the Krakn. Maybe the wildies would distract them and he could make it to Super and Lightpole in time after all!

Suddenly something happened that totally changed the situation from bad to worse. Another screech echoed in the air, but it didn't come from the pit! Misterwizard spun around, searching with his eyes for the source of the new sound.

Then he saw it. Coming towards them were two

more Krakn!

"Confound our persistent calamity!" Misterwizard thundered, his face clouded with anger and frustration. "We traverse from one dilemma to another!"

The wildies saw the new Krakn coming. They all shrieked, pointed and took off running, the leader caveman at the front of the pack. The new Krakn were a block away but moving fast.

Misterwizard glanced at the Krakn in the pit. It had heard the others and now screeched back and glared up at Misterwizard, happy it had allies coming to its aid.

Misterwizard turned his eyes to Super, who finally seemed to be moving. Even Lightpole began to stir, though Misterwizard knew Lightpole would need help to free his leg. Super stood up on shaky legs, but she was still moving way too slow!

With no choice, Misterwizard aimed at the free Krakn in the pit, hoping he could hit it before the other Krakn arrived. He took careful aim, looking through the site glass on the scope, but the Krakn kept moving its head, making Misterwizard have to move the gun and aim gain.

"Stay stationary so I can eliminate you, you creature from a horrifying nightmare!"

Then Misterwizard heard a new sound, one that stopped him, filled him with hope and made him very curious. It was the sound of a Harley in the distance! Could it possibly be Johnny? Or maybe Starbucks?

Misterwizard grinned, hoping with all his might he was right. He took aim once again at the Krakn and fired a shot.

The two Krakn ran fast, scrambling over old cars and rubble by grabbing things with their tentacles and sliding over. Watching them made Starbucks feel queasy, for it was like watching a giant spider-beastie scamper along.

The monsters were fast, Starbucks had to constantly rev his engine, slowing down to work around old rusted hulks then speed up again until he reached the next old car. The constant maneuvering made his progress slow, and he worried impatiently that he was going to fall behind and lose sight of the Krakn.

He glanced back and saw his two companions, Jewelrydept and Bargainbin pedaling as fast as they could on their man-powered vehicles. Because they all had to weave around the junk, the two men weren't that far behind Starbucks, in fact it seemed like they were able to get around the obstacles faster. Still, Starbucks wasn't going to worry about leaving them behind. His main concern was not losing the monsters, and if he had to fight them alone, at least until they caught up, then that was what he would do.

Soon Starbucks and his companions left Pelpia behind, and now the horizon opened to where Starbucks could see beyond the houses that lined the sides of the concrete path they rode on. As he traveled south, in the distance on his right, he saw mountains far in the distance. On the left, just more flat land and houses that seemed to go on forever.

Despite the urgency of his present task, a fleeting thought danced through his mind as he gazed at the distant mountains. *What is out there?* he thought. "Will Johnny and I go in that direction someday, and find out what lies at the foot of those mountains? What monsters or strange civilizations will we find? And will we ever really unite this country back together under 'Mocracy, as Johnny and Misterwizard want? Or will we really die someday, somewhere, far, far away?"

Starbucks forced himself to stop musing and concentrate on catching the Krakn. He realized with dismay that even his quick pondering had helped the Krakn to put more distance between them and Starbucks. They were almost two city blocks away! It wouldn't be long before he lost them! He gunned the engine and finding a relatively clear spot, shot forward.

Now that he was on the long concrete strip between cities, he was able to move faster, and Jewelrydept and Bargainbin began to fall behind. He glanced back and could barely see them, dots on the horizon, pumping their legs as fast as they could. Starbucks grinned, for it was a funny sight, and he mentally thought how grateful he was that Johnny found their Harleys. What the other two men rode on looked like a lot of work.

Starbucks began to gain on the Krakn again! And

just in time, for in the distance, he saw the tall square shapes of the buildings of Ballmor. If the monster reached there first, he would surely have more than two monsters to fight, and he had no idea where Super was, if she even made it this far. If he lost the Krakn, he'd just have to stop looking for them and start searching for Super again instead.

Starbucks decided he'd better decide just what he was going to do when he reached the Krakn. Was he going to try and knock them over with his Harley? Would he slash at them with his sword? Or just yell at them, trying to get their attention? He realized he had no real plan, and would just have to "play it by ear", as he'd heard Misterwizard say.

They were almost at Ballmor! They couldn't be more than two blocks away! Starbucks grabbed his sword out of its scabbard on the side of the Harley and readied to attack. But then he shook his head, thinking he must be dreaming. There in the distance, he swore he saw Misterwizard in his flowery shirt and shorts, with a rifle in his hand. Had the Red Eye's heat done something to his mind? Or were the recent fighting and his exhaustion simply too much for him? This was no time to start losing his senses. Starbucks shook his head to clear it, and gave the Harley gas. Now more than ever, he had to get to the Krakn, and fast, before he was so incapacitated, he couldn't fight.

Moxie stumbled along in the darkness, his skin trying to crawl off his body. Everywhere, people shuffled slowly forward, whispering, crying, moaning. They sounded like they were Lurkers. Some were Nork soldiers, but there were also prisoners, Moxie could no longer tell. It was hard going, because the tunnel was choked with old cars and trash. And so hot and stuffy! Every breath felt like a fight just to get air in his lungs, and each one made him afraid he wouldn't be able to breathe in the next one.

The people in front would constantly be stopped by some huge obstacle, making the whole crowd stop, run into each other and wait. Then people would yell in anger or cry out in panic, until the whole crowd moved again, only to repeat the same process a few minutes later. They were all so loud! Why didn't they all shut up, so those things wouldn't hear them?

It was not only hot and airless but so, so dark. Somebody had finally found a torch, but the darkness still seemed to be a living thing, grinning at him from the places just beyond the torch's light. Shadows danced everywhere, and everywhere imaginary Lurkers hid. The sounds of so many voices bounced off the walls, creating a deafening din, so you couldn't even hear what anyone was saying or yourself think. And Moxie was sure he'd peed his pants. He didn't really care though he just wanted the nightmare to be over.

Moxie began to realize they were stupid letting the prisoners go first, for now the prisoners would be the first to get out, and the Lurkers from the other tunnel were surely right behind Moxie and his men following. Even worse, the stupid people ahead would stop again, blocking the escape, just long enough for the Lurkers to reach them and start feeding! And it was all because he listened to that stupid Bugsy!

They all stopped again, and Moxie, his mind still full of the image of the Lurkers behind them, felt panic rise up in him like hot water in a kettle. He turned and peered back in the utter darkness behind them, for the one torch was to the side, and only lit up ten or twelve feet around itself. It was so dark back there, anything could be coming, and they wouldn't see it until it was on top of them. He turned back around and willed the people in front of him. Hurry up!

Moxie turned and yelled, "Get moving!" but his voice was quickly absorbed in the din of all the other voices. He decided that he wasn't going to be the first to get eaten. He grabbed a soldier in front of him by his suit shoulder and pulled the man backwards, making him stumble and fall to the ground. Quickly Moxie stepped over him and ran to grab the next man in line to do the same thing.

A moan sounded somewhere in the darkness behind them. The sound was faint, distant and soft, but it was enough. Immediately screams of terror filled the tunnel as everyone glanced back fearfully towards the end of the tunnel, then turned back and in a panic bolted for the far entrance.

Moxie's mind stopped altogether, to be replaced by sheer terror and panic. A big bus was right in front of him, and the light of the nearby flickering torch made it look like a giant dead beast. It was so long! Moxie ran along its side, trying to find the end, feeling the cold steel. Inside, he saw skeletons, sitting in the seats as if they were still riding it on the way home. Some of them wore grisly grins, as if it was all a big joke. Others looked almost happy, as if their struggle was now over. Could one of them turn out to be a Lurker? The door to the bus was open. Was a Lurker going to stumble out at any moment?

The torch was getting too far ahead! Moxie would soon be left in the dark with those things coming! He felt his hands along the side of the bus faster, almost running, trying to find the end. Something sharp stabbed his hand and a sharp pain shot through it. The wetness of blood pooled on his hand and then dripped into the darkness. Cripes! How bad was he hurt? He cradled his hand against his stomach as pain shot up his arm and ran on, unthinking like a wild animal.

He finally made it around the bus. Two men were right behind him, stumbling along in the dark. Moxie saw one disappear out of the corner of his eye. He turned quickly to see what happened, but there was no sign of the man. Had a Lurker grabbed him? Moxie hurried around the bus only to run into a two-wheeled biciclee lying on the ground with his feet. He fell headlong onto it, his arms getting tangled in the bars. He hit the palms of his hands on the hard concrete, scraping them and hurting both of them some more.

Another moan, this one close! Moxie struggled desperately to get up, pushing against the concrete and trying to free himself from around the biciclee's bars.

He didn't make it all the way up, but still managed to crawl away on all fours, his knee landing for a moment on one of the biciclee's metal bars and sending a stab of pain up his leg. It was harder to see over the cars from the ground, and so dark it was like swimming through mud, but he didn't have the time to stand up, he had to get out of there!

A light appeared ahead, faint and small. It was the other side of the tunnel! Moxie almost sobbed with relief. Joy flowed through him like water to a man dying of thirst. Maybe he wouldn't die after all!

He crawled like a man possessed, his bleeding and scraped hands getting dirty from the blood mixing with the grime from the street. His whole body and suit were filthy from the dirt on the ground, but he didn't care. He realized suddenly that he'd lost his tommy gun somewhere, but he didn't care. Let the Lurkers have it. He wasn't going back for it, that was for sure! He realized he'd left that Harley he'd found behind too. Who cared? He just wanted to escape!

He heard a joyful sound, happy people shouting as they poured out of the tunnel. Moxie giggled, his mind gone, crawling along like a beastie, dirty and bloody, happy to be free.

Moxie saw something ahead of him, under one of the cars. Two glowing green eyes peered back at him. Moxie's joy dried up, as if it had never been there. Moxie froze, for the eyes were right in front of him. He tried to back up, but it was hard to do on all fours.

A hand grabbed his wrist! It was a woman's hand, but wrinkled and with flesh hanging off it. A Lurker! Moxie spun around on the ground and looked up. There she was! A sightless corpse in a tattered purple dress. She wore a shiny gold bracelet, and looked like she was about to go to some kind of show, not dead. Moxie screamed and pulled his hand away violently, but the creature had him in a vise-like grip. He howled with terror, his throat tightening up. He kicked up at the hand with his foot and then smashed his other fist on it.

A monstrous visage floated up out of the darkness under the nearest car. A skull with skin and ragged long black hair moved towards him, crawling from under the car. Moxie's breath caught, he could no longer speak, and he sat like a beastie caught in a trap.

As Moxie watched in silent fright, the creature under the car opened its grisly mouth, showing rotted, yellow teeth and a horrible dark hole behind them. With sick fascination, Moxie saw a mouse-beastie sitting in the creature's mouth, staring out at him! As Moxie watched helplessly as the creature bit down on his leg, mouse-beastie and all.

He felt the teeth sink in, past his suit and into his leg. He finally found his voice and screamed again, flailing around as he felt the teeth sink in. He felt his skin break and pain shot up his leg, and more wet blood began to flow.

A Nork soldier ran in front of him, luckily for Moxie, for it ran into the arm of the woman monster, knocking Moxie's hand free. The creature under the car let go to get a better bite. Moxie scampered away on his bottom, whimpering in fright. His head felt hot and his leg and both hands throbbed with pain.

Finally reaching the tunnel entrance by crawling backwards, Moxie was able to stop long enough to stand up. The soldiers and the prisoners wandered about, as if they were too dumb to think about what to do next. Moxie's vision blurred for a moment, and he felt as if he was going to fall down. He stumbled out on shaky legs. Bugsy ran up to him.

"What do we do?" Bugsy yelled, looking as mindless and terrified as Moxie was.

Moxie had to act like he was in charge again, no matter if he felt like falling over, throwing up and passing out. "Call them dumb guys at the wall," Moxie mumbled in a slur. "We got to get inside, fast!"

Bugsy nodded though and ran to do what he said. Moxie looked back. Almost all of the soldiers and prisoners had made it out now, only a few stragglers running from the entrance. Moxie wondered how long until the Lurkers poured out? It couldn't be long, for they had been right behind him!

Moxie hurried to the gate to see Bugsy arguing with the gate guards, Tiny and Larry, who peered out the opening. Tiny was so short all Moxie and the others could see was the top of his head and his eyes. Larry was so big; all Moxie saw was his chest.

"Who are all you people?" Tiny said, grinning, enjoying a little joke, not aware of the danger not far away. "We didn't order no entratainment."

"Yeah, the Boss said to bring back supplies," Larry said, "not a whole crowd of clowns wit ya. I don't think we should let you mugs in. Go back where you come from."

"*Let us in!*" Moxie screamed, his head throbbing and sweat breaking out on his forehead. "Or I'm going to see the Boss makes a special case of you idiots!"

Tiny's eyes peered down at him, looking a little scared now. "We was just having a little fun, Moxie?" he said. "Hey, you don't look too good."

"Shut your mouth and open the gate! Lurkers comin', brainless morons!" Bugsy yelled.

"Lurkers?" Tiny said, his eyebrows arching. "There ain't no Lurkers out here. They're all inside the subway."

"Let us in, or I'm gonna full you full of holes!" Moxie yelled, forgetting he lost his tommy gun.

Tiny and Larry just stood there. Moxie began to feel like he was in some sick, twisted joke.

Suddenly Tiny saw something and pointed, his little finger sticking out the opening. Moxie looked. Lurkers poured out of the tunnel.

"It is Lurkers!" Larry yelled. "Whattya know!"

"Hurry!" Bugsy yelled. "Before we're all eaten!"

"Okay," Tiny said and he disappeared. After a few moments to Moxie's relief, the huge wooden door swung inwards.

Another panic ensued, and everyone pushed to get in at once. People fell down and were trampled by others in the rush to get inside. The crowd forced the door open wider and poured in, spreading out inside. A fleeting thought came to Moxie that he'd better get the guards to corral the prisoners before they all ran off, but he didn't really care at that moment. He couldn't remember feeling so rotten before, and he wasn't sure if he'd ever care about anything again.

The Lurkers shuffled out of the tunnel. Five, ten, fifteen of them, heading right towards the gate.

"Close the gate, fast!" Tiny yelled.

Moxie found himself once again at the back of the crowd and cursed his luck. It was taking too long for everyone to get inside! The Lurkers were slow, but they never stopped and they were getting closer every second!

Finally, after what felt like days and days, the last of the crowd ran in. Moxie finally ran inside. He leaned against the other closed door on the inside and breathed a shaky sigh of relief.

Moxie watched Tiny, Larry and others, guards and prisoners, push on the door to close it. Watching little Tiny try to push the door would have been funny to Moxie, if he was feeling better. Just then, it didn't even make him smile. In fact, Moxie scowled with hatred. These two idiots almost got him killed! The door was almost closed. Moxie ran over and grabbed Tiny, lifting him up in the air like a rag doll.

"Hey, what you doin? We let ya in!"

Moxie grinned with evil intent and threw Tiny out the opening just before it slammed shut. Tiny's shrill scream could be heard falling away as he hit the ground and started rolling.

"Close the gate!" Moxie yelled angrily. His men, having seen what he did, grinned at each other and slammed the door shut. Then they and Moxie laughed darkly. Moxie looked at Larry, but Larry was too slow to think of what to say, so he just stood there, looking unhappy.

"Hey," Bugsy said. "Let's go up top and see what happens to him!"

Moxie, Larry and Bugsy all nodded and hurried up the wooden steps on the back of the gate to the small opening. Moxie was in the lead, chuckling merrily with an evil joy in his heart, like an evil child who is enjoying torturing a small beastie. Maybe things were all gonna turn up roses after all.

CHAPTER 20

Johnny watched in amazed fright as the ground grew smaller and smaller and Johnny and the strange winged being rose high up into the sky. Without realizing it, Johnny held his breath and then when he started breathing again, it came in gasps. The young man Mantayo held Johnny in a firm grip around the waist, and silently Johnny hoped the boy was strong, for the ground was now far below.

The strange teen Mantayo flapped his wings, and each time he did, they swooped upwards again with a jerk, higher and higher. They flew straight up, as if Mantayo wanted to get some height before moving forward. Soon Johnny could see everything below. He saw both sides of all three tunnels and the gray ribbon of road stretching off back towards Pelpia. With interest, he saw that not only the clansmen were on the other side of the tunnel now, but the whole crowd, prisoners and army, poured out of the middle tunnel. Johnny knew what had happened. They too had run into the strange monsters with their decaying flesh.

Mantayo flew so fast, soon Johnny couldn't see the crowd anymore and he wished Mantayo would stop for a moment so he could see what happened. He worried about the people of Pelpia, if the monsters would get them, but from where he was way up in the sky, there was obviously nothing he could do to help them. And it was better that Mantayo get them wherever they were going before he began to tire and dropped Johnny. The thought of falling from the sky, screaming in fear, only to splat on the ground made Johnny queasy.

He could see the far side of the concrete road now, and houses, none more than one or two stories, dotted the landscape on both sides, seeming to go on forever. Johnny looked to his right and saw an amazing sight. In the far distance, there was a shoreline, and beyond it, water, as far as he could see. He'd never seen so much water in his life. It seemed as if the world stopped and the water took over. The water continued all the way to the horizon.

All these things Johnny saw in an instant, for there was so much to see, and they kept flying, moving fast, soaring like an eagle-birdie. Johnny grinned. He had to admit, flying through the air was pretty exciting. What it must be like to have wings! Johnny tried to look up at Mantayo, but the young man was behind him, so it was impossible. He contented himself with enjoying the amazing view below.

As if reading Johnny's mind, the boy who called

himself Mantayo spoke, and Johnny heard humor in his voice. "Do not fear, Jonni Pocklips. I am used to carrying animals and younger Sky and not dropping them. I am very strong."

"It's A-pock-a-lips!" Johnny yelled over the sound of the wind rushing by his ears.

Johnny grinned darkly, recognizing a sense of arrogance and bravado in the teen that while annoying, reminded Johnny of himself, and made him feel a sudden kinship and affection for Mantayo. Maybe this young man wasn't a bad person at all, but a friend.

"Where are we going?" And how high are we going, Johnny wanted to add, but he didn't. And what happens if I get sick?

"All your questions will be answered when we arrive back at our kingdom."

Kingdom? That sounded a little ominous to Johnny, but having no choice, he settled in and turned his attention to looking down at the world as it passed below.

As Johnny watched with fascination, they passed over the high wall that just moments earlier he and Deb stood in front of. After the wall, it looked like the buildings had been leveled, leaving a block of nothing but rubble. Then the city of Nork started. First there were two and three-story buildings for what looked like miles, as if the whole world were nothing but buildings, broken up by streets of gray. Johnny had never seen so many buildings crammed together. Then far in the distance, he saw the "skyscrapers". There were so many of them, and they were so far away! They huddled together like a giant steel and brick jungle, dark and impenetrable. Johnny was amazed. He'd never seen such a place before. The city seemed to stretch on forever, as if the whole world was made up of buildings.

Worry filled Johnny's mind, for he never expected they were taking on a foe with such a big fortress. If the whole massive city was full of Norkers, Johnny figured they must be as numerous as ant-beasties. There was no way the people of Letfreedomring, or even his own tribe, would have a chance of defeating them.

How could they free the people of Letfreedomring once they entered such a vast land? They would be swallowed up and disappear. It looked impossible. The thought made Johnny feel discouraged. His tribe might be making a big mistake even bringing themselves to the attention of such a big enemy, at least until they had a chance to grow in numbers themselves. He started to have a really bad feeling, as if they'd made a huge blunder, and would end up losing everything because of it.

He gritted his teeth and forced himself to stop thinking such negative thoughts. They had Misterwizard, and a whole tribe of courageous men. They had the Undergrounders, and the wildies who had joined them. Together, they would find a way, just like they always did, to win.

As they flew along, Johnny was amazed at how strong the boy seemed to be. He held Johnny in a tight grip, and every few seconds flapped his wings again, causing them to surge forward. They grew closer to the huge "skyscrapers", and Johnny began to see something strange about them. What looked like spider-beastie webs looped between tops of the buildings. It connected the buildings together by web from one side of the city to the other.

Johnny's head began to spin from so many new sights and weird experiences. What kind of a world had sprung from the mushroom monsters? It was so different than the pictures and stories Misterwizard shared with him. Surely none of these strange things existed before the war, did they? Misterwizard never mentioned them. Misterwizard spoke of the "radeeashun altring the sisting kemistry" of living beings, whatever that meant. As with most of what Misterwizard said, Johnny just filed it away, not really understanding.

Johnny thought about Deb again. He grew impatient to get this flying adventure over so he could find her again and Deecee too. He hoped this boy was taking him to the same place they were going.

They flew so high! Johnny managed to see Montayo's face. There was strain from the hard work of flying, and he had a sheen of sweat, but he smiled and looked confident. Johnny wasn't sure if he felt more confident or not, for they'd been flying for a long way. Surely the other boy must be growing tired.

Johnny looked down. The ground seemed so far below, and yet Johnny could see the landscape clearly.

He was getting a bird-beastie-eye's view of Nork, and it was massive.

He looked behind and saw an island with a strange, tall white statue of what looked like a woman in a robe on it. She wore a crown with spikes on her head. The statue's arm had broken off, leaving a gaping hole where the arm had been. On the ground far below, Johnny saw the arm and hand, holding a torch.

He looked ahead and saw the land of Nork was actually on a massive island. The huge buildings of Nork lay straight ahead. He began to pass buildings that looked beautiful and strange. One looked like the buildings in Deecee, with huge stone steps, large stone columns and spires rising up into the sky. Another rectangular building seemed to be made entirely of glass, though many of the windows were shattered, exposing the skeleton-like structure underneath.

To the right of the island, he saw a ribbon of water, and then a huge land mass, also full of buildings as far as he could see. Far beyond that, Johnny saw a large strip of land, almost like a Krakn tentacle, stretching out into the far distance, and beyond it, nothing but the blue of water. On the horizon in that direction, it seemed like the world came to an end, and he wondered if it truly was the end of the world.

They drew closer to the giant buildings, and Johnny couldn't help but smile, for despite the danger, he was having an exhilarating experience flying over the city. He had a fleeting feeling of jealousy for Mantayo. What it must be like to fly wherever you wanted, as if you were the lord of the skies.

They approached one of the tallest buildings. It looked to Johnny like a giant long square box with a needle at the very top. It seemed to be one of the tallest buildings, standing so tall the rest of the building around it looked short in comparison.

With fright, Johnny saw two giant spider-beasties clinging to the sides. What looked like spider webs draped from the building to the others around it. As Johnny looked around, he realized that most of the tall buildings had the webbing connecting them, all near the very top.

His eyes opened wide with apprehension, and Mantayo must have noticed. He yelled down to Johnny with an effort, "Don't fear the Piders. Our goddess Pantina controls them. They protect us from the Groundworms."

The Groundworms, Johnny thought. *Is that what these people call the Norkers?* It seemed as if there was not exactly a love shared between the people of Nork and the people of Sky. Johnny filed the information away, for it might prove very useful in the future.

As they drew closer, Johnny saw that some of the material connecting the building was indeed spider-beastie webs, but some other bits were rope and even wood fashioned to make walkways from one building to another. The whole city of buildings as far as he could see was connected by the webbing and ropes, making it look as if a giant spider-beastie web had descended from above and dropped on them. He thought it was no wonder the people of Nork were afraid to climb up and attack the Sky, for as he gazed around, he saw other spider-beasties clinging to other buildings.

They drew close to the building with the needle. It wouldn't be long before Johnny could find some answers, and find out if he had to fight to rescue Deb and Deecee.

As Monsta limped along, his mind was absorbed watching the sights and sounds around him, he almost forgot about his aches and pains. Nork was a bustling place, with people everywhere, running, playing, or just walking down the streets. Many seemed deformed, with their faces twisted or missing limbs. It looked to Monsta like the Mushroom Monsters must have hit this place pretty good, causing the people to be so affected. They all looked wild or mildly waksy too, and Monsta wondered if that was also caused by the Mushroom Monsters. A nervous fear gripped him, hoping they didn't attack him again. It seemed as if as long as he was with a guard, they left him alone. He definitely didn't want to face the crowd alone again, not unless he had a head start running away.

Not many had the fancy clothes of the Nork guards. Most had what looked like clothes sewn together from the rags of old clothes left over from before, and they were all dirty, as if bathing never occurred to anyone. But they all seemed as if they were trying to look like the pictures on the buildings of the guy in his striped suit and the girl in her dress and pill-shaped hat, as if it was a rule they had to follow.

Sometimes he'd see couples who did look just like the posters, and they had crisp clean looking suits and dresses. Monsta figured these were the rich people, for everyone else stayed away from them and treated them with respect. The rich people always seem to have a guard following them, who looked like he was ready to beat up anyone who even breathed in the rich peoples' direction. Monsta figured the rich people must be friends of the king or high up in the right circles. Monsta noticed that not even many of the guards had the tommy guns, but all had some kind of gun or rifle. Monsta figured out most of the tommy guns were just for show, to look like the posters, and some of the rich guys even had ones covered with glitter or jewels that obviously didn't really shoot.

As Monsta strolled along with his guards, he marveled at how many buildings there were. They were everywhere. And the blocks between streets went on forever, one broken down building after another, gray, dirty and broken building. Inside some of them, Monsta saw people huddled around fires, or lounging under makeshift tents made of blankets draped over old rubble. Through one doorway he saw a family watching a dog-beastie roast over a fire on a spike, the father slowly turning it over and over. It looked tasty, and Monsta realized how hungry he was.

The buildings soared up into the sky. Monsta looked up at them, and saw something else that chilled him to the bone. There on the side of a tall building, way up near the top, sat one of the giant spiders-beasties.

Monsta looked at the men with him, and realized with grim satisfaction that they too stared up at the spider-beastie warily.

"Do them things attack?" Monsta asked.

Wheezy-man looked at Monsta with a scowl, as if he was a bug-beastie, but then he answered Monsta anyway. In a wheezy voice he said, "If we leave the Angels alone, the monster spiders stay up there. It's how the Angels keep us from going inside the buildings and rub 'em all out."

"Yeah," Mustache-man, the short one with the black curly hair said. "It's what you call a 'truce'."

"But they still attack you guys Sometimes!" Monsta said. "They attacked Charly, Tick-tock, Lady Stabs and me!"

Wheezy man chuckled darkly. "We didn't say we was their friends with them or nothin'. They was probably payin' us back for somethin' we did. We find ways to take 'em out once in a while, and then they return the favor."

"They act like they own Nork," Mustache-man grumbled, "One day the Boss is gonna find a way to kill them spiders. Then we take flying freaks out, permanently. The king will own it all. Then we'll start expanding our territory."

"Flying freaks is right," Wheezy-man agreed.

"Unnatural. People with wings. They're as creepy as them people with weird slanted eyes or black skin, like Tick Tock."

Wheezy-man's words made Monsta curious. "You guys don't like black people?"

"The Boss says they're all freaks, changed by the bombs," Mustache-man said. "Them, and the yellow skin with slanty eyes, and anyone who don't look like us. They live in across the water in Booklin. They used to own Keens too, which in on the same island as Booklin, but on the north side, but we took it over. We fight them all the time, too. One day, the Boss is gonna wipe everybody who don't look like us out. Then nobody but us will be around."

For some reason, hearing the last thing from his guards made Monsta like the king and his people even more. They weren't just evil, they were bigoted too. Monsta remembered how Ripper had a rule about not letting anyone but white people in the Doomsday Prophecy. It was just another fun way of hating people and being exclusive. Monsta began to feel almost happy the Doomsday Prophecy had been destroyed, for now he felt like he'd really found a home.

"Hey. What's your names?"

Mustache-man glared at Monsta suspiciously. "Why you care?"

Monsta shrugged. "I like you guys, you're my kind of people."

The two men chuckled and grinned. Wheezy-man said, "You're not a bad guy, with your black hair and beard, and big as a gorilla. But you got to prove yourself before we let you in, and that means get the Boss's okay," Wheezy-man pointed to himself and then Mustache-man. "But I guess it won't hurt nothin' to tell you who we is. I'm Frank. And this here is Antonio."

"I'm Monsta," Monsta said.

"Monsta," Antonio said. "There's a lot of monsters nowadays. You got to earn a moniker like that. So far, you look like a mouse-sta."

Both men laughed, and Monsta grinned, not taking offense. He knew the routine. He'd have to prove himself, just like he did with Ripper. He'd show them who was a monsta, and very soon. All they had to do was give him a chance.

They passed an open space where there was only a pile of rubble where a building had been. Monsta looked closely and saw bloody rags, bits of bones and trash. He decided it must be where they threw the refuse from meals. The bones were from beasties, but also people. Skulls lay on the ground, human skulls, and leg and arm bones, picked clean. *These people here were crazy,* Monsta thought. Once again, he felt his skin crawl. He wondered what this king was gonna be like, if the people were this weird. He started to really love Nork.

He turned and gazed ahead. There in front of them surrounded on all sides by larger skyscrapers he saw a beautiful vision. Smaller than the buildings around it, it still commanded a person's gaze for it was elegant and beautiful. To Monsta it seemed to be some ancient structure from some ancient time, when the world was magical and full of beauty. It almost looked like it wasn't really there, just an illusion, and if you drew too close, it would disappear.

It was a square golden building with large rectangular windows curved to a point on top from which light poured forth, giving the building a glow that seemed to emanate from its core. Three pointed spires rose from the top, two taller ones on either side of a shorter one in the middle. Below the smaller spire, a huge rectangular door, ten-feet-tall and curved at the top stood. Sweeping stone stairs led up to the door, and they were full of people, all crowding around and talking to each other. Most seemed to be talking to the two guards at the entrance, as if asking for permission to enter. As far as Monsta could tell, not many were getting in.

Monsta knew immediately this must be where the king of Nork held court. It reminded Monsta of Misterwizard's castle, but this one was even more magical and beautiful than Misterwizard's place.

Just as Monsta expected, they walked towards the imposing building. Monsta glanced at Frank and Antonio and saw with surprise they looked nervous. *The king must be really scary,* Monsta thought. He began to wonder if it was possible there was a leader even more fearsome and wonderful than Ripper, and that he was about to meet him. Without even seeing the king yet, Monsta began to feel a love for him. He had to find a way to impress the king, make him see Monsta was not just a great new soldier, but the best, fiercest and most ruthless one the king had ever seen. Monsta decided he'd do anything, kill anyone, do whatever it took to impress the king and make the king like him. Monsta committed himself to not only being accepted, but becoming the king's new right-hand man.

Monsta, Frank and Antonio walked up the steps towards the huge, wooden door, and Monsta's meeting with the king.

CHAPTER 21

isterwizard turned to see a welcome sight. Starbucks rode towards him on his Harley! But the two new Krakn were ahead of him, running right towards Misterwizard!

The cowardly wildies were now nowhere in sight. Misterwizard knew with his limited skill with the rifle, he'd be very lucky to hit one of the new monsters with a bullet from it let alone both, especially since they were fast moving targets. Still, he knew he had to try.

Quickly Misterwizard swung his rifle around in the direction of the two Krakn. He didn't take time to look through the scope, but simply pointed at the closest one and fired.

The crack of the rifle mixed with the sound of Starbuck's Harley. And then an amazing and totally unexpected thing happened, but one that was very welcome. At the sound of the rifle shot, the two Krakn immediately changed course and ran off in another direction!

Misterwizard laughed. "Cowardly curs!" he yelled. "Though I do appreciate your lack of internal constitution!"

Starbucks saw the Krakn run off, but now he had also seen Misterwizard and sped towards him. Misterwizard didn't have time for a greeting however, for he knew Super and Lightpole were still in imminent danger.

Misterwizard aimed the rifle at Krakn in the pit again, concentrating with all his might and squinting through the small scope, but the infernal Krakn wouldn't stay still!

He squeezed the trigger, but didn't hear any sound, in fact nothing happened. He'd forgotten to reload the rifle!

"Curse my stupidity and haste!" Quickly he lowered the gun, pulled back the bolt and chambered a new round in the barrel.

The Krakn moved again! It shrieked, filling the air with horrible sound, waved its tentacles in the air and crawled towards Super. Misterwizard had no time to lose!

To Misterwizard's relief, Super looked up at him, eyes not focusing. He yelled in a high frantic voice, "Arise and avail yourself of the means of escape my dear! Expeditiously!" Misterwizard scolded himself mentally. This was no time to use elaborate words the girl wouldn't understand. "Climb the curtain!" He yelled.

Super nodded woodenly and looked at the curtains. She didn't move toward them though, but instead rubbed her head and looked confused. She saw the Krakn, which was no only five feet away, its giant black body towering over her, Super's eyes widened with realization and fright.

Misterwizard looked to see Lightpole had managed to free himself from the spike. He leaned against the wall of the pit, looking faint and with his leg covered in blood. Misterwizard's mind filled with dismay, for surely there was no way Lightpole would be able to climb the curtain. The only way to save Lightpole would be to shoot the Krakn, wounding or killing it. Super was closer however, and his first concern was with distracting the Krakn long enough for her to escape.

The roar of an engine filled the air, and Misterwizard heard and registered it, but he had no time to think about it. He steadied his hands, squinted through the scope and fired again.

The rifle bucked, swinging wildly in the air. He looked down. He'd missed again! The Krakn was momentarily distracted though, and it glared up at him, its mouth open showing sharp teeth. It snarled at him, waving its tentacles around.

Then one of its tentacles flew off! Blood spurted from where it had been cut! Misterwizard was dumbfounded for a second, then he looked to see Lightpole a stern look of bravery on his face, holding his katana sword with both hands. The katana dripped blood.

"Most commendable, my brave Asian friend," Misterwizard said with a smile of respect and admiration. Despite his wound, Lightpole was still a warrior, and a fierce one.

Super saw what Lightpole did and she grinned. She grabbed the curtain! She was going to climb out!

But now the Krakn spun on Lightpole and advanced. Misterwizard loaded the rifle again as he watched helplessly, unable to do anything until the gun was ready again.

He caught something out of the corner of his eye, and looked. It was Starbucks! He had jumped down into the pit! Misterwizard's spirits soared crisis seemed to be turning in their favor. Starbucks ran and stood in front of Lightpole, his own sword raised. Together both men faced the monster. Misterwizard chuckled, feeling less urgency now. He knew his main concern now would be to ensure if he tried to shoot again that he wouldn't miss and hit the wrong target. He pulled the bolt back on his rifle, and took careful aim, taking his time.

Moxie, Bugsy and Larry ran up the wooden steps on the inside of the wall, giggling like little children, eager to see what happened to Tiny when the Lurkers reached him. Larry was big and ponderous so he was slower than Moxie, but his excitement gave him speed. Larry's big boots made clunking sounds on the wood steps. Bugsy was behind both of them, and Larry's huge bulk kept Bugsy from getting around him. When Larry arrived at the opening in the wall, he saw Moxie already peering out. He slammed into Moxie, knocking him to the stair floor.

"Hey, ya stupid ape!" Moxie yelled. He stood up, glared at Larry, and rubbed his sore bottom. Larry looked sorry and afraid, and finally Moxie stopped looking at him and went back to looking out the opening.

Bugsy arrived, and soon all three jostled each other for space to see out the little window. From the ground, the soldiers and prisoners watched with tired interest.

Tiny stood with his back to the wall, his hands pressed against it, a look of absolute terror on his face. He turned his head first left then right, looking for a way to escape.

"Hey, let me back in! This ain't funny guys!"

Moxie and the others looked past towards the tunnels, and they all grinned with dark delight. The Lurkers shuffled forward, slowly but steadily. There were more now, thirty or forty of them, from ragged men and shriveled, ghoulish women to creepy little scrabblers. All had missing skin, or eyes, or limbs. Some had no teeth, or hair. All of their skin was shriveled and gray, as if it had long ago started to rot. And they sported a soft, green glow.

"Oh, this is gonna be good," Moxie said, really enjoying the sport, for after the last few days he needed something fun to make him feel better.

The Lurkers moaned and cried out, as if in pain, their faces twisted in frozen agony. Tiny shrieked with fright and ran down the right side of the wall out of sight.

"Cripes! We can't see him anymore!" Moxie yelled. He turned and ran up the stairs, hoping to get to the top of the wall where he could get a better view. Larry lumbered after him, but he was slow, and it would be a long time before he reached the top, if he made it at all. Bugsy once again was too slow to get around Larry, so once again he was in last place.

Moxie could hear the moans and shrieks from outside as he ran, up one set of stairs, on one side of the wall, then down the walkway to the other side of the wall where the next set of stairs led to the next platform and on and on, growing winded and sweaty. *It's worth it though*, he thought, *to see what happened to Tiny!*

He thought as he ran from the sheer number of Lurkers. *Where did they come from?* The Boss had made sure they were all trapped down in the underground where the old long cars used to run. They must have found a doorway that led to the tunnels. That was a bad thing, for now they were out. And anyone who was bitten by them got the strange green sickness and became just like them. How far could they spread? Could they take over the whole city of Nork? The whole world?

Moxie thought about where they came from, and remembered the old story of how everything happened, though no one knew how much of it was true. The story went that one of the stars that was supposed to fall on Nork fell up north in a lake instead. It blew up, making the weird cloud the stars all made, and the blast from it wiped out half the buildings in Nork and everywhere else for miles. The lake started glowing green, and the rivers from the lake all got filled with green goo too. The rivers flowed into the underground subway, and everyone down there died and became Lurkers.

Chaos took over Nork, and there was fighting and killing and death everywhere, until the Boss's great grandfather took over. Every generation of the Boss's family had ruled since, each one weirder than the last, until the present Boss.

Now nobody drank from the green waters, and the subways were all blocked off. The only water was from the tanks that got their water from the big water to the East, treated so it was drinkable. And nobody went anywhere near the subways, or the green goo filled rivers.

Moxie reached the top of the wall and looked out at the wide expanse. Suddenly Moxie felt strange and like he was going to faint. He realized everything had a red tint. He shook his head to clear it. He felt like any minute he was going to fall over the top of the wall, all the way down on the other side. He gripped the top of the wall and almost threw up.

Then he turned and saw something terrifying. It was a Lurker, right there on the stairs with him! Moxie yelled and put his hand to his face!

It was Larry, but he was a Lurker now! Half his face was gone, exposing the skull beneath. His right hand was nothing but bone, and his shirt hung open, showing a cavity where Moxie could see his ribs.

Moxie realized how stupid he was to run around without his tommy gun, for he had no way to fight Larry the Lurker! Moxie forgot all about Tiny as he gripped the top of the wall desperately, his heart beating wildly.

Larry stared at him with a frown of curiosity. "What's wrong with you, Bub?

"Get away from me!" Moxie surged forward, grabbed Larry and flipped him over the wall.

"AAAAH!" Larry screamed, his eyes wide with surprise and terror as he tumbled in space down towards the ground again.

"What'd ya do that for, Moxie?" Bugsy asked, a look of confusion on his face. "Why'd ya do it?"

Moxie felt sick. "Didn't you see? He was a Lurker!"

Bugsy grinned, then he laughed. "Are you feeling okay, Moxie? You don't look so good."

Bugsy hadn't seen it! Was Moxie having delusions? Was Larry not a Lurker?

"I'm fine, I was just havin' some fun, is all."

"The Boss ain't gonna like you killing all his guards," Bugsy said. "One's maybe okay, but...

"Let me worry what the Boss thinks, got it?" Moxie said with almost a snarl.

Bugsy shrugged, looking uncomfortable.

They both gazed over the top of the wall. They saw the entrances to the three tunnels. Moxie looked over the side. He stared down at the wire and mangled steel embedded into the wall, and the dead bodies hanging there. Some had bird-beasties sitting on them, eating the flesh, their skin hanging in rags and their skulls and bones exposed. Others moved feebly, and Moxie felt a cold tingle run up his spine. Were they alive still, or were they Lurkers too? He couldn't tell.

Moxie looked down at the ground, and a chill filled his heart. The whole area in front of the tunnels was filled with Lurkers! If even one of them got in, it would mean they would turn everybody inside to Lurkers too. The thought made Moxie so scared he found it hard to breathe.

"Look! There's Tiny!" Bugsy yelled, pointing to the ground on the right. Moxie looked, and sure enough, there was Tiny. He was at the edge of the highway, frantically clinging to the wall, trying to climb up. He was so short he was having a hard time.

Moxie and Bugsy laughed. "You better hurry Tiny," Bugsy said, "those guys look hungry!"

Moxie forgot all about Larry and the strange delusion with the fun of seeing Tiny, and he grinned happily. "I hope they get him!"

One of the Lurkers headed towards Tiny! Soon a whole crowd of Lurkers heading Tiny's way! Tiny turned, his back against the wall, and screamed in terror, his hands in front of him as if to ward off the monsters.

The Lurkers reached Tiny.

"They got 'im!" Moxie said with dark glee.

Tiny disappeared from sight behind a crowd of Lurkers. Moxie didn't think he'd ever seen anything so grisly and horrible before, and he studied the scene, wanting to freeze its memory in his mind. Soon blood flowed under the Lurkers' feet, and Moxie and Bugsy knew they were tearing poor Tiny apart.

After a few moments of pure horror, the Lurkers dissipated, each carrying pieces of Tiny in their hands or in their mouths. All that was left was a dark red stain on the side of the wall, a small skull with some meat left on it and Tiny's ribs.

"Wow, that was amazing!" Bugsy said with a voice full of awe. "I ain't never seen nothing as cool as that before! I'll be talkin' about that until the day I die!

Moxie and Bugsy laughed some more, enjoying the grisly spectacle. Then Moxie had an evil idea, he didn't know why. As Bugsy Larry leaned forward, most of his body leaning out over the wall, Moxie walked up behind him.

"Why don't you join him, Bugsy?" Moxie grabbed Bugsy's legs and pulled them up. Bugsy screamed in surprise. Pushing Bugsy with all his might, Moxie flipped him over the wall as Bugsy screamed in terror.

Moxie watched as Bugsy tumbled down the wall, the steel and wire cutting him. Moxie was afraid Bugsy was going to get stuck on the wall, but his weight pulled him free of the wire, and down he fell.

Moxie watched with dark excitement as Bugsy hit the ground, part of him shattering into a bloody pulp. The Lurkers immediately turned and shuffled towards the new food source, and as Moxie watched with sadistic pleasure, the Lurkers surrounded Bugsy and began tearing him apart.

As Moxie watched the new grisly scene, he tried to think. Why did he do that? Bugsy was his second-in-command. Why did he have the overwhelming urge to kill him? The realization that he didn't even think about it scared Moxie to his core. What was happening to him? Was he losing his marbles? Terror filled Moxie again, this time a darker, colder type that seemed to fill his bones. He wanted to get home fast, before something else happened. He had to get home!

CHAPTER 22

As Johnny and Mantayo grew close to the building with the long needle at the top, Johnny gazed at it. The needle sat on top of a thicker column, which then connected to the rectangular vertical blocks of the building below. The building soared above all the buildings around it, and Johnny knew that this must be an important place for the winged people. Johnny had settled down and accepted his condition, and the initial fear had subsided a little. Now he simply stared at all the amazing buildings below him, each one different, of different sizes and shapes, and each one strangely beautiful.

Johnny didn't know much about Nork, but he was beginning to love the city, for it was vast and amazing and looked like a place with a million adventures, one around every corner.

It seemed to Johnny as if a gray carpet of buildings had been laid down, intersected by streets, creating a giant maze. The Red Eye, slipping towards the distant horizon as late afternoon began, glinted off the buildings and created shadows that bathed some of the streets in gray. On Johnny's right he saw the big water, with small islands in the near distance. On his left he saw more city, and then more water, for it looked like the water curved around the city and met it on both sides.

Ahead of them in the near distance Johnny saw a large rectangular strip of grass two blocks wide and at least ten blocks long, full of trees and shrubs. It looked like a pleasant oasis in the middle of all the stone and brick.

Johnny couldn't believe any city could be so huge. How were they ever going to rescue the people of Pelpia from it? The Nork army could hide them anywhere, and Johnny and his friends would never find them. Johnny thought, that even if they didn't try to rescue them, how long before the people of Nork came south to Pelpia, and then to Washington Deecee? He realized at that moment how small his tribe still was. The last time Misterwizard counted them, he said there were a little more than a "thousand", which didn't sound like very many compared to Nork.

He knew that even if the people of his tribe came to help, they would have to do it secretly, sneak in, rescue the people of Pelpia and get out. There was no way they could take the people of Nork on in a battle. Right now, the people of Nork didn't even know Johnny's tribe existed. If that changed, it might mean big trouble for Johnny and his tribe.

All this Johnny thought about in the last few

moments before they reached the building. When they grew close, Mantayo flew down the side of the building until they were what looked to Johnny ten floors from the top. The building seemed to be built in stages, with a smaller rectangle sitting on a slightly larger one, and that one sitting on a bigger one that went all the way to the ground. In the middle rectangle, Johnny saw an opening where the brick had crumbled, revealing the interior. Not far below the open space, the webbing and ropes connected to another building nearby. The webbing hand pointed downward, for the building they were heading for was much taller than the one the webbing connected to. With mild alarm, the giant saw a giant spider-beastie clinging to the side of the building, but on the right side, not the side with the opening. Johnny was glad they were not flying next to it.

Johnny was relieved they were landing, for Mantayo looked tired and covered with sweat. Johnny would be glad to get on a solid surface before the teen from the Sky lost his grip and dropped Johnny to the ground far below.

As they grew close, Johnny could see inside. The room was large and looked like it took up half the floor of that level of the building. Couches with gold colored cloth and gold-colored cushions filled the room. Gold statues of winged women with no arms stood in all four corners. A lush black carpet covered the floor. Men, women and scrabblers lounged, talked and ate on the couches, the younger ones with wings. Everyone was white, and most had pure white hair, though a few had hair that was brown. On either side of the room a dark wooden table lined the walls. The tables were filled with delicious looking food and pitchers of something to drink. Johnny's stomach rumbled with desire, and he couldn't remember when he'd last had a good meal.

Mantayo fluttered his wings to slow down, making a loud rushing sound, and for a second, they rose up again in preparation for landing. To Johnny's relief he saw Deb smiling up at him, with Deecee next to her. They looked happy and unharmed. Behind them, the two members of Sky who had flown Deb and Deecee to the building stood. They also looked like young teens Mantayo's age; their huge white wings folded onto their backs. They stood, joked and watched Johnny and Mantayo approach.

Mantayo flew into the opening and landed softly. Johnny grinned, for it had been an exhilarating ride, and now that it was over, he could reflect on how amazing it was. He looked at Mantayo with respect, for the young man was definitely confident and strong. He would make a good ally.

Johnny turned, eager to reunite with Deb, but to his surprise, he saw someone else standing there! It was someone he was definitely not expecting to see, but seeing her nonetheless filled him with joy. It was Lady Stabs! Johnny's spirits lifted. It looked like they might in the presence of allies, not enemies. Maybe with a little help, they could rescue the people of Letfreedomring after all.

Monsta strode up to the doors of the beautiful castle-like building, with Antoinio and Frank right behind him. He looked up at the words above them and saw "Saint Patrick's Cathedral" written in stone letters high on the side of the building. He didn't know why he bothered to look at all, he couldn't read any of the old words, but it seemed the right thing to do before entering

Two guards stood at the sides of the door, both dressed in crisp fancy suits that looked brand new. The tommy guns they had looked shiny and new, and Monsta had no doubt that their guns worked.

The guards were also two of the biggest lugs Monsta had ever seen, with square jaws and dark eyes that stared ahead at nothing.

The guards didn't move, so Monsta grabbed the long, copper handle on the door on the right. Suddenly the butt of a tommy gun smashed into his hand and he yowled and pulled his hand back. One of the guards had hit him! The guard now pointed his tommy gun right at Monsta's heart, and Monsta's heart froze in his throat. His eyes opened wide, and he wondered if he'd made another big mistake and was about to get filled full of holes.

"You ready to die, Bub?" the guard said, in an icy, cold steel voice that showed he meant business.

Antonio stood in front of Monsta, shielding him, and looked at the guard in a friendly way. "Hey, Stogie, it's me, Antonio, and Frank. This guy don't know any better, he ain't from around here."

The guard, Stogie, turned and glared at Antonio. "Nobody touches the golden handles but us. You all want to die?"

"Hey, Stogie," Frank wheezed, "we got to see the Boss. We got to introduce this guy to him and tell him what's going on? You get it?"

"I don't care," Stogie said, turning his glare on Frank. "I break arms and legs of people who touch the golden handles."

"Sheesh," Monsta said with irritation. "This guy's touchy about his door handles."

"Shut up, you," Antonio said hurriedly to Monsta. Then he turned back to Stogie. "Look, Stogie. We're sorry about the door. Can you let us in?"

Stogie stared at them for a moment, then reluctantly pulled his gun back, as if disappointed. Antonio, Frank and Monsta all wilted a little with relief. The other guard chuckled.

"You better be tellin' the truth. If I get in Dutch, I'm comin' to find you, Antonio."

Antonio grinned in a jaunty manner. "Relax, it's all on the up and up."

Stogie grabbed the handle and opened the door. Frank and Monsta walked in. Antonio smiled one more time at Stogie, who glared back at him. Antonio's smile disappeared as he hurried inside and shut the door.

As soon as Monsta walked in, he knew he was in a place full of beauty and style. This was the Boss's pad, for not only was it classy, but also very dark and twisted. They entered a small room with golden walls and beautiful golden statues. A rich red carpet lay on the floor, and fancy chairs and tables lined the walls. On the walls were paintings of naked ladies and mythical creatures. And dead bodies on hooks.

"Geez!" Monsta said, his eyes wide. "What'd these guys do?"

Frank chuckled. "Maybe nuttin. The Boss was just feeling mean that day."

At the end of the small door there was an archway. The room beyond was hidden by a thick, elegant red curtain that hung down over the archway. In front of the archway on either side, two more big guards, but these guys were dressed in long golden robes. Instead of tommy guns they held long poles with wicked looking swords at the ends. They stared forward with dark scowls like statues, not even noticing the three men entering.

"We got an appointment," Antonio told the guard on the left. The guard didn't move or look down.

"Not a good time. The Boss is in one of his moods."

Frank and Antonio glanced at each other with nervous expressions. Then they turned back to the guard.

"He'll like what we have to say," Antonio said, hopefully. "We got news of a new place to conquer."

"It's your neck." The guard continued to look forward, but with his left hand he pulled the curtain back. Monsta looked beyond it to see a room out of a dream. The walls were covered in gold, and the floor was covered with animal furs. Tables lined the walls with all kinds of food and drink on them. Men and women in scant clothing lounged in chairs or on the rugs, drinking and eating. Beautiful girls in furs danced in place around the room.

Then he saw the bodies in hanging cages around the room too. The cages hung from the ceiling by black chains and were square in shape. Inside the cages were skeletons, rotting corpses, and live people, all who looked like they had been tortured or beaten and were on the point of starvation. The people were filthy, their hair and beards long and unkempt, and they stared out of the cages with looks of fear and resignation, as if they were just waiting to die.

At the far end of the room on a raised platform Monsta saw an elegant throne. And on it sat the King of Nork! The King had long black hair that flowed down his shoulders. He had a long face, a sharp chin and a large, pointed nose. His eyes were black and he wore a bored, cruel expression. He wore a sparkly gold outfit that looked like pajamas and little brown slippers with fake bear-beastie heads on the ends. And he held a pure black cat-beastie on his lap which stared out at Monsta and his guards, as if irritated at the intrusion.

At this moment right in front of the throne, a man stood, dressed only in rags. His head and arms were stuck through holes in a box on poles so that he faced the king. Behind him, another man in a black hood stood with a whip. As Monsta watched in amazed horror, the man with the hood swung the whip. A loud crack sounded as the whip hit the man's back, and the man shrieked in pain.

Monsta grinned, for he already liked this king. And he was going to meet him at last!

Super slowly inched her way up the curtain as both Starbucks and Lightpole faced the Krakn. The Krakn was next to Super however, and as Starbucks and Lightpole looked in dismay, it plucked Super out of the air with one of its tentacles and held her high. The tentacle wrapped around her like a snake's coils. Misterwizard saw her struggle, and hoped it wasn't crushing her in its grip.

As Starbucks and Lightpole moved towards it, the Krakn held Super in front of it like a shield. This creature was not so dumb after all! With alarm, Misterwizard saw the Krakn scrunch down and look up. It was about to leap out of the pit with Super!

Misterwizard it was his turn now to aid the fight. He took careful aim, and fired. This time his shot was true. The bullet hit the Krakn in the side, just below its huge bulbous head. It shrieked and waved its tentacles in the air, this time in pain, as green blood poured from a bullet wound. It dropped Super, who fell to the ground, dangerously near the spikes.

But now Starbucks and Lightpole had their

chance. Like angry lion-beasties, they sprang on the Krakn, slashing at its tentacles that waved about, trying to catch them. The Krakn snarled fiercely, but there was fear in its eyes, for it knew it was outnumbered and might soon be dead.

"Don't dismay, I am coming to your aid!" Misterwizard yelled, and cocked the gun again. He raised it to aim, but now Starbucks and Lightpole were right in the way. He had to make sure he got a sure shot, or he'd hit one of his friends, most probably killing them with the force of the rifle bullet.

Starbucks slashed at the Kraken, forcing it to back off. He slashed at one of its legs, cutting it off a foot from the ground. The Krakn reached out tentatively with a tentacle, trying to grab Starbuck's sword, but afraid of being slashed again. Lightpole slashed! Another of the Krakn's leg tentacles went flying! It tilted to the side, wounded and defenseless.

Just then Super stood up, bit hard into one of the Krakn's tentacles, ripping and tearing with her teeth. Misterwizard laughed, for she was like a wild beastie in her anger.

The Krakn's turned weakly to face her, but it was now outnumbered. The wounds from Starbuck's and Lightpole's swords and from Misterwizard's rifle began to take their toll.

Crack! Misterwizard shot again! Once again, he found his target, but this time it was one of the Krakn's eyes! Green blood instantly oozed out of it as the Krakn howled in pain. The Krakn crawled backwards only to find the spikes waiting for it. It impaled itself on the spikes and flailed around, as Starbucks and Lightpole continued their attack. Soon it was all over. Starbucks and Lightpole continued to slash at it, and Super kicked it, until it stopped moving, dead.

Starbucks grinned and was about to let out a war whoop, but suddenly something pinned him to the ground! It was a beautiful dark-haired girl, kissing him again and again. Starbucks tried to laugh or even catch his breath, and soon he was kissing her back. They held each other and lost themselves in the pleasure of being together again, of the feel of their bodies touching and just the wonderful joy of knowing they were alive and safe.

Misterwizard saw what was happening and chuckled. "Once again, Love vanquishes the denizens of evil!" He walked over and looked down at them. They continued to kiss and hold each other, until Misterwizard began to feel slightly embarrassed. Lightpole looked slightly uncomfortable too, and with a smile he began to climb the curtain.

"Starbucks? Super? I understand your romantic enthusiasm, however..."

Starbucks and Super didn't seem to hear him.

"If you plan on continuing this course of action, you might want to find a location with a bit more sequestration."

Finally, Starbucks and Super seemed to stop, or at least slow down. They smiled up at Misterwizard and waved. Misterwizard looked down at them ruefully. "I must make it an imperative to find for myself a significant other in the not-too-distant future. It does appear to be a very entertaining and worthwhile endeavor."

CHAPTER 23

Moxie couldn't remember being so scared before, but then he'd been in so many scary situations lately, he really couldn't tell for sure if this was worse than the other times or not. Moxie just knew he had to get back down to the ground and get the prisoners stowed somewhere. Then he could go to the Boss, and tell him about it and take a nice, long rest. Maybe he wouldn't even tell the Boss about the prisoners, he'd just leave them somewhere and come back later to tell the Boss. Or maybe he'd just take a powder and leave the Nork soldiers and prisoners to take care of themselves and just get the blazes out of there!

Moxie started back down the first set of wooden steps, his breathing heavy, his face drenched in sweat and his heart aching. All he could think was, 'gotta get down, gotta get down'!

Suddenly he stopped and peed his pants. There standing in front of him was Tiny! Tiny's whole face and body were covered in blood. Half his skull was exposed, and he was missing both eyes.

"This ain't real!" Moxie yelled. "It ain't stinkin' real!"

Tiny reached out to him with a hand missing flesh, his tiny skeleton hand palm up. "Why'd you do it, Moxie? Why'd you push me outside? I was gonna let you guys in. Look what they did to me!"

"No!" Moxie yelled. Waving his hands in front of himself, he ran at the horrible visage. Just as he suspected, once he reached Dead Tiny, Dead Tiny disappeared.

Moxie ran down the stairs, almost falling until he reached the next wood landing. He raced across the planks until he reached the stairs on the other side. Then he raced down them. He jumped a few steps, two at a time, and finally fell, tumbling down to the next level. Not even thinking about the pain from the fall, he leapt up and ran across the next landing, his mind screaming at him.

After what seemed an eternity, he reached the ground with a relief so immense he almost cried. The soldiers stood around, watching the prisoners, who sat in the street, looking discouraged and bored.

Moxie tried to come up with a story about what happened to Bugsy. Another of his soldiers, a man named Alcopoon, walked up. He looked confused at not seeing Bugsy. Alcopoon was of average height, with curly black hair, stubble on his chin and a lower-than-average intelligence.

"Hey, Moxie," Alcopoon said "What happened to Bugsy?"

Moxie scowled, trying to act like he was in charge again. "The dummy got too close to the wall. He fell over!"

Alcopoon looked sad. "Gee, that's a bad break."

"Not for you," Moxie said, "'cause now, you are number two."

Alcapoon smiled and stood up a little straighter. "Gee, thanks Moxie. You won't regret it."

Moxie scowled. "I already do."

After the mistake at the gate, Monsta didn't know what to do, so he waited for Frank and Antonio to make the first move. Frank and Antonio looked more scared than Monsta had ever seen them, and he got the idea that if you made the wrong move here, it could mean curtains.

Frank and Antonio glanced at each other then moved forward really slowly, like it was the last thing they wanted to do. Monsta walked behind them slowly, to the screams of the man being tortured.

They all stopped on the side of the man being whipped and waited. On the right side of the room against the wall near the throne, a rich red curtain hung from the ceiling all the way to the floor. In front of it a table full of food and drink. Gazing at it made Monsta almost faint, and realize how hungry he was. He wondered what delicious things the king of Nork got to eat. His stomach grumbled and his knees felt wobbly.

Frank and Antonio got on their knees. Monsta watched them for a moment. He didn't like the idea of bowing to this "king", of bowing to anybody. They'd all treated Ripper like he was a king, but even he never expected anyone to bow to him. Still, if Monsta wanted to get in the king's good graces, he realized he'd better play along.

Antonio whispered, "Get on your knees, stupid, unless you want to be hangin' in one of these cages."

With deep resentment, Monsta complied, but he thought to himself, someday, maybe they'd all be bowing to him instead. Monsta gazed at the king, taking his appearance in. The king held some kind of tasty looking meat in his hand, and he tore pieces off and fed them to the cat-beastie.

Two gorgeous women lounged in elegant green chairs on either arm of the throne; the most beautiful women Monsta had ever seen. One was a blond in a black robe with red roses on it, with long blond hair that fell over her shoulders. The other was a brunette with short hair wearing a red robe and white silk pants underneath. They looked bored, their eyes half closed, as they watched the man being tortured. *Man*, Monsta thought, *someday I want to have dames hanging around me like that!*

This was luxury, thought Monsta. Eating good food, watching some guy whipped for your entertainment, while beautiful women waited at your beck and call. This was Monsta's dream, but in reality! Monsta swore total allegiance to this new king, and fell under his spell completely. He forgot all about Ripper. Who was Ripper, compared to this guy?

Next to the king stood an old man in a long black robe. The man looked weak and frail, but carried himself with an air of dignity that said he was someone important. The old man clasped his hands together and stared at the king in an imploring way. Monsta instantly didn't like him, for he'd seen men like them before. Guys always spoil your fun, telling you to face "reality", telling you that you was out of the funny water for the vehicles, or the town you wanted to attack was too far away, or other annoying facts like those. They were the kind of guy you listened to, nodded, and then slow roasted over a fire for fun after they got on your nerves just one too many times.

The man was at least fifty seasons old and bald, with wrinkled skin, a hook-like nose and beady eyes. He was downright ugly! He spoke to the king in a commanding voice that wasn't respectful at all, as if he was the king. "Your majesty, you simply must address the food situation. The people are complaining that they are starving. They are threatening riot and attack the castle if they don't get more food."

Monsta was right about the guy! Just like he'd thought, he was some kind of annoying adviser. The king didn't even look at the man, which made Monsta grin. The king continued to break off pieces of meat and feed it to his cat-beastie, and smiled as the whip came down again and again, and more screams of pain filled the air.

"Please, your majesty," the annoying man said. "Listen to reason!"

Finally, the king raised his hand without looking. "You are so boring, Ferdinand! Always trying to spoil my fun. I tell you what you say to them. Tell them to eat each other. That way, they are fed, and there are less of them to complain. Let the strong eat the weak and the frail. It's the best way to fix the situation."

Ferdinand replied, "Your majesty, If I were to go tell them that, there would definitely be a riot. You do realize how many people there are now? The numbers keep increasing every day. We are running out of room and food!"

The king grew irritated and frowned. Without looking at the old man he said, "Ferdinand, if you would work with Horatio, the head of my military and come up with a way for us to destroy the annoying angels living in our skyscrapers or the unclean living in Booklin, we would have more room. And as for food, the leader of my army, Moxie, should return soon with the offering of food from the city to the south. Then the people will be able to gorge themselves until they throw up. Will that satisfy you?"

The old man looked slightly mollified, but not completely. "That food will be a drop in the bucket of what we need. We need to come up with a new food source, in an area where someone is not trying to kill us."

The king waved his hand impatiently. "Enough!

Can't you see I'm trying to enjoy my entertainment? We will discuss this later. If you don't leave now, you will be tomorrow's fun."

Ferdinand frowned with disappointment, obviously not satisfied. He frowned with displeasure at the king, shook his head and walked away. Monsta chuckled. *Good riddance, you annoying bug-beastie,* Monsta thought. *Off with your head!*

A servant dressed in strange clothes, a frilly shirt and shorts and long white socks, walked up carrying a tray. Monsta spied what was on it. There were round, brown mounds that looked like something delicious and a fancy glass with yellow liquid in it. As Monsta watched with hungry fascination, the king took one of the candies and popped it in his mouth. Monsta's stomach churned again and made a noise. Suddenly he was famished, and those candies looked like the most wonderful thing he'd ever seen. He ached inside, wishing he could sneak one.

The king picked up the glass of liquid and took a sip with his free hand. Then he set it back on the tray. He picked up one of the brown things and held it down for his cat-beastie! It looked at it with mild interest and started nibbling on it.

Suddenly the man doing the whipping said, "I'm sorry your majesty, it seems he has died."

The king frowned with unhappiness. "Pity. Oh well. Take him away."

Two men hurried up, released the dead man from the wooden stocks and dragged him away. The man with the whip bowed and also left.

The king finally seemed to notice Frank, Antonio and Monsta. He looked down at them with happy curiosity. "What have we here?"

Frank and Antonio rose, so Monsta did too. They approached the king.

Antoinio bowed and lowered his head. "Hello Boss. Please beg our indulgence. We are lowly worms, come to bring you worship."

The king looked at them and waved an impatient hand. "No longer call me the Boss. I'm tired of that story." The king picked up a book from the floor next to him. "You see this?"

All three of them looked at the book. It was green, and had a man in a green outfit with a pointed hat with a feather. The man held a bow and arrow in his hands.

"This is Robin Hood. A wonderful story. From now on, we will all dress and act like people from Sherwood Forest."

Frank and Atonio looked confused. "Sherwood Forest?"

The king looked annoyed. "You all must learn to read, like I do. I so tire of having to explain everything. We will no longer be gangsters is what I'm saying. I shall put out a decree tomorrow. Meanwhile, from now on, call me King Richard or simply, Your Majesty."

Frank looked at Antonio and they both shrugged. "Yes, Your Majesty."

"And speak quickly. I grow tired."

Frank wheezed, "Your majesty, this here is

Monsta. He comes from a place a long ways to the south."

"Don't talk that gangster gibberish anymore. From now on, you will talk like English lords and ladies. South?" The king said, grabbing the glass from the tray and taking a sip again.

"Hello, Your Majesty," Monsta said. "I come from Pill-a-delpia. I was a member of a gang, the best one in the world. We was the Doomsday Prophecy."

The king grinned, amused. "Monsta. You don't look like a monsta. And Pill-a-dalpia? Pill-a-delpia? What an odd name. You are an amusing fellow."
The king burst into laughter, and everyone in the room followed suit.

"Doomsday Prophecy. You are very entertaining and so refreshing. Someone with something new to say."

"We was the toughest," Monsta said with pride.

Antonio spoke in an excited voice. "Moxie told Charlie and Tick-tock to bring him here to you, but they got attacked by the Angels. Monsta says Charlie got killed and Tick-tock ran off. We caught him trying to leave the city."

The king looked more interested, and turned to sit straight on his throne.

"Moxie and Tick-tock attacked? And that Tick-tock fellow is running loose in my kingdom? I told Moxie not to trust one of those dark-skinned fellows, but Moxie vouched for him, said he was worth giving a shot."

"Yes, Your Majesty," Antonio said.

The king took the hand of the lady on his left, and held it to his face. He smiled at her and she beamed back at him. The King said, "We shall put out a decree. They are to find Tick-tock and bring him here for our entertainment, for not reporting in to me."

"Tick-tock's a good soldier, Your Majesty," Frank wheezed.

The king glared at him. "What did you say?"

"He didn't say nothing, Your Majesty. He's stupid, is all," Antonio said hastily. Antonio tried to change the subject. "This Monsta guy has some news."

"Yeah," Monsta said. "I can tell you stuff you don't know, like your guy Moxie is headin' into trouble. He's attacking Pelpia, but he don't know there's a guy there who helpin' 'em, a guy named-"

The king interrupted in a bored voice. "You said you were with this Doomsday Prophecy. Are you here representing them?"

"My gang was," Monsta's face colored with anger and embarrassment. Hatred and fury made him speak in stilted words. "They was all killed by Johnny Apocalypse."

The king laughed again, in a waksy way. "Johnny Apocalypse. Another funny name. You are becoming very entertaining. I'm glad you came to me after all."

Everyone else laughed too, and Monsta got the notion that when the king laughed, everybody else was supposed to too, or suffer the consequences.

The king stood up, laid the cat-beastie on his

throne and walked over to the table full of food. He turned to Monsta. "Hungry?"

Monsta grinned with joy. He was winning the king over! He hurried over to the table and eyed the food and drink greedily. Then he tried to get control of himself and said casually, "I could do with a bite."

The king grinned, seeing how hungry Monsta obviously was. "You could do with a bite! That's funny!"

Everyone laughed, including Monsta. The king motioned with his hand for Monsta to join him. "Come. Eat, while we talk."

Monsta didn't need a second invitation. He grabbed a leg of some bird-beastie and bit down on it, like a man who hadn't eaten in days, which was the truth. He tore a piece off with his teeth and chewed as fast as he could, wanting to swallow the meat as fast as possible. Frank and Antonio walked up behind them and stood silently, having had no invitation from the king to indulge themselves.

The king grabbed a piece of cheese and said idly, "So, this Johnny Apocalypse killed your gang. Was your gang weak?"

Monsta stopped in mid-bite and moved the bird-beastie leg away from his mouth. He snarled, "Of course not! We were the best gang in the world!"

The king smiled, pleased at the reaction he had caused. He motioned with his hand. "Eat, please."

Glowering at the king, Monsta went back to chewing on the bird-beastie leg.

The king studied Monsta's face as he spoke.

"And yet this Johnny Apocalypse killed them all."

"That's right!" Monsta said, his mouth full of food. "He got lucky, is all. He's one of those goody-good types, always spouting junk about something he calls, "jussice" and "mocracy". Him and that crazy old man who helps him are always talkin' about makin' the country like it was in the old days. He looks down his stupid nose at everybody, like he's superior. And he's only a scrabbler!"

The king smiled darkly, amused. His eyes and Monsta's met. "A scrabbler, you say? How old."

Monsta shrugged, chewing. "Fifteen seasons, I guess.

The king picked up his cat-beastie and walked back over to stand next to Monsta. As he talked the king stroked the cat-beastie's head and it purred and closed its eyes.

"I know something of this 'mocracy', you speak of. Unlike most of the rabble I rule over, I have been well taught. My father saw to it that I learned to read and write the old words, and gave me a good education. So, I know about the government that used to rule these lands."

The king picked up a piece of cheese and fed it to his cat-beastie, who didn't eat it, just swatted at it with his paw.

"But good fortune has brought us to a new world, one without laws or morals, where men like you and I can dispense with the more nauseating ideals of the past and live as we wish, ruling the weaker fools with an iron fist."

Monsta stopped eating, for he was struck with a deep love and affection for this king. He was everything Monsta had dreamed he would be. Monsta tried to keep his adulation from showing, for it would look like weakness. He went back to eating nonchalantly, but a silent understanding occurred between Monsta and the king.

"So, this Johnny Apocalypse. What happened to him?"

Monsta grew excited again. "That's what I'm trying to tell you! He's fighting your guy Moxie right now!"

The king frowned. "Does this mean my man might not be supplying us with food?"

"Your guy will be lucky to survive!" Monsta said. Then he realized how stupid he sounded, as if Johnny was some kind of God. "I mean, he's got a good fight on his hands."

"Tell me about him," the king said.

"He has a tribe," Monsta said, finishing the bird-beastie leg and grabbing a bowl of peas, "and he's got this crazy old man who they call Misterwizard, who is always helping Johnny with his magic. They live in a place called Washington Deecee, and they are always sticking their nose into everybody else's business."

Concern creased the brow of the king, as he looked down in concentration. "You are so full of strange names. And you think Moxie and the whole army will be defeated by this one boy."

Monsta scooped peas in his mouth greedily while talking. "This Johnny ain't no ordinary boy. He's smart, and knows the ancient words, like you. Misterwizard teaches him. And his people are feisty, not afraid to fight. And he's got this girlfriend, named Deb."

The king's eyes twinkled with interest. "Girlfriend, you say? Is she beautiful?"

"The beautifulesst, your majesty. And he's got this friend, a black boy named Starbucks, who has a girlfriend named Super."

"A black boy you say? Hmm, this Johnny Apocalypse does seem to be the type I tend to hate with a passion. He is appearing to be more and more intolerable."

"Don't you worry about him, your majesty, 'cause I'm gonna kill Johnny and his friend someday for what they did to the Doomsday Prophecy. Then you can have both their girls."

The king dropped his piece of cheese and picked up a piece of fish, which the cat-beastie seemed more interested in. "Why are you not there, killing this amazing young man right now?"

Monsta, growing bolder, turned to the king in anger. "I was trying to do it when your guys grabbed me. They made me come here. Or he'd be dead already!"

The king turned to Antonio and Frank. "Shall we trust this strange clown, men, or should I use him for tomorrow's entertainment?"

Antonio and Frank just shrugged, too afraid to say anything.

"I tell you what we are going to do," the king said, his dark eyes twinkling as he petted his cat-beastie. "We are going to put you in our deepest, darkest prison."

Monsta looked scared and surprised, for he thought the king and he had developed a friendship. He realized this king was devious, and not one to easily trust.

"And when Moxie gets back, we will ask him if he met this Johnny Apocalypse you speak so passionately about. If your story rings true, we will speak again."

"But your majesty!" Monsta sputtered. "I thought we were, I mean…"

The king smiled. "Never assume what you do not know, fine fellow. Truth is found in actions, not words. We will talk again, after you have discovered what happens to men if they displease me."

The king motioned to two of his guards, and they hurried forward and stood on either side of Monsta. One of them took the bowl of peas from Monsta. The other grabbed Monsta's shoulder and spun him around.

"Hey, wait a minute!" Monsta said, his voice rising in fear.

"I'd do what the king says, if I was you," Frank wheezed.

"That is," Antonio added, "if you don't want to be tomorrow's entertainment."

Monsta looked sad and dejected, his face in an unhappy pout. The king moved to where he could see

Monsta's face again. He pointed a piece of fish in front of Monsta, who looked at it longingly, wondering when he would get to eat again.

"As you ruminate in our foulest pit, think on this, Monsta. If I find out you have been lying to me in the slightest way, the pit I have left you in will seem to be a paradise compared to what happens to you next. I will devise a particularly fun and painful way for you to die. Too-da-loo."

The guards marched Monsta out as the king and his cat-beastie returned to the throne. Frank and Antonio bowed their way out, following Monsta and the guards.

Monsta began to wonder if it was such a great thing to meet this king after all.

CHAPTER 24

As soon as Mantayo landed, Deb, Lady Stabs and Deecee ran over to Johnny with smiles of joy. Mantayo had barely let Johnny go when Deb leapt into his arms, hugging him and holding her face close to his. Johnny's heart filled with happiness as well, and relief, knowing Deb wasn't hurt and was back in his arms. Deecee barked cheerfully and wagged his tail, and kept barking until Johnny finally reached over and patted his head.

Lady Stabs stood by with a warm smile. Once Johnny and Deb had sufficiently greeted each other for the moment, Johnny walked over to her.

"Lady Stabs! I'm so glad you're all right! We were so worried when we saw that ganger kidnap you!" Johnny took Lady Stabs in his arms and gave her a big hug, which touched her deeply, and her lower lip trembled.

When Johnny let her go Lady Stabs spoke, her voice husky with emotion. "I'm so glad you and Deb are all right too," Lady Stabs said, her voice husky with emotion. She wiped a tear from the corner of her eye, hoping Johnny and Deb didn't notice.

They stood in a circle, holding each other's hands, enjoying the moment. Behind them, Mantayo sat on a soft golden couch and watched them, waiting patiently, wings folded behind him and arms folded. A sheen of sweat covered his face and body, and it seemed the effort of carrying Johnny was more than he wanted to admit. He looked tired, but he smiled with pride at having done the feat and enjoyed their reunion.

Johnny looked around the room. Soft pillows and couches in bright colors filled the space and tables laden with food and drink lined the walls. Men, women and scrabblers grabbed food from the tables or lounged on the couches. Johnny noticed most of the older men and women did not have wings, but were just pale with white hair and blue eyes. The younger males and all the scrabblers had wings, and Johnny wondered what had changed to make the younger people different.

There was even one little girl Sephie's age, eight or nine seasons, with long white hair, a white cloth dress and large white wings that started a little above her shoulders and reached almost to the floor. It seemed that when the Sky weren't using their wings, they could conveniently tuck them in close to their back, almost flat against their bodies.

There were so many strange and amazing sights Johnny felt overwhelmed. He gazed out the large hole in the building, and could see they were way up in the sky, almost up to where the Red Eye traveled, and the ground looked so far below he could barely see it. The thought of being so far up made Johnny's head woozy. He steeled himself against the feeling of being afraid, thinking how Deb and Lady Stabs had accepted it, and how silly he would look if he was the only one who showed fear.

"Who are these people?" Johnny asked Deb and Lady Stabs.

Lady Stabs started to answer, but Johnny cut her off. "Where are we?"

Lady Stabs began to answer that question when Johnny hit her with another one. "How did you get away?"

Deb laughed. "Give her a chance to answer one first, before you ask her another!"

They all laughed, and Johnny stopped asking questions so Lady Stabs could talk. "These people call themselves the Sky." Lady Stabs pointed to the people in the room, and then at Mantayo. "They are warm and friendly, as long as you are not an enemy. They fight the people of Nork, because the people of Nork are led by an evil king who wars with everyone, trying to kill them and take over their lands. From what the Sky tell me, the king is always sending his soldiers up the insides of the buildings, trying to get to them. Luckily the "Groundworms", as the Sky call the people of Nork, are afraid of the giant spider-beasties. Otherwise, they'd try harder. The Sky live in the top parts of the "skyscrapers", and the people of Nork stay below. It's an uneasy standoff that surely can't last."

Johnny looked at Mantayo. "Hello, Mantayo. Thank you for bringing us here to meet you. May I ask, why do some of them have wings, and others don't?"

Mantayo stood up and walked over. "It is the blessing of our goddess Pantina. We were ground worms ourselves, barely surviving. Then she was born, and since then, all those born have had wings. When she came to us, everything changed."

"What is a 'goddess'?" Johnny asked.

"A goddess is someone sent from the heavens. She is not of our world, but is perfect and holy. She leads us and tells us how to live."

Johnny, Deb, and Lady Stabs glanced at each other, all thinking the same thing, that Mantayo and his people had some strange beliefs and they'd better be careful not to cause offense or they might be in trouble.

"Have you met Pantina, Lady Stabs?" Johnny asked.

"No outsider may meet Pantina!" Mantayo said, his voice with a tinge of anger at the very thought. "Only the high priest talks to her. We the Sky only get to gaze on her beauty on the night of Perceptival, when we worship her and give her our gifts."

Johnny, Deb and Lady Stabs stole a glance at each other again, each wearing a slight grin. Yeah, the Sky were a little waksy. They'd all better be careful.

Johnny turned to Mantayo. "We didn't mean any harm. We just don't know your traditions."

Mantayo nodded, mollified. He frowned at Johnny with mild contempt. "You are outsiders. It is only natural that you would not know. Soon you too will learn to love and worship Pantina."

Mantayo began walking. He motioned with his hand. "Come! All outsiders must meet Lord Flaggalon, our high priest. He will tell Pantina about you. Then she will ultimately decide your fate."

"That sounds ominous," Deb said.

Mantayo walked through the room, but he heard her words. Johnny, Deb, Lady Stabs and Deecee followed. "Don't worry," Mantayo said, "Pantina is wise. She will surely realize you are good people, and friends."

In a low voice so only Johnny and Deb could hear, Lady Stabs said, "You're going to love this Lord Flaggalon guy, Johnny. He's going to remind you of someone I think you'd really like to forget."

"Who?" Johnny whispered back.

"Leader Nordstrom!"

With a smile and a feeling of grim satisfaction, Misterwizard watched Starbucks, Lightpole and Super kill the second Krakn, stabbing it until it also stopped moving. Then Starbucks helped Super and Lightpole climb the curtain out of the pit. When they were safely out, Starbucks followed.

When Lightpole was out, Misterwizard examined him. The Asian warrior was weak and covered in sweat, but smiling with the quiet pride of victory.

"I was lucky," Lightpole said as Misterwizard examined his wound. "The spike did not go through the muscle, only the skin. My leg will give me considerable amounts of pain, but should eventually heal."

"Excellent!" Misterwizard said. He grabbed the curtain hanging in the pit and pulled it up, intending to use some of it to bind Lightpole's wound.

As Starbucks and Super held each other gazed at each other like long lost lovers, Misterwizard worked on Lightpole's leg wound.

Suddenly Misterwizard saw something out of the corner of his eye. He turned and looked to see a very curious sight. Two men rode up on two-wheeled metal contraptions. One seemed big and muscular, with black hair and wore black pants and a white shirt. The other was slender with long brown hair down to the shoulders and wearing a black ankle-length dress, white socks and shiny black shoes. The vehicles seemed to be powered by pushing pedals with their feet. They seemed tired and the vehicles moved slow, as if they had been riding the vehicles for a long time.

"I do believe those are called bi-cycles!" Misterwizard said with a jaunty grin. "One cannot possibly have any precognition as to what bizarre new spectacle they will observe next in this strange, new world."

Bargainbin and Jewelrydept rode up until they reached Misterwizard, then they stopped pedaling, and they did look exhausted. They slowly climbed off the bicycles stiffly, as if their legs were very sore. Both wore big grins however, for they both recognized Misterwizard.

"Misterwizard!" Jewelrydept, the muscular one with wavy black hair said, hurrying over to Misterwizard as fast as he could on his sore legs. "We never thought we'd ever see you again!"

Misterwizard frowned, as if recognizing Jewlerydept, but not sure where he'd met him before. Misterwizard pointed a finger at Jewelrydept and wagged it, scrunching up his face to try and remember. "I do recognize you! Don't tell me, I'll get it! My mental faculties don't retrieve data from my brain as quickly as they used to, but they eventually complete the task I assign them, if I simply cogitate and use patience and perseverance."

"Misterwizard!" Bargainbin said, the one with the shoulder-length brown hair and the dress, walked up and put an arm around Jewelrydept.

Seeing this triggered the memory in Misterwizard and his face lit up with recognition.

"Bargainbin! I named you Bargainbin!

Bargainbin smiled with pleasure at being remembered.

"And you are Shoedept!"

Jewelrydept frowned. "Jewelrydept. Yes, you named us when we were just scrabblers."

"Oh yes!" Misterwizard said with a smile, nodding his round head. "The synapses in my brain are recreating the pathways to the memories as we speak. You too were banished from Sanctuary, as I recall, by

Leader Nordstrom, simply for your choice of affections."

Jewelrydept and Bargainbin frowned at the memory. "Yes. And we almost didn't make it, Misterwizard. We came close to starving, or being eaten by beasties."

"I am sorry for that, my friends. Bigotry and prejudice are the traits of small, unintellectual minds, and the former leader of Sanctuary, Leader Nordstrom, was a man whose cognitive ability fit the description of a person with such faculties perfectly."

"We wandered the wasteland for a while," Jewelrydept said. "Then when we came back, you and the people of Sanctuary were gone, and Letfreedomring had taken over the city."

"They welcomed us without the slightest hesitation," Bargainbin said. "It was good too, for we had almost given up all hope."

Bargainbin and Jewelrydept saw Lightpole, and their faces brightened with pleasure. But then they saw Lightpole's condition and they both frowned with concern. "Our great general has been hurt!" Bargainbin said.

Lightpole smiled up at them. "A mere flesh wound. I will be as good as new soon!"

"That is a possibility," Misterwizard said, "However, prudence dictates you should repose yourself in one of our vehicles for some restoration of the remainder of our sojourn, brave warrior."

Lightpole scowled, but he nodded sagely. Starbucks and Super joined them.

"Hey!" Super said. "What are you two doing here?"

They all laughed. "They followed me," Starbucks said. "We were hunting those two Krakn, but it looks like they didn't have the stomach for Misterwizard's magic gun!"

"Indubitably, this is a most enjoyable reunion," Misterwizard said. "Nothing cheers the heart like rejoining old friends you thought were dissolved in the mist of time forever."

"Speaking of friends, Misterwizard, we have a lot to talk about," Starbucks said.

"I think it may have to wait for a little more suitable moment in time, dear Starbucks," Misterwizard said, for he saw something that gave him concern. "It appears our aborigine friends have returned."

Misterwizard was right. Having seen the Krakn killed, the wildies had regained their courage. Pouring out of every doorway and building, they advanced on the small party. They held clubs and sticks, and dark scowls, showing that they definitely were not looking to be friendly. Little scrabblers scampered amongst them, holding rocks or sticks of their own. The wildies eyed Misterwizard and his party with malice, and hunger.

"Are these people friendly, Misterwizard?" Starbucks asked, as they all studied the growing crowd of wildies.

Misterwizard set his short legs and tried to look as intimidating as possible with his short round body. He held the gun in front of himself pointing in the air, in case he had to shoot a warning shot.

"I must regrettably reply in the negative, Starbucks, for that has not been my experience to this moment. They seem to be totally preoccupied with where to find provender for their next repast, and they are not above eating human flesh to satisfy their cravings!"

As Misterwizard watched with dismay, the cavemen leader with the matted black hair showed up again, waving a club with sharp nails on it. He looked even fiercer now, emboldened by the dead Krakn and his superior numbers. He stared at Starbucks and his eyes opened wide, as if he'd rarely seen a black man before. He put on a dreadful scowl and grimaced, showing yellow teeth.

"Now you or kill!"

The wildies behind him laughed and cheered in very unpleasant ways. They advanced on Misterwizard and his party.

But just as if they were the cavalry coming to the rescue, the car cavalcade from New Sanctuary roared up behind them, rumbling down a side street. Their engines whined and groaned, and the springs in the old buses creaked. The buses belched smoke, sending plumes into the air.

The effect was magical on the cave men. Thinking they were seeing some evil apparitions, their eyes opened wide with fear and they all turned and ran, their hands in the air and yells of fright on their lips.

The cave man leader's eyes opened wide too,

and showing he was really quite cowardly when the odds were against him, he turned and meekly hurried away. He began to run and quickly overtook his followers, knocking some of them down in his haste to get away.

Misterwizard and the others laughed and grinned, relieved at the perfect timing that got them out of a tight spot.

Misterwizard walked over to Starbucks and Super, who held each other in their arms. "Quite a serendipitous turn of fortune, wouldn't you agree, Starbucks?"

"It was sure lucky they came when they did," Starbucks said.

The buses and cars ground to a noisy halt a few feet away. With loud cranking noises, the doors of the buses opened and the men and women of New Sanctuary piled out, all talking excitedly at once. Starbucks, Super and Lightpole ran over to the group and greeted them with smiles and warmth.

Sephie ran out of one of the buses. She ran up to Starbucks, who knelt down to greet her.

"Is Johnny with you?" Sephie said, looking anxious to see him.

"No, I'm sorry, he's not Sephie," Starbucks said.

Sephie looked disappointed. She turned and walked back on the bus. Starbucks and Super grinned at each other. "I think Johnny has a female admirer waiting for him to return," Starbucks said.

Misterwizard turned to Jewelrydept and

Bargainbin. Stroking his white beard and bunching up his white bushy eyebrows he said to them, "So, Starbucks tells me your people are in need of a little assistance."

Jewelrydept and Bargainbin looked at each other sadly and then back at Misterwizard with defeated looks.

"The Nork soldiers took our people captive, Misterwizard," Jewelrydept said. "By now, they are surely already inside Nork."

"Hmm," Misterwizard said, looking into the distance as everyone watched him. "On my one trip to "Nork", as you call it, I observed quite a few different social groups existing within a very small area of geography. They were varied and socially isolated. At the time, there seemed to be much conflict between them. I heard some talk of a king who ruled the main section of the city, but also that he was at war with many of the others living in the same vicinity.

I avoided entering the city, for it appeared to be in a constant state of war and upheaval. If this king has somehow managed to win his wars and unite the various indigenous groups, he could indeed have quite a formidable population at his command."

"What did he say?" Bargainbin asked Starbucks.

"He said, there might be a lot of people living there under this king," Starbucks said.

Super put her free hand up in the air, the one not holding Starbucks. "So, what can we do, Misterwizard? We can't just leave the people of Letfreedomring to die."

Jewelrydept frowned with conviction. "We won't let that happen. Our people will fight alone, if we have to, to the last scrabbler."

Misterwizard walked over and put a comforting hand on Jewlrydept's arm. "Don't despair, dear friend. Now that the people of New Sanctuary and Letfreedomring are allies, nothing will prevent us from standing shoulder to shoulder with you in your defense."

Jewelrydept smiled and nodded, touched. So did Bargainbin.

"So, what should we do, Misterwizard?" Starbucks said. "If they've already taken the people into Nork, how can we get them back?"

"It does appear to present an insoluble conundrum," Misterwizard said. As they all looked at him waiting for his next words, he took a cigar and his small metal box out of his shirt pocket, put the cigar in his mouth and flipped the top of the box open. Jewelrydept and Bargainbin looked amazed as Misterwizard rotated a small wheel at the top of the box and a flame once again leapt to life.

"You truly are a wizard!" Bargainbin said with conviction.

Misterwizard chuckled good-naturedly and put the flame to the end of the cigar. Soon smoke rose lazily into the air. Misterwizard took a few puffs, then took the cigar out of his mouth and pointed with it north, towards Nork.

"My predilection is to move in a generally northward direction towards the city until we find some indication of the presence of Nork inhabitant occupation. Then we shall procure a spot of concealment and perform a reconnaissance mission to ascertain the current location and predicament of our incarcerated allies."

Jewelrydept turned to Super with an exasperated look of confusion. Super laughed. "He says we'll go take a look, and see if we can find your people, without being spied on."

Starbucks laughed. "You're actually starting to understand him!"

They all laughed. Misterwizard led them back to the buses and cars. "First, we will pass through Pelpia, as you call it. Then we will proceed to a particular location just outside the city. There we will discover three tunnels. The tunnels are without illumination and span a considerable distance. They will be advantageous locations to ensconce ourselves and use as a base for dispatching spies and investigators."

"Let's go!" Starbucks said. "I'm ready for some action!"

"Me too!" Super said

Misterwizard grinned at them. "Oh, the flame youthful exuberance!"

Starbucks and Super helped Lightpole onto one of the buses. Then with belches of smoke and the cranking of old engines, the strange cavalcade continued their journey north. Starbucks and Super headed for Starbuck's Harley.

CHAPTER 25

Johnny, Deb, Lady Stabs and Deecee followed Mantayo as he walked across the room, past the tables and couches where Sky people lounged, laughing and talking. Mantayo turned to them. The Sky saw them and soon they were surrounded by a crowd eyeing them with friendly curiosity.

Mantayo turned to the Sky surrounding them. "Everyone, this is Johnny Apocalypse, his friend Deb, and their doggy Deecee. You have all already met Lady Stabs. They come from a land far away, but they are friends."

The people murmured friendly hellos and smiled at Johnny and his friends. Johnny and Deb smiled back, and Deecee wagged his tail.

"I am sorry. I am a terrible host. Before I take you to Lord Flaggalon, are you hungry? You are welcome to eat first. We have lots of food and drink available." Mantayo put his hand up towards the tables.

The mention of food made Johnny realize how

long it had been since he'd had a decent meal, and his stomach churned with hunger. He looked at Deb, and could see on her face she was starving as well. Thinking more of Deb than himself, he said, "We are very hungry, Mantayo. We haven't eaten in a long time. And you really are a great host."

They walked over to the tables. Johnny had never seen so much food all at once, and it all looked delicious. Deecee eyed it as well, and whined. Johnny grinned and looked at him. "You're pretty hungry too, huh, Deecee?"

They all laughed, including Mantayo. "Please, help yourselves. Even your doggy."

Johnny and Deb didn't have to be asked again, for it was all they could do to keep from grabbing at the food like starving animals. With barely contained restraint, they grabbed plates from a stack on the table and began loading up food.

Deecee looked longingly at Johnny, but he didn't have to worry. The first thing Johnny did was grab what looked like a bone belonging to some large beastie, loaded with meat. He tossed it to Deecee, who grabbed it happily in his mouth, lay down with the bone in his paws and started ripping pieces off in happiness.

There was so much food, and such a wonderful variety, Johnny didn't know what to grab first. There were different types of fruits than Johnny had never seen before, and four or five different types of beastie meat, and a light brown rectangular thing with round corners that looked delicious.

Johnny picked up the brown square thing and found out it was soft. He tore it in two and discovered the inside was white. He pulled a piece of the white stuff inside out and popped it in his mouth. It was tasty!

Mantayo chuckled, watching them. "You have never eaten bread before, Johnny?"

Johnny felt embarrassed, and shrugged, hiding his reaction.

"I'm sorry, I didn't mean to make fun of you. Most people haven't. It comes from a strange long plant that we found far away. We learned how to shape it and cook it." Mantayo swelled with pride. "We know a lot of things."

When Johnny and Deb had filled their plates, they sat down on one of the couches. Lady Stabs sat next to them with a glass of red liquid. Johnny looked at her quizzically, and she said, "I've been here awhile. I've been eating their food for a few days. I'm actually stuffed!"

Johnny turned to Mantayo, who sat on a couch next to them, chewing on a beastie leg lazily.

"How do you have so much food, Mantayo?"

"We fly all over the land, and have studied it for as far as one can go before the light of day is gone. We know where to find all kinds of special things. I've seen things too, amazing things."

Johnny believed that. As he chewed on some more bread, he wondered what it must be like to be able to fly, and once again felt a pang of jealousy. *To soar with the clouds, high above the world,* Johnny thought. *What would Misterwizard think?* Then Johnny thought of something he needed to tell Mantayo.

Mantayo, his large wings folded onto his back and looking relaxed, stood next to Johnny sipping on a glass of red liquid.

"Mantayo, just before you found us, something happened, something very strange."

Mantayo turned and looked at Johnny quizzically. "Strange?"

Deb broke in. "Weird men attacked us in the dark tunnels just before the gate."

Her words seemed to trigger something to Mantayo, for his eyes opened wide with alarm. "Tell me what these men looked like."

Johnny and Deb glanced at each other, then back at Mantayo. Johnny spoke in a serious tone. "They looked dead."

His words had even more effect on Mantayo, and he looked very concerned. "Did they seem to have parts of their flesh gone, missing arms, or legs?"

"Yes!" Johnny said, picking up on Mantayo's tone.

"That is bad, very bad," Mantayo said. "That means Lurkers have escaped from the subways."

"Lurkers?" Johnny asked, his inside tightening, for something told him a very bad thing was happening.

"The undead. They are the ones who drank too deeply of the magic water, and it killed them. They were the ones trapped in the subway when the magic water flooded it, drowning them. The magic water killed them, but gave their bodies magical power to keep going, as if they were still alive."

Deb looked skeptical. "You mean they're dead and yet still walking around? How is that possible?"

"We don't know how, it just is," Mantayo said. He turned to them and looked them up and down. "We have asked Pantina, but she had not told us. You were not bit, were you?"

Johnny and Deb both shook their heads. Mantayo sighed with relief. "Good. If they bite you, they spread the magic water inside you, and before long you die and become one of them."

"How do you stop them, Mantayo?" Johnny asked.

"The only way is to shoot them in the head or cut them to pieces so they can't attack you anymore. Then you must burn them. They do not stop moving until there is nothing left of them. Even their heads keep moving when cut from their bodies."

"They were coming out of the dark tunnel, just ahead of the Nork army and all the prisoners from Letfreedomring," Johnny said in a worried voice. "Then when we were flying, I saw the Nork army and the prisoners running from the tunnel. If those things caught them…"

"I hope they did not," Mantayo said. "Even the groundworms do not deserve to be turned into one of those things. I must fly there and see what is happening. If the Lurkers are free, we must destroy them and seal up their way of escape, or they will spread their death everywhere."

"Let me go with you!" Johnny said. "Our new friends are there!"

Before Mantayo could reply, suddenly the friendly atmosphere in the room changed. Everyone seemed to tense up. They all stood and turned towards the door with serious frowns. Even the little scrabblers looked scared as they clung to their mothers.

Johnny turned to see what had caused such a sudden and alarming reaction. There in the doorway stood an old man in a shimmering gray robe with a hood. He was bald with a long, thin face, and dark eyes that hid under bushy black eyebrows. He wore thin, pointed black boots scuffed and old.

His right hand held onto the top of a twisted wooden pole with the skull of a small beastie on top of it. The skull was long and thin and had sharp pointed fangs. The old man leaned on the pole, as if it was the only thing keeping him from falling down.

The old man wore a scowl of displeasure that looked like a permanent feature of his face, and a piercing gaze that scanned the room, piercing through anyone it fell upon.

Johnny noticed that even Mantayo, who seemed so strong and courageous, showed worry and fear in his eyes. Johnny knew this man must be the high priest, Lord Flaggalon.

Johnny braced himself, and filled his mind with courage, the way he always did when faced with a new challenge. He placed a protective arm around Deb, who didn't seem to notice, for she was also looking at the old man. Johnny noticed Lady Stabs was the only one who didn't seem mesmerized. She simply gazed at the old man with a look of dislike. Deecee quietly growled, and Johnny smiled inside, thinking how dog-beasties always seemed to have a sense of what kind of person someone was as soon as they met them.

The old man searched the room with his eyes, as if sure someone was doing something they were not supposed to. His eyes stopped on Mantayo, Johnny and his friends. His face showed interest at seeing someone new, and a smile played at the corners of his mouth briefly before disappearing. He strode towards Mantayo and Johnny in stiff little steps. The rest of the Sky quietly walked away and took protective positions on the couches.

"Hello, Lord Flaggalon," Mantayo said nervously. "These are new friends. This is Johnny Apocalypse, his girlfriend Deb and their doggy Deecee."

A dark twinkle shone in Lord Flaggalon's eyes. He gazed down at Deecee, who stared back with danger in his eyes. Johnny quickly put a hand on Deecee's head, and Deecee looked up at Johnny, then seemed to relax slightly.

Lord Flaggalon strode to stand within inches from Johnny, which Johnny didn't like at all, for it felt like a challenge. Johnny didn't flinch or move, but simply stared back at Lord Flaggalon without fear.

For a brief second Lord Flaggalon and Johnny simply stared at each other, as everyone else unconsciously held their breath. Then, sensing Johnny was not going to wither under his gaze, Lord Flaggalon backed up and bit and smiled. Then turned on Mantayo with a voice of disapproval. "Why did you not bring these intruders to me at once? Instead, you feed them and show them around, as if they members of the Sky already."

Mantayo looked uncharacteristically confused and shy, and Johnny wondered if this Lord Flaggalon could enact punishments for behavior he didn't like.

Mantayo answered Lord Flaggalon in a reverent but confident voice, which cheered Johnny up. Mantayo wasn't totally under this old man's spell, "They are friends of Lady Stabs, who you have already met and approved of. They come from the same tribe. They were very hungry and hadn't eaten in days. I know it's not your intention to lose good allies, by making them think we are not good hosts."

Lord Flaggalon knew a challenge when he heard one, and he stared at Mantayo, who stared back without flinching.

Giving up with displeasure, Lord Flaggalon turned his attention back to Johnny and his companions. "We are letting quite a few strangers into our homes lately. And all from this so-called tribe. And yet they say they are our friends."

Mantayo replied in a petulant tone, "We have no reason not to believe them. Until they prove themselves false, we should take them at their word."

Lord Flaggalon spun on Mantayo and moved to

within inches of his face. Mantayo, despite his bravado, was taken aback and he and his face showed tension.

"How dare you speak for 'we'? I know you young Sky think you are smarter and stronger than your elders, especially you, Mantayo but you are barely older than a little child and still know nothing of the real world. You need to learn to listen and not think, for only then will you truly gain any wisdom. And Pantina alone decides important matters, for she alone is all-wise and all-knowing."

Johnny decided it was time to interject. "Lord Flaggalon, we want to be your friends. We have a tribe that lives in a city not far from here, and they are coming this way to save our friends from the city of Pelpia who have been taken captive by the Nork army. If there is a way we can prove to you our good intentions, please tell us. We want you to be sure about us."

Lord Flaggalon spun on Johnny, and Johnny instantly agreed with Lady Stabs opinion of him, in fact Johnny began to dislike the old man. Deecee growled again, staring at Lord Flaggalon, this time more menacingly. Johnny quickly put a hand on Deecee's head again, for the last thing they needed was Deecee to bite the high priest of the Sky. Deecee looked up at Johnny, as if to say, "I'm ready to attack, just give me the word."

Lord Flaggalon looked down at Deecee with a scowl and then back at Johnny. "You needn't concern yourself, Johnny Apocalypse. Pantina can always see the truth, for she can see right into a person's soul."

Johnny tried to hide the smile that came to his

face, for he was sure Lord Flaggalon wouldn't like it, but he was beginning to think all the god worship stuff was getting silly. He even began to wonder if the Sky were a simpler people than he had at first thought.

Lord Flaggalon turned his attention back to Mantayo. "From now on, bring all strangers to me before you treat them like friends." He fastened his laser-like gaze on Johnny. "We don't want to waste precious food and drink on enemies."

"Yes, Lord Flaggalon," Mantayo said, barely hiding his contempt.

Lord Flaggalon turned to Johnny, Deb and Lady Stabs. "Follow me. I will show you to Pantina. She will decide your fate."

Once again, that phrase, thought Johnny wryly. *Hopefully, this Pantina could really tell friend from foe.*

Lord Flaggalon spun around and walked away, as if confident that he would be obeyed. Johnny turned to Mantayo. "I'm sorry if we got you into trouble."

Mantayo grinned, his bravado fully back. "Don't worry, he's always like that. Old people love to make big speeches." Mantayo lowered his voice so only Johnny, Deb and Lady Stabs could hear. "He's a real blowhard."

They all smiled and chuckled quietly. Lord Flaggalon turned suddenly, and Johnny worried that he had heard their comments. But Lord Flaggalon just looked down at Deecee. "Your animal must stay here."

Anger rose up in Johnny, but before he could reply, a young girl of ten seasons with small, dainty wings walked up and started petting Deecee's head.

"Don't worry, Johnny, we'll take care of him while you're gone, if that's okay. We'd love to get to know him!"

Johnny smiled at her, and so did Deb and Lady Stabs. Johnny walked over and bent down to the little girl. "Thank you. He really likes pretty little girls. I bet you and he will be good friends."

The little girl smiled with hope and looked at Deecee. "Come along, Deecee, we'll feed you."

"Not too much!" Johnny said, laughing.

"Come!" Lord Flaggalon thundered, and he turned and strode off again.

"You better follow him, or he'll get angry," Mantayo said. "Meanwhile, I will go and find out about the Lurkers. I'll return and tell you what I see. And don't worry about your meeting, Pantina is all wise. She will know you are good right away."

Johnny watched Mantayo spread his wings and fly out the opening in the wall. Johnny wondered just how much influence this Pantina had, and what would happen if she decided they were not good? Would Johnny and his friends still have a fight on their hands?

CHAPTER 26

Antonio and Frank bowed as they backed towards the entrance. Monsta backed out too, but he didn't bow, for he was too busy frowning and thinking about his future.

"So, what's this prison like I'm going to?" Monsta whispered to Antonio as he walked in front of them.

Antonio answered. "Oh, it's a nice place." Then he grinned cruelly. "The subway, the darkest, dirtiest place in all of Nork."

"Yeah," Frank, the big round one, wheezed. "They march you down the stairs, and all the while, you can hear the Lurkers waitin' for ya. Then they leave ya alone, and ya better get ready to run."

"And all you got to do is survive in the dark, with them Lurkers all around ya. But don't worry, there are rats down there to eat."

"How many people has he put down there?" Monsta asked unhappily.

"Fifty or sixty," Antonio said. "But most of them are Lurkers now. Any that's still alive have found someplace in the dark to hide."

"You ain't never gonna survive long enough to see the king again." Frank wheezed with laughter. Antonio laughed too.

"Wait!" As Frank and Antoinio watched in surprise, Monsta ran back to the king. Frank and Antonio stared at each other. No one had ever done something like that before. Monsta was really asking for it! Antonio and Frank looked terrified at each other and followed, waiting to see what happened to Monsta now.

Monsta bowed in front of the king. The king had one of the girls on his lap, and she had the cat-beastie on hers. As Monsta looked at the king, the king didn't look angry, just delighted and amused.

Antonio reached Monsta first, for Frank was fat and out of breath. He stopped a little way back. Antonio looked at the king with a sorrowful look and pleading eyes, afraid Monsta was going to get him into trouble too.

"We're sorry, Boss. Please don't blame us. This guy's crazy as a loon! He don't even know what a Schmoe he is!"

Frank struggled to his knees, wheezing. He stared at the king imploringly. "He's dumb in the head, Boss! We tried to stop him, but he's nuts!"

The king didn't look angry at Monsta, but he glared at Frank and Antonio in fury. In a slow voice dripping with poison the king said, "Didn't I say I wanted you to call me King Richard?"

Frank and Antonio looked at each other in fright, then back at the king.

"We're sorry, King Richard!"

"Guards!" The king motioned with his hand. The girl on the king's lap smiled down at Frank and Antonio. "You guys are in Dutch now."

Frank and Antonio's eyes went wide and their faces turned white.

The guards ran up.

The king pointed at Frank and Antonio. "Take these men. Prepare them for tomorrow night's entertainment.

As Frank and Antonio yelled in terror, the guards grabbed their arms and dragged them away. Then the king turned to Monsta.

Monsta knew this was his last chance.

"Please!" Monsta said, forgetting his pride. He put his hands out in supplication. "All I want to do is serve you. You're the greatest bad guy I ever met! Let me prove what I can do. I'll do anything! Just name it!"

The king gestured to the girl and she climbed off his lap. The king stood up and walked over to Monsta with an amused smile.

"You have what in the old gangster book they called, "moxie". I find you pathetic, smelly and dirty, but I do sense a level of authenticity in you."

Monsta gazed at the king, hope springing up inside him.

The king looked around at his subjects, who all

smiled back at him, enjoying the game. "You say you will do anything for me."

"Oh, yes, your majesty!" Monsta said, hope rising in his voice.

The king poured some red liquid from the pitcher on the table by his throne into a glass, picked up the glass and took a sip. "No matter how difficult?"

"Just name it!" Monsta said with sincerity.

"This is what you must do. Come with me."

The king walked over to the side of the room. Monsta stood up and hurriedly followed. The king pointed out a small window in the wall.

Monsta looked at what the king was pointing to. He saw a tall black glass building, made up of two thin black glass buildings next to each other. The furthest building was the tallest, and it had strange, small wings on either side at the top.

"You see that building in the distance?"

"Yes, your majesty."

The king looked at Monsta. "That is where Pantina, the creature that the Angels worship as a goddess lives. If she were to die, it would bring the Angels terrible sadness."

Monsta studied the building. The king put an arm around Monsta, surprising everyone. "If you truly want to win my affection and be part of my kingdom, find a way to the top of that building and her. Then bring me her head and her wings. When I see them, I will make you a lord and give you anything you desire."

Everyone in the throne room watched in amused

amazement, for they knew the king was giving Monsta an impossible task.

Monsta smiled with grim determination. "Consider her dead already, your majesty. How do I get up there?"

The king smiled, and everyone in the room chuckled. "Dear Monsta, if I knew that, I'd do it myself. You said you'd do anything, even the impossible."

"I will!" Monsta said with conviction, making them all laugh again. "But if I do, you gots to promise me you'll do one other thing for me in return."

The king, and everyone in the room looked at Monsta with curiosity.

"And that is?" The king replied with a dark smile.

"Help me kill Johnny Apocalypse, and his friends."

The king chuckled. "You must really detest this fellow."

"I hate him more than anything in the world," Monsta said, clenching his fists and gritting his teeth. "He killed all of my friends. He killed Ripper. And if you don't stop him, he'll take you down too."

The king looked interested and mildly concerned. "Hmm. I'm beginning to tire of this Johnny Apocalypse, and I haven't even met him yet."

The king chuckled, and everyone else grinned. "I give you my promise. You bring me Pantina's head, and wings and I will personally hand Johnny and his friends over to you, to do to them whatever makes you happy."

"That's a deal!" Monsta said.

Starbucks walked over to his Harley and motioned to Super. "Hop on!"

To his surprise, Super shook her head. "I ride my own now."

"Where is it?" Starbucks asked. Super grinned and pointed a thumb towards the pit. "Down there."

Starbucks laughed, and Super grinned wider. "A lot of good it's going to do you, too," Starbucks said. "We don't have time to get it out. Hop on!"

Super shook her head again stubbornly. "I'm not leaving without it! You wouldn't leave without yours."

They stared at each other, at an impasse. Finally, Starbucks chuckled and gave in. "Okay, if you want to ride alone. It's much more fun with two."

He walked past her towards the pit, but his words had affected her. Starbucks looked back at her, his eyes twinkling because he knew it.

Super frowned. "It's not because I don't want to ride with you."

"That's okay. If you don't want to put your arms around my waist and your head on my back, if you'd rather be all lonely on your own Harley…"

Super looked torn d, so Starbucks let her off the hook. "It's okay, I understand your wanting to ride your own. We can always cuddle later."

Starbucks walked to the edge of the pit and

looked down at the Harley at the bottom of the pit. It didn't look like it was in that great of shape. The back wheel looked bent, and the handlebars were buried in the mud.

He looked back at Super, and was surprised again, this time pleasantly. She sat on his Harley, her arms folded.

"Well, let's go! What are we waiting for?"

Starbucks grinned, his whole inside filling with love and affection for the dark-haired beauty who had won his heart. He hurried over and sat on the front of the Harley, and a warmth filled him as Super wrapped her arms around his waist. She laid his head on his back.

"I missed you so, Starbucks. Let's never be apart again."

Starbucks felt his throat constrict with emotion, but he managed to croak out, "We won't. I promise."

His Harley roared to life, and Starbucks took off. Once again, he felt like the world was a wonderful place, as long as Super was in it.

Suddenly they heard a high whining sound. They turned to see Misterwizard ride up next to him on his little scooter, goggles over his eyes. His short round frame filled the little bike and Starbucks and Super couldn't help but grin at him and try not to laugh, but Misterwizard didn't seem to mind in the least.

"Tell me, Starbucks," Misterwizard yelled over the sound of their engines as they barreled along. "When did you last see Johnny?"

"He was headed north towards Nork," Starbucks

yelled back. "He was following the Nork army that had kidnapped Deb and the people of Pelpia."

Misterwizard nodded and looked even more grave. "He might have already found himself in the thick of a dangerous hornet's nest. We have a monumental task ahead of us, friends. We are but a small contingent compared to the population of the city we are proposing to engage. Discretion and stealth will be our only paths to victory."

"Yeah," Super yelled. "It's going to be tough!"

Misterwizard looked at Starbucks through his goggles and pointed a finger ahead. "Lead us on, oh Moses, to the Promised Land."

Starbucks chuckled, not having a clue what Misterwizard meant, but he got the general idea Misterwizard wanted him to take the lead. He gave the Harley gas and sped out in front of the strange cavalcade, Super shouting with pleasure as the wind blew back her hair.

Moxie took the lead as the strange cavalcade wandered down the street leading from the wall. Surrounding them was nothing but rubble, for the buildings for the first few blocks next to the wall had been leveled to create no hiding place for enemies.

In the distance, they could see where the buildings began again, and they all looked empty and forlorn, with dark empty windows. The people of Letfreedomring, tired and sore, stumbled over the bricks and rock. They looked sad and defeated. Even the guards looked gloomy, for the Red Eye had begun its descent on the other side of the horizon, and the somber half-light made the world seem even more desolate.

And Moxie didn't feel so good. Sweat beads rolled down his hot, flushed face. Why was he so hot? And why did he feel so angry? His stomach twisted and churned and he thought he should feel like throwing up, in fact he wished he would, because then he might feel better, but instead there was just the constant aching inside. His eyesight grew blurry and then clear again, and back to blurry.

His condition scared him. He glanced at Alcapoon, and suddenly he realized it was all Alcapoon's fault! He should grab a gun and blow the guy's head off! What was he thinking? He was off his marbles! He had to get home and find out what was wrong!

"All right, listen up!" Moxie yelled, trying to sound confident. "Start hoofin' it, on the double! Get the lead out!"

Alcapoon walked up. "Where we takin' em, Moxie? To the Boss? There's a lot of 'em!"

Man, this guy is stupid, Moxie thought. *I really should shoot him right between the eyes.* "No, stupid," Moxie said, taking his hat off, wiping his forehead with his sleeve, and then putting his hat back on, trying his best to keep his voice from betraying how sick he felt. "Whaddya got, straw for brains?"

"Then where?" Alcapoon said, his face looking confused. "If we don't find a place where we can watch 'em, they're all gonna escape."

Restaria walked up, the last person Bugsy wanted to hear from at the moment. For some reason, Moxie didn't want to kill her, instead he felt a strange terror inside just looking at her. What was wrong with him?

Restaria placed her hands on her hips and glared at Moxie with anger. "Our people are hungry. There wasn't much food last night. And some are dying of thirst. Your king won't be happy if we all die before you take us to them."

Moxie wanted to ball her out, but he was suddenly too scared. "Tough beans!" Moxie said. "You'll get fed when we get where we're going, if you're lucky. Now get back to your rabble before we decide to start eating you!"

Restaria glared at him again, but fear showed in her eyes as well, for she knew they were his prisoners. Reluctantly she turned and walked away, to Moxie's relief.

Moxie tried to think fast, because he knew Alcapoon was waiting for an answer, but his brain didn't seem to want to work. He concentrated as hard as he could, but it was like his brain had shut off. All he could think about was killing something, ripping someone's head off and sucking the blood out of their neck. His head started to hurt, bad.

"I know!" Alcapoon said. "Let's take 'em to that

big round building, you know the one with all the seats. I heard the Boss call it Madson Skare Gardem. We can seal it up so there's no way they can get out."

Relief washed over Moxie at having been given a solution, for his brain was like a dead weight at the top of his head. He didn't want Alcapoon to know it though, so he pretended like that was his plan all along. "That's just what I was gonna say, if you would'a shut up for a moment. Madson Drabon, dabble da plus."

Alcapoon's face scrunched up as he stared at Moxie with concern. "You okay, Moxie?"

Moxie just nodded and waved towards the crowd. "Gettle dum movlin'" Spittle dripped from Moxie's mouth, and he wiped it on his sleeve.

Alcapoon didn't look convinced, but he turned to follow Moxie's orders. What was happening, Moxie wondered. He was feeling confused and when he spoke, what he thought didn't come out of his mouth. He began to get really scared. He wasn't bit by that Lurker; the guy didn't break the skin. That girl, she grabbed Moxie's hand. Did she scratch it? Why did he go in that stupid tunnel in the first place?

Moxie hoped he wasn't making a big mistake bringing all these prisoners right into Nork. If they all escaped, they could hide out in the buildings, and they'd never find all of them! And didn't the king say he wanted supplies? Moxie forgot to get any, he was too busy gathering up the prisoners.

Moxie tried to quell the fear that fluttered inside him like a birdie, then two birdies, then more and more, as if they kept multiplying. He began to wish he'd never taken the army south, that he'd instead run away that morning when they left, and never returned. Maybe it was the biggest mistake of his life.

It was all that kid's fault, that Johnny Apocalypse. *Yeah, that's right,* Moxie thought and now all his hatred and desire to kill concentrated on the image of that boy in his mind. Johnny had messed up everything. Johnny has sicced those monsters on them, and caused everything to go haywire. If it wasn't for that stupid yellow haired kid in his black leather and army boots, Moxie would have gotten the supplies and went back home, and none of the terrible things that happened later would have happened.

Moxie only hoped he could hold onto his hatred until he ran into that kid again. Then he'd really let it all out. *Just you wait, kid,* Moxie thought. *I'm gonna get ya.*

CHAPTER 27

Johnny, Deb, and Lady Stabs were led through a doorway into what looked like a long, dingy hallway. There were no 'lectric lights, so gloom permeated the room. Lord Flaggalon strode down the hall without looking back, expecting them to follow. He walked in stiff, purposeful strides as if stomping on the floor with each foot in anger. With each step, he banged the bottom of his pole on the floor, making a loud cracking sound, which seemed to punctuate his anger.

Lord Flaggalon walked slow, so slow Johnny had to pace himself to stay behind him, something Johnny was sure the old man was doing just to be more irritating. Lord Flaggalon would even stop every few seconds to see if Johnny and his group stopped, not turning around, pause for a second, then continue on. It made Johnny smile. The old man loved control, and being dramatic as well, and a twinge of sympathy touched Johnny. It seemed to Johnny Lord Flaggalon felt old and frail, and was trying his best to remain important and noticed.

They reached the end of the hallway and Johnny saw the wall in front of them was gone, just like in the other room. Next to the opening, four tall winged young men stood, waiting.

From the opening, Johnny could see the city again. It seemed to stretch forever, and in front of them in the distance stood a cluster of buildings. In the center of them stood one building taller than all the others. It was made up of two thin, rectangular buildings standing against each other, one taller than the other, both covered in black windows. The taller building's roof ended in a triangle shape, and a little way from the top small black wings protruded. Much of the glass on the bottom half of all the buildings was gone, exposing the metal beams underneath. It made the buildings look like their skin was removed to expose their bones.

Lord Flaggalon turned to them haughtily and pointed with his finger. "You see that tall building in the middle? That is the holy place where Pantina, our goddess resides. There we go to worship. You will of course not see her, no matter how much you worship, but she will see you."

Johnny thought to himself, *Don't expect us to do any worshiping, Lord Flaggalon*, but he didn't say anything.

Lord Flaggalon said, "It is too far for a rope bridge, and so we will need to be carried."

Suddenly Lord Flaggalon looked embarrassed and uncomfortable as he raised his arms and one of the winged young men grabbed him from behind. Johnny realized something else then, Lord Flaggalon was also jealous because he didn't have the ability to fly and felt as if it made him seem less powerful than the young men. Johnny was sure it irritated Lord Flaggalon to no end to have to be carried by the young men as well. It made Johnny grin inside.

Johnny didn't relish another flight either, being held by a teen again, this one not much older than himself and wondering once again if the young man was going to drop him. Even more, he didn't like the idea of Deb being carried by one of them again. He didn't like anyone touching her but him. There were too many people around her lately for Johnny's liking.

"Lord Flaggalon. May I please ask that my Deb and Lady Stabs be allowed to stay here? I'll go and see Pantina alone and tell her about our tribe."

Lord Flaggalon frowned irritably. "You may not. Pantina will want to see all of you. You will just have to endure your friends in the arms of my young guards. Trust me, they will be safe."

As if on cue, the young men walked behind Johnny, Deb and Lady Stabs. Without asking they wrapped their arms around the companions' bodies and clasped their hands together.

With a rushing of wings, the four young teen men rose into the air, and once again, Johnny felt unease as he lost contact with the ground. He could see in the eyes of the others that they also felt the same, even Lord Flaggalon.

The young men were strong, however, and their wings were powerful. Johnny assumed they were chosen for this duty for their ability to carry people around, but it didn't give Johnny much comfort.

Once again, Johnny sailed out over the open void, his heart in his throat. They left the safety of the building and were totally reliant on the young man's wings for support. Johnny looked down and wished he hadn't, for the ground was so far below, he could see the tops of the other buildings. The buildings looked like toys he used to play with when he was a scrabbler.

Wind rushed past Johnny's ears, and once again along with the fright came a quiet exhilaration. *To soar into the sky, any time you wanted to, to fly anywhere, it must be wonderful,* Johnny thought. He glanced over at Deb, hoping she wasn't scared, but to his surprise, she was smiling brightly, having a wonderful time. It made Johnny feel happy, knowing he was enjoying it with her. Doing anything with Deb next to him was always a hundred times better.

He looked down again, with less fear and more pleasure this time, at the ribbon of streets intersecting all the buildings of all different sizes. Then he saw something that filled him with excitement!

A huge crowd moved slowly through the streets. At the distance, he couldn't see their faces, but he knew it was the Nork army! And there in the center were the people of Letfreedomring!

Johnny turned and yelled at Deb, pointing at the ground but the wind was too noisy and she was too far away. Deb looked everywhere, taking in the sights. Johnny looked at Lady Stabs, but she didn't look like she was having fun at all. Her eyes were shut tight, as if just waiting for the ride to be over.

Johnny looked down again and studied the crowd, trying to see if he could figure out where the Nork army was taking them. As Johnny watched, the whole turned down a street on the left, going away from where Johnny and his companions flew high above them. Johnny looked down the street to see if he could see some kind of destination, and then with excitement he did. There in the distance he saw a huge round building of only ten stories that looked like a big bowl turned upside down. It must be where the Nork army was taking them!

Joy filled Johnny's heart, for sheerly by accident he'd found out where the people of Letfreedomring would be. Now all they had to do was find a way to rescue them! As Misterwizard would say, "piece of cake"!

The young men approached the strange building with the triangle roof and the wings on the sides. It seemed to Johnny like they'd only been flying for a few minutes, he'd been so occupied with his thoughts.

They approached an opening in the side of this building three floors from the top of the shorter building in front. Once again, the flying teens flapped their wings loudly and all slowed to a stop, rising up slightly as they prepared to land. With amazing grace and agility, the young man floated through the opening and landed, setting their passengers down gently.

Lord Flaggalon had already landed and waited for them, his ever-present scowl still on his face. As soon as their passengers were free, the young winged men moved to the sides of the room and took a waiting position. They all looked hot and tired, and Johnny noticed they availed themselves of a pool of water nearby. The young winged men talked quietly to each other, joking and pushing each other, like teens everywhere.

Johnny surveyed the room. Once again it was one giant space. The floor and walls were covered with rich, black, furry carpet. The room was empty except for padded black benches lined up in rows with an aisle down the middle of them. The walls were lined with burning torches, and soft music played. Johnny looked for the music's source, and saw three older male Sky members sitting in a far corner, playing some sort of small wooden instruments. They wore soft white robes and sat on black cushions.

The instruments they held were brown and oblong, with a hole in the middle and strings running attached, running vertically over the opening and up a stick attached at the top. The men dragged another thin stick with a ribbon attached across the strings on the instrument, and this made the melodious music that came from them. The music was soft and pleasant, but then suddenly there would come a loud screech that hurt the ears. Then the soft music would start again, until another one of the men made a loud screech. The men wore no expressions and looked tired, as if they'd been playing for a long time. Johnny wondered if they had to do it all the time and never got to leave. It seemed like an unpleasant way to have to live.

A pleasant aroma that Johnny didn't recognize filled the room, and Johnny saw it came from an open pot with burning coals. The smell was wonderful, but not in a way that made you want to eat something, just enjoy it with your nose.

On the far side of the room, Johnny saw what the benches were lined up to face. There stood an amazing display, and it was towards this that Lord Flaggalon moved. Johnny and the others, after having taken in the strange room, followed him.

On the far side of the room curtains hung down on either side of a curved raised platform. On the platform there were more lit torches and flowers in the stand. And in the center of the platform Johnny saw a giant statue of a giant winged creature, made entirely out of gold. It didn't look like a bird-beastie, for it had a body like a lion, but with scales, and a head like a lizard-beastie. Johnny remembered pictures Misterwizard had shown him in stories he'd read to Johnny. The creature was called a dragon. Its long golden tail curled around its feet and its eyes were made of some kind of red stone that glinted. It was beautiful and awe-inspiring.

Next to the dragon statue sat a golden chair, the most beautiful chair Johnny had ever seen. The gold was metal, and encrusted with stones of every color. The seat and the back of the chair were made of a soft, red cushion.

In front of the raised platform where the dragon statue and the chair were, different objects were scattered all over the floor, from food to round circles of gold to flowers of all colors and shapes. There were even toys, and types of clothing. Behind the dragon statue and the chair, Johnny noticed large black curtains going all the way up to the ceiling

As Johnny and the others watched, Lord Flaggalon walked up the aisle past the benches and knelt in front of the raised platform on black pillows on the floor. He turned and scowled at Johnny and his friends.

"Come worship Pantina with me, or die as enemies!"

Johnny looked at Deb, and saw she was thinking the same thing he was. Both of them had been taught about freedom and 'mocracee from Misterwizard, as well as about kings and dictaters. Though neither of them had heard of a god before, they both cherished their independence stubbornly and were proud to fight for it.

Still, Johnny knew they needed the friendship of the Sky, and deciding to be stubborn at that moment would only end up getting them killed. They both looked at Lady Stabs. She shrugged and said in a low voice, "It makes them happy. You and I know it's all nonsense."

Johnny and Deb grinned at each other and silently shrugged as well. Watching each other, they both walked up and knelt on pillows next to Lord Flaggalon. Lady Stabs joined them.

Johnny wondered if this strange golden statue was Pantina. If that was so, the Sky were more primitive than Johnny had thought. It might be hard to deal with them, for the real power would then be Lord Flaggalon, and he seemed to be a hard man who liked to be in control.

But just as Johnny was wondering these things, Lord Flaggalon spoke in a deep, loud dramatic voice which Johnny instantly found overdone and annoying.

"Dear Goddess Pantina, it is your lowly servant Lord Flaggalon again, come to worship and adore you. I bring strangers who have heard of your beauty and excellence, and have come to worship you as well."

Lord Flaggalon grew silent, and Johnny and his friends waited. Time seemed to pass slowly with no response. Johnny began to feel uncomfortable, for he doubted the dragon statue was going to answer any time soon, which meant that Lord Flaggalon would pretend to get a special "message" from it. Johnny braced himself for what that message might be.

Lord Flaggalon turned to them with eyes of fire. "When Pantina appears before us, keep your head down and eyes lowered. No one may gaze on Pantina, especially not an outsider. I warn you again, do not look at her, or you will instantly burst into flame."

Lord Flaggalon's last words instantly made Johnny want to laugh, but he quickly stifled the urge. He glanced at Deb and saw her smiling secretly too. Even Lady Stabs hid a grin. *What mumbo-jumbo nonsense,* Johnny thought. But at least it might mean maybe

Pantina wasn't the dragon statue after all.

A soft bell chimed. The men playing instruments stopped and bowed their heads, shaking with reverence. Seeing them made Johnny's skin crawl, it was all too creepy.

Suddenly there was a fluttering of wings from behind the curtains. Johnny, Deb and Lady Stabs waited with excited curiosity, their heads down, wishing with all their might they could look up and see what was coming.

They heard something land softly behind the curtain. Then it was silent, but Johnny glanced at Lord Flaggalon. He looked mortified with fear. Pantina was there!

Johnny sensed someone sit in the golden chair. Johnny smelled a pleasant perfume, and somehow knew it was a woman.

There was a silence for a few moments, and Johnny could tell the being was staring at them, sizing them up. Then a soft, melodious female voice spoke.

"These are strangers?"

The words from Pantina made Johnny very curious, for they didn't sound like those said by some majestic being, and definitely not from a powerful god to worship. They sounded like they came from just an ordinary woman and one not much older than Johnny and Deb. It dawned on Johnny she sounded lost. She sounded sad. She sounded lonely.

Lord Flaggalon to drone on. "Oh, high goddess, lovely being from the place beyond the lights at night, I bring you travelers from a distant land. They say they are friends to us. Please use your infinite wisdom to tell us if they be friends or foes."

There was a moment of silence. Then Pantina the goddess spoke again.

"Where do you come from? Is it far away?"

Before Johnny could answer, Lord Flaggalon interrupted. "They say they come from a place to the south, a place they call Washington Deecee. There are only three of them here, with a doggy. But surely more are coming."

"A doggy?" Pantina said. "What kind of doggy?"

Johnny chuckled silently. This Pantina seemed like just an ordinary girl, more interested in Deecee that anything else.

"The doggy is not important, oh great goddess. You must tell us whether to trust the strangers or not."

"They seem nice. Bring me this doggy, for I would see it as well."

"Your holiness," Lord Flaggalon said, and Johnny sensed Lord Flaggalon was growing irritated, "I sense that you want us to watch the strangers carefully, and see if they prove to be false. Now we will leave you, for we do not deserve to be in your presence any longer."

There was another silence, and then Johnny sensed a profound sadness. Then Johnny felt Pantina stand up and walk away quietly.

Johnny glanced over at Lord Flaggalon. Lord Flaggalon wore a dark grin. Johnny understood now what was happening. The evil man was controlling their "goddess", manipulating her. What kind of prison did the "goddess" live in? Was she just a puppet for Lord Flaggalon to take out when he wanted to impress the Sky? At that moment, Johnny developed a true hatred for Lord Flaggalon. This man was cruel and devious, the type of person Johnny disliked the most. He knew now that he and his friends would have to watch Lord Flaggalon closely, for he was a snake-beastie, not to be trusted.

There was another fluttering of wings, and Pantina was gone.

CHAPTER 28

The king of Nork lounged in his throne, watching idly as two combatants fought to the death in front of him. The couches and chairs had been removed, and a ring set up with makeshift walls three feet high of pieces of metal. The two fighters were each given sharp stick to start with, and as the battle progressed, the king would decide what other weapons they were given. Guards watched from outside the ring, making sure the fighters didn't try to get away. On tables next to the guards lay other weapons to be handed in at the king's word.

The men in the ring both wore dirty rags and their faces and bodies were filthy, for they had spent the last three moon cycles in chains, feeding on scraps the king and his servants threw to them. Nork peasants who had found a way to irritate the king, they were both told if they won, they would be set free. What neither of them knew was that the winner would be set free all right, but inside the subways where he would meet his fate with the Lurkers. The thought of seeing the face of the winner when they were told what was going to happen was one of the king's favorite moments to anticipate.

The king idly chewed on some grapes and stroked his pet cat-beastie which sat on his lap. His eyes were lit up with an evil fire, for there was nothing the king liked more than to see someone die.

One of the men was short and slight, and he wore a terrified expression, for his opponent was a large, muscular man with a bald head who grinned back knowing he had the advantage. The small man spent most of his time running away while the big man chased him, which made the king and all the people in the throne room laugh. For the moment it was amusing to the king, but soon he would grow impatient for some fighting.

One of the girls pointed to the men fighting and whispered in the king's ear. The king nodded and smiled up at her. She leaned down and kissed him. The king turned and motioned to one of the guards. The guard hurried over and the king whispered in his ear. The guard nodded and hurried away. The king smiled up at the girl, and she smiled back, pleased that the king had listened to her.

As the king and the crowd watched, the guard picked up a sword. The combatants ran around in the ring, the larger man laughing and not really hurrying, knowing the little man would tire soon and he would be able to kill him swiftly.

As the larger man passed by the guard, the guard reached over the wall and slashed at the larger man's leg. The man screamed in surprise and pain and fell to the floor. The smaller man smiled darkly, knowing that the odds were being tipped more in his favor.

The king smiled up at the girl. "Do you feel better now, Maid Marion?" She nodded with a big grin. The king chuckled as she kissed him on the cheek. He held her hand, and went back to watching the battle, which just grew more interesting.

The smaller man now advanced, full of a new courage at seeing his opponent on the ground. But the larger man managed to get up, though his leg was bleeding from a large slash on it that dripped blood. The larger man was incensed now, and knew he had to protect himself. He pointed his stick out in front of himself towards his opponent and glared, daring the man to attack him.

The king motioned to the table and to the smaller man, and the guard near it nodded in understanding. He picked up a sword and reached over the wall, handing it to the small man. The man grinned even wider. The large men looked frightened and waited for him to be handed a sword, but neither of the guards moved again. The larger man realized that it was the king's wish that he be at a large disadvantage, and he faced his opponent again, but this time with an obvious look of worry behind his eyes.

Just then Ferdinand, the king's advisor, walked up from behind him. He stood for a moment for the king to see him, but the king was too busy watching the fight. Finally, Ferdinant cleared his throat, and the king heard it and looked up at him.

"Not now, Ferdie, can't you see I'm enjoying the battle!"

"King Richard, forgive the intrusion, but your army has returned from the south. The leader Moxie wishes to give you a report on the war, and bring you the spoils."

The king's eyes lit up and he smiled with interest, but then he frowned again. "Tell him to wait until the entertainment is over."

Ferdinand frowned crossly himself, and spoke in a serious tone. "Your majesty, he is very insistent. These are matters you must attend to at once."

The king turned and glared at Ferdinand, his eyes blazing with fury. "You go too far, Ferdie. Since my father passed away, you have been my trusted advisor. But sometimes you act like I am still a little scrabbler and you run Nork instead of me. You would be wise to remember, at any time I can put you in the ring."

Fear flashed in Ferdinand's eyes, but only for a second. "You know you could not rule without me, 'your majesty'. If it wasn't for me doing the actual task of keeping your kingdom intact, you would have been killed and tortured yourself, long ago."

The king frowned with anger, but he knew Ferdinand was right.

"Just remember who is king."

"I only wish to serve and help you in any way I

can, 'King Richard'. Sometimes, even kings have to face reality…"

"Oh, all right, shut up!" the king said, waving a hand. "Guards, take the combatants away, we'll finish this fight later. Bring in Moxie and let's get this over with."

The guards opened the gate in the ring, and led the two men, who both looked happy and relieved, out and towards the door of the palace. The larger man couldn't walk, so he crawled out on all fours. The other man hurried, as if afraid the king was going to change his mind at any second.

The king watched them leave, a look of regret and unhappiness on his face. The girls on either side of him bent down and whispered to him, trying to make him feel better, but he didn't smile. He stroked his cat-beastie nervously.

From a side door behind the king, two guards led Moxie and Alcapoon in. Moxie's face looked white, and he was covered in sweat. Alcapoon, who had never been in the presence of the king, looked terrified.

Moxie stumbled forward and fell at the king's feet. The king's cat-beastie hissed and jumped off the king's lap, irritating the king greatly. The king stared down at Moxie, wondering if Moxie was sick or something. Alcapoon stayed in the background, wringing his hands. He looked at Moxie with an alarmed expression, as if Moxie had been acting strangely.

Moxie stared forward, not seeming to see anything, and rocked back and forth sideways. He didn't look like he even knew where he was. Spittle dripped from his lip to the floor.

The king looked at Ferdinand.

"Ferdie, what's wrong with this fellow? Is he sick?"

Ferdinand stared down at Moxie gravely, wondering the same thing.

Moxie felt so hot, he was burning up. Here he was, in the presence of the Boss, wasn't he? He couldn't really tell, for his eyes refused to focus.

"Well?" The king said. "Give me your report. Did you bring the food like you were told to, so my people can stop complaining all the time? Say something, you wretched creature, and then get out of my sight!"

Suddenly Moxie's eyes cleared. He felt better. He looked around, saw where he was and the king sitting in front of him. He was home!

Moxie grinned; confident the king was going to be pleased with his next words. "I brought ya slaves, Boss!"

The king, surprised, thought for a second. He looked at Ferdinand standing behind him, but Ferdinand looked as puzzled as the king was. "Slaves? Whatever do you mean, you brought me slaves? Did you bring us food?"

Moxie grew angry at the question. Was this king stupid or something?

"I brought you slaves, stupid! Slaves! You know what slaves are, you ignorant hippopotamus? Are you always this lame-brained?"

The king looked dumbfounded for a moment. No one had ever spoken to him like that, and for a minute his mind went blank. Then a dark scowl of fury came to his face. He got ready to speak and fill this arrogant, idiotic soldier with terror at the thought of what the king was going to do to him.

But just before the king spoke, Ferdinand strode forth. He put a hand on the king's shoulder. The king looked at him with surprise also, for it was the second time in the last few moments something totally unexpected and unprecedented had happened.

"Your majesty, call your guards," Ferdinand said, looking at the king with alarm and gravity.

The king caught Ferdinand's meaning; there was something seriously wrong with this fellow. The king nodded quickly and signaled for his guards, who hurried forward.

Moxie stood up. His eyes smoldered with a red fire. His whole face seemed to sag, as if it was wax melting in the hot sun. "It's all your fault," Moxie said, staggering slightly, gnashing his teeth. "You sent me out there! You made me go in that tunnel! You killed me!"

The king jumped from his throne and stood behind it. The two girls screeched and ran to the back of the room. The cat-beastie hissed from under the table.

"I'm gonna eat you!" Moxie screamed. He raised his hands in front of him and advanced on the king. The king's eyes went wide with panic.

"Grab him!" The king yelled, as Moxie advanced on him.

But nobody moved! The guards seemed frozen in place.

"What's wrong with you?" The king yelled.

One of the guards, looking terrified, managed to say, "He's a Lurker!"

Everyone's eyes in the room opened wide with panic and fright, especially the king. They looked at Moxie. He was dead, but still moving.

The king's voice rose in panic. "A Lurker? Keep him away from me!"

Moxie shuffled towards the king, and a slow but gruesome chase ensued.
Ferdinand and the other guests all ran as far away as possible.

Ferdinand pointed to the guards. "Grab him, fools! Or you will be fed to the Lurkers!"

The guards, terrified, saw they had no choice. They ran up and grabbed Moxie's arms. Moxie turned his head and snapped at them.

"Put him in the cage!" Ferdinand yelled. The guards dragged Moxie, who snarled and snapped at them, over to the cage. One of the guards got too close, and Moxie's teeth sunk into his arm. The guard screamed in terror as Moxie bit down hard, holding on. The other guard grabbed Moxie's legs and flipped him into the cage. The other guard, still attached to Moxie by Moxie's teeth, went over and into the cage as well.

Now that Moxie and the guard were contained, the panic died down slightly. Everyone walked over to gaze at the grisly spectacle

Another guard joined the one who was left. They picked up long steel poles with sharp points on the end to keep Moxie at bay, but they didn't need to worry. Moxie was busy eating the guard, who screamed in terror as he slowly died.

The king's courage had returned now, and he grinned with dark delight as he, Ferdinand and the girls walked over to watch the fun.

"Wow," one of the girls said. "A real Lurker. Gee, I ain't ever seen one before."

The king turned to the girl. "Yes, isn't it exciting?"

Alcapoon walked up to watch too. "Poor Moxie. You was a jerk, but you didn't deserve this."

Ferdinand wore a dark smile as well, enjoying the horrible show. "We should really take them to the subway at once, your majesty, before he is able to infect anyone."

The king was silent for a second, thinking. "No, I think maybe, as long as we're careful, we should keep them." The king looked at Ferdinand. "We may just find a use for them."

The king turned to Alcapoon. "Now, since it seems your leader is no longer able to speak coherently, tell me everything that happened."

The king gazed at Moxie and the remains of the dead guard. "And especially, tell me if you've met a character named Johnny Apocalypse."

CHAPTER 29

Johnny, Deb and Lady Stabs were flown back to the first building again, away from the goddess Pantina. Lord Flaggalon stayed behind, making Johnny suspicious. Johnny hardly knew the man, but already he mistrusted everything Lord Flaggalon did.

As they landed, Deecee greeted them, wagging his tail and wearing a big grin. Johnny was glad to be done being carried through the air for he hoped was a good long time, and solid ground never felt so good to him before.

The Sky surrounded them. A woman took the lead, looking to be about forty seasons old, with brown hair and wearing a soft purple gown. She smiled at Johnny.

"Hello, Johnny Apocalypse. What did you think of our goddess, Pantina?"

Johnny, Deb and Lady Stab turned to the woman with interest. Johnny, not really sure who this woman was or if she was in league with Lord Flaggalon took care in responding. "We did not gaze on her, but she sounded wise and kind."

The woman laughed. "You are a wise for your age, Johnny Apocalypse. You will make a good leader someday."

"Who are you?" Deb asked.

"I am Layla, Mantayo's mother. I watch over the young Sky. I teach them schooling and help them learn to use their wings."

"Nice to meet you, Layla," Johnny said. "Mantayo is a very nice and caring person. I'd like to think we are now his friends."

"Come," Layla said, motioning with her hand. "Let me take you to our learning room. I can tell you some things, and you in turn can teach me."

Layla turned and they all followed, including Deecee, who padded along next to Johnny.

As they walked with Layla, they left the other Sky and soon were alone in the hallway as Layla led them to the Learning Room.

Johnny sensed that Mantayo's mother was a wise woman herself, and he found it hard to believe she thought the girl in the other tower was a god. Now that they were alone with her, Johnny took a risk.

"Layla, do you really think Pantina is a god?"

Layla stopped and turned, and Johnny saw a smile of admiration on her face. "You are a smart boy, Johnny. Wiser than many of our older people."

Layla glanced around, and made sure they were alone. "We will talk when we get to the

Learning Room."

Johnny looked at Deb and Lady Stabs, and they all smiled at each other. Deb gave Johnny a look that said she complimented for being so good at reading the signs.

Layla continued to talk in a conversational tone, as if to fool anyone who might be listening. "Mantayo tells me he really likes you as well, and thinks you and your people are to be trusted."

"Is Mantayo back from checking on the Lurkers?" Lady Stabs asked with concern.

Layla glanced at Lady Stabs but kept going. "No, he is still gone. I was hoping he misunderstood you, and what I thought he said wasn't true."

"I'm sorry, Layla," Deb said. "There were Lurkers there. We almost got eaten by them!"

Layla stopped in front of a doorway with no door. "Then the world just became much more dangerous."

Layla entered the room and Johnny and the others followed. This room looked like it took up the other half of that floor, for it was also very big. This room had puffy cloth covered bags set up in rows, all facing a large map and elegant chair at the front of the room. At the back of the room Johnny saw what must have been where the Sky practiced flying, for there were platforms jutting out from the walls, and handing down from the ceiling.

As the companions gazed about in interest, Johnny saw something that instantly excited him. There on the walls next to the map were colored drawings made by my children. They all showed a female with red hair. And Golden wings. Johnny was sure he was looking at depictions of Pantina, their goddess

Deb knew it too. She poked Johnny with her elbow. "Johnny."

Johnny, mildly irritated, frowned at her. "I see it."

Layla noticed too. "Yes, that is Pantina. Our goddess."

Johnny turned to Layla, wondering if she was going to continue their conversation from the hallway.

Layla glanced about furtively, as if though they were alone, ears were everywhere. Then she looked at Johnny and his friends. "When Pantina first was born, Lord Flaggalon was young. He convinced the Sky, especially the younger ones, that she was a goddess sent from the lights above. Most of the elders didn't believe, but soon Lord Flaggalon made sure anyone who didn't go along was too afraid to say so. Lord Flaggalon gathered enforcers around him who hurt and intimidate anyone who doesn't agree with Lord Flaggalon. Now we worship Pantina as a goddess, but it is really Lord Flaggalon who is in control."

It was just as Johnny suspected. The Sky had more problems than just the Norkers trying to kill them.

Deb and Lady Stabs nodded at each other in understanding.

"There's always one jerk in every crowd, isn't there?" Lady Stabs said.

They all chuckled, even Layla.

"But come, let's talk of more pleasant things." Layla led them over to the large map on the wall. Deecee padded around the room, sniffing at things.

As they reached the map, Johnny saw that there were actually two maps, a smaller one of the city of Nork, and a large one showing the land surrounding it. The larger map was so big, it even included Washington Deecee and lands far to the north of Nork. Johnny saw there were words on the map, which surprised him. They were the names of cities and places.

Johnny turned to Layla. "Do your people know how to read the ancient words?"

Layla smiled. "We are learning. The king of the Groundworms is fluent in the old language, and so we must learn to protect ourselves. I teach the young Sky, but I am just learning myself."

"Misterwizard will love you!" Deb said. "He knows all the ancient words. When he gets here, he'll help you!"

Layla smiled, curious. "You must tell me more about this Misterwizard. Johnny, please look at this map. Where do your people live?"

Johnny pointed to Washington Deecee, which at the moment said only, "White City".

"This is where our tribe lives, in Washington Deecee."

Layla nodded. "So, you are just past the place called Pelpia, where the Letfreedomring live."

"They did," Johnny said. "The Groundworms, as

you call them, captured them. I was trying to free them when Mantayo brought me here."

"But not all of them, Johnny," Deb said. "There were still some people left behind."

"And I think Starbucks and Super are going back home to our tribe. When Misterwizard and my tribe find out about the people of Letfreedomring, they will come help us to free them." Johnny added.

Layla nodded. "The people of Letfreedomring were good people. We had just begun meeting with them and learning to be friends. If the Groundworms have them, we will help you set them free. But it will not be easy."

"What about Lord Flaggalon?" Johnny asked. "Will he agree to help us?"

Layla smiled, once again impressed at Johnny's intelligence. "Of course not. That is why we will do it without him."

Johnny pointed to the map of Nork. "Can you tell us about Nork, and the people around it?

"Of course," Layla said. She pointed to areas of the map as she talked. "To the northwest, on the mainland live the Clan. They are a nomadic people who are willing to fight for whomever pays them the most.

As you know, the land we are on now is an island called Mattan, occupied by the Groundworms. They also have conquered the land on the next island across the river called Booklin. But the land on the south of that island called Keens is the home of what the Groundworms call the Unclean. The Unclean are a wild, fierce people. They are the ones who legend says were burned and disfigured by the death stars when they fell. They have the black skin, the strange slanted eyes and yellow skin, the brown skin and dark hair."

Johnny, Deb and Lady Stabs looked at each other with concern.

"So, anyone who is not white," Deb said in anger.

Johnny thought about his friend Starbucks. Then he turned to Layly somberly. "Layla, you don't believe that, do you?"

"Of course not," she said bitterly, "but once again, it is something being taught to the young Sky by Lord Flaggalon and his cronies. He wants us to hate everyone who is not Sky. Sometimes, I think he is worse than the king of the Groundworms."

Johnny, Deb and Lady Stabs all looked angry, especially Deb. "Well then, he's not going to like Starbucks, is he the creep?"

"Starbucks?" Layla said.

"He's my best friend, and Super's mate," Johnny said. "He is also black skinned. And anyone who hates him, has me for an enemy."

Layla nodded. "Mantayo is a good judge of character. He was right about you. You are good people."

Johnny pointed to the south, to the island just below Mattan. "Who lives here, Layla?"

"That is Satin I-land. The Gants live there. Huge creatures as tall as some buildings. No one dares cross that land, for the Gants eat anyone who comes too close. The king of the Groundworms feeds them members of his own people to appease them so don't come across the water."

"Wow!" Lady Stabs said, shaking her head. "There are sure a lot of different types of peoples in the world now."

Layla pointed to a spot far north of Mattan. "This is where we came from. Here a death star fell, meant for the city of Nork. The land was laid waste, but the waters were made magical. Our ancestors drank of the waters, and then Pantina was born."

Suddenly Mantayo burst into the room, in a state of excitement. He ran over to Johnny. Everyone turned towards him, eager to hear about his trip.

Mantayo looked grave. "Johnny, you were right! The Lurkers have escaped! There are too many to count! Luckily, they're trapped at the moment in the road because of the high walls, but if we don't do something soon, they will climb up and spread everywhere!"

"We must tell Lord Flaggalon," Layla said. "We have to kill them and seal up the opening where they escaped, or soon they will spread everywhere!"

"Will Lord Flaggalon listen?" Johnny asked.

"Of course," Layla said. "Even he doesn't want the whole world to be destroyed."

"There is something else, Johnny," Mantayo said in a breathless voice of excitement. "I saw a group of old vehicles traveling down the same road. There were old, long yellow ones and a few odd-looking ones at the back."

Johnny, Deb and Lady Stabs all smiled at each other with excitement.

"It's our tribe, I know it!" Johnny said.

"There were also two other smaller things that made a lot of noise. One had two people on it, a young man with black skin and a girl with long black hair."

"Starbucks!" Johnny yelled with happiness.

"And Super!" Deb yelled, just as joyfully.

"And there was a strange, round little man with a beard on a funny little vehicle that made a funny sound."

"Misterwizard!" Johnny, Deb and Lady Stabs all said it at the same time, which made them all laugh.

"These are the members of your tribe you spoke of!" Layla said, wearing a big smile. "Just as you said, they are coming to help your new friends."

But then Mantayo frowned darkly. "I'm afraid there's some bad news, Johnny. They're far away, but they're heading right for the Lurkers."

"Oh no, Johnny!" Deb said, the smile on her face fading and being replaced with a look of concern.

"We have to stop them before it's too late, Mantayo!" Johnny said. "They have no idea what they're heading into!"

Mantayo looked at his mother. She nodded. "Go with them! I will talk to Lord Flaggalon. We will bring others soon to help you."

"Hurry!" Mantayo said with a motion of his hand. "There's no time to waste!"

Restaria and the people of Letfreedomring settled into a large, weed-filled area in the middle of the round building. They were tired and hungry, but relieved to finally stop walking and have a moment to rest.

The large dome at the top of the building was broken and crumbling, and huge holes let the last rays of the Red Eye in. As the people of Letfreedomring gazed about, they saw rows and rows of empty seats, rising up from the field on ramps. There seemed to be thousands of them, all empty, some broken and laying on their sides. The seats rose almost to the edges of the roof, and some were so far away, they could barely see them.

The building was cold, for holes not only above but in many places in the walls let in the cold breeze. Surrounding the people near the ramps, bored guards sat and talked. Some looked half asleep, but they all held tommy guns and other weapons. The people of Letfreedomring were too tired to fight back anyway, they were simply glad for a chance to rest.

A little brown scrabbler of four seasons with dark hair walked up Restaria where she sat on the grass. Restaria smiled at her, picked the little girl up and set her on her lap. "This place is scary," the little scrabbler said. "Where are we, Restaria?"

The little scrabbler's name was Starlite. Restaria hugged her, and Starlite put her head on Restaria's chest. "It looks like a place they watched people perform, Starlite."

"Perform?" Starlite asked. "What does that mean?"

"That means they did things to entertain people, while the people watched."

"Did they do tricks?"

"Some of them probably did."

Starlite looked up at Restaria, who turned to look back at Starlite's face. "What's going to happen to us?"

Restaria wished she had the answer. "We're going to be fine. We will stay here for a little while, then some of our people will come and take us home," Restaria said wishfully.

"I'm hungry," Starlite said.

"I'm sure they'll bring us food soon." Restaria couldn't remember being so tired before, and all she wanted to do was to lay her head down and sleep, but she knew the people were relying on her. She looked at Starlite.

"Go back to your mother now. She's probably looking for you. I'll come see you later."

Starlite nodded wearily and crawled off Restaria's lap. She shuffled away, and Restaria watched her sadly, wishing she had been a better leader. Maybe if she had, they wouldn't be prisoners, at the mercy of the king of Nork.

Restaria rose up with an effort, for every bone in her body ached, and made her way over to her second in command, Johnthebaptist. Johnthebaptist stood at the edge of the prisoners, frowning deeply, watching the guards with a look of concern. As Restaria approached, he glanced at her.

"I don't like the way the guards are laughing and smiling. They have something evil planned for us. And where did their leader, this Moxie fellow go?"

Restaria nodded, her head feeling as if it weighed fifty pounds. "To tell the king of Nork about us, no doubt."

Johnthebaptist folded his arms and put on a serious frown. "We have to find a way to escape, if not from the city, then someplace in it where we can hide until we can find a way out."

"The people are too tired right now. Let them rest. Meanwhile, you and I will see if we can come up with something. The guards have weapons, and we have nothing. And we have only a few soldiers."

"We can't just sit here and wait until they do whatever they plan with us," Johnthebaptist said with passion. "Who knows what kind of men these are? We may be their next meal!"

"I agree. But any plan must be a sure one. If we try something and it doesn't work, we will only get people killed."

"One is for certain," Johnthebaptist said, "We are on our own."

Restaria put a hand on his arm. "That is certainly not true. Our people who were left behind are surely working on a way to rescue us. And the young man Johnny Apocalypse…"

"Johnny Apocalypse!" Johnthebaptist almost spit Johnny's name out. "Everyone speaks as if he is some kind of a god. He didn't save us from being captured, did he? And where is he now? Surely, he has returned to his own tribe to save his own skin."

Restaria felt a deep sorrow try to well up in her, but she stubbornly refused to let it. "No. I know men like Johnny. He is what they used to call a hero in the ancient times. They fight against evil, because it is what they believe what they must do, and they don't stop until there are no more bad men to fight. Or until one of the bad men kills them."

Restaria gazed around at the drab, gray interior of the building, all the empty seats that seemed to be filled with ghosts watching them. "I know we will see Johnny Apocalypse again, and it will be when he comes to help us fight our enemies."

Johnthebaptist smiled grimly. "I hope you are right." He looked around too. "Hurry Johnny Apocalypse. We don't have much time."

Join Johnny Apocalypse for the thrilling, action-packed conclusion of Johnny's New York adventures in *Johnny Apocalypse and the Battle of New York!*

And sign up for Mark Robijn's newsletter so you don't miss any Johnny Apocalypse news. You might even get a chance to read the next Johnny Apocalypse book for free as a reviewer! You can also go to Mark Robijn's website, www.markrobijn.com, where you can find all of Mark's other books. And don't forget to check out the Johnny Apocalypse and the Nuclear Wasteland Facebook page!

See you next time in the Wasteland!